Crescendo

A MUSICAL LOVE STORY

LORI THORN

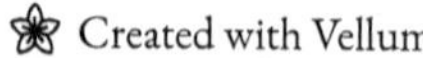 Created with Vellum

This book is for anyone who thought they knew what they wanted but changed their mind.

You are allowed to pursue new passions.

Note to the Reader

Within this work lies topics of a certain nature. If you could use a content warning, it is available for you in the book description on my website at www.authorlorithorn.com, or scan below.

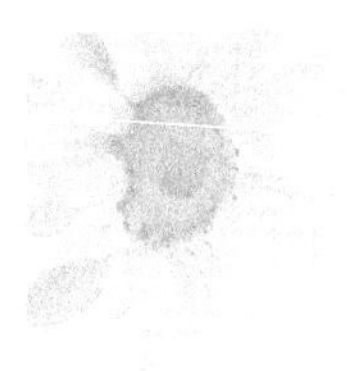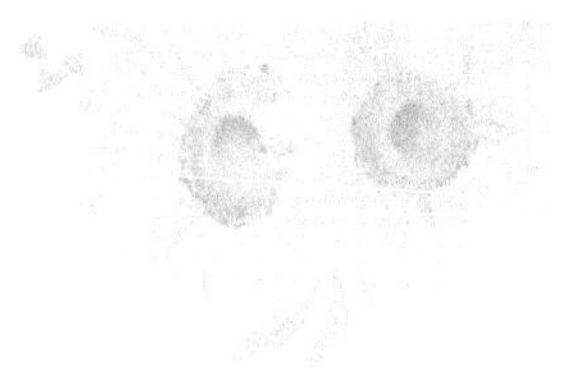

One

28% OF BAND DIRECTORS ARE WOMEN. MOST
OF THOSE WORK IN ELEMENTARY GRADES
WITH DECREASING REPRESENTATION AS
GRADE LEVEL INCREASES.

As retirement parties go, this one had the thrill and all the feeling of a deflated balloon. A smattering of teachers from the nearby Middle and High Schools milled about the First Baptist Community Hall. Their faces were smiling as they chatted with each other, but it didn't feel like a celebration. Though they spoke in clusters, it was strangely quiet. Nobody had arranged for music, the streamers and decor had the battered signs of being reused, and Derek found himself wondering how hastily this was pulled together.

Part of him felt sorry for Al. *Shouldn't retirement merit some livelihood? Al has been at Everest Middle for his entire career. Shouldn't there at least be music at a director's retirement?*

Al didn't seem to care as he made his way to the front of the room. He was wearing a straw hat and Hawaiian button-down with cargo pants. As he turned to face the audience, the gin blossoms on his cheeks betrayed the rate at which he'd been enjoying his would-be-clandestine stash of alcohol located in a cooler in the back of his pickup truck. Derek had joined Al and the other area directors (Greg, Matt, Billy, and

Chuck) the first time they snuck out of the hall for their hidden libations. It was expected that they would stick together. Luckily, he'd found excuses not to join them on their following three excursions.

Al cleared his throat loudly. "I don't need a microphone if everyone can give me your attention." He paused as conversation lulled, and the crowd turned their heads toward him. "Now, I've been conducting at Everest Middle for forty years, and it's been a joy in my life teaching the kids of our small town how to play an instrument. Now I'm old, and times are changin'. People are changin'. I've seen it happen." Al's tone indicated his opinion regarding these observations. "When I started, if two boys were at odds with each other, I could just take 'em out back and tell 'em to fight. A couple punches, and they'd be friends again. Can't do that anymore." He chuckled. "Nowadays, something like that would get me fired instead of retirin'. I guess what I'm sayin' is things ain't what they used to be, and this good ol' boy is passin' the torch for someone else to figure it all out. Thanks for coming, all y'all." He waved his hand at the room, hiccuped, and returned to the table.

The abrupt ending of Al's speech caught the crowd off guard. Their polite applause didn't begin until several awkward moments after he pulled out his chair and slowly lowered into it. He rolled his eyes as chatter picked back up.

"What are you going to do now, Al?" Greg Howard asked from across the table.

"Probably go to the bowling alley."

Greg shook his head. "I mean in life, like, instead of teachin'."

Al winked and adjusted his hat. "Probably go to the bowling alley." The men laughed. "Honestly, I have to tell you boys somethin'. Now, don't make a fuss, but me and Sue are moving up to Tennessee. She wants to be closer to the kids."

Billy reared his head back in shock. "I wouldn't have

guessed you one for moving." Chuck, never a man of many words, nodded along.

"The missus is mighty insistent about it." Greg scoffed. Al slapped Derek's knee and continued, "The real question now is what you'll do. I know we haven't always seen eye to eye, but I have always given you the best feeder for your band. The new middle school director will be an important factor for Everest High's talent. You'll need to show 'em how it's done."

Derek leaned back in his chair. When he started directing Everest High's band three years ago, he had found it difficult to befriend this group. They had a way of doing things and weren't exactly open to new ideas. As a young new director, he dreamed about how he would teach and how his band would be. Ultimately, it had been easier to survive by adapting to what was already established. "I'm sure I can train them up. I know your methods well. I wonder who it'll be."

"Not many folks applyin' from what Steve says. Last I heard, only some woman from up north."

Greg sneered. "A female! It's not woman's work, I'll say that. Can't coddle musical talent out of folks." Chuck shook his head and looked at the table.

Matt rapped his knuckles against his seat and added, "Never met one of them before."

Al replied. "Don't get too excited, boys. I'm sure it was a mistake. No city girl would move to the sticks. Wouldn't last long if they did, hah!" He sucked his teeth. "Let's go back out to the truck."

Derek knew he was obligated to join this round; there would be no out. The group rose, their chairs scraping against linoleum, and exited the hall's back door. The night air was cool, and puffy clouds soared swiftly across the sky. They stood in a semi-circle around the open truck bed. Greg poured each of them a heavy shot of Wild Turkey, raised his plastic cup, and said, "To Al!" They all toasted and downed the brown liquor.

Derek was privately grateful when the side door of the church opened, and a middle-aged woman in a maxi dress appeared. She didn't approach but did call to them, "Y'all can't be drinking on the church property. Everyone knows what you're doing out here!"

Al grumbled, then lifted his voice, "Calm down, Judy. We ain't hurtin' nobody. It's my retirement, isn't it?" There were snickers from the men. Even Derek found his mouth quirking up.

Judy's blessed interruption provided an out for Derek. He tipped his cup toward Al. "I think I'm going to head out. It's been a pleasure working with you, Al. I hope you love it in Tennessee."

"Thanks, Derek. You're a good kid. Jus' remember who's in charge now." With a clipped nod, Derek withdrew from the circle.

Elle Foster closed her laptop. Her shoulders slumped as her eyes adapted to the lower light. Though she'd lived them, the last few weeks were hard to imagine. She'd just graduated from Penn State's prestigious Music Education program. A feat in itself, but as if it wasn't enough, the well-funded High School in Allentown, where she performed her internship, offered her a permanent position. It was unprecedented. Preposterous. The alignment of their director leaving and her graduation was uncanny enough, but a school like that making an offer to a fresh grad? It was a dream job. Anyone with her background, her goals, would see it as such. And she turned it down.

Every application she submitted to music positions in rural areas made her wonder if she was utterly derailing her life. In truth, she had never been less confident about a decision. Still, she knew she didn't want to be in a city anymore. Settling down after an upbringing of disruption had been her dream for as long as she could remember. *I could grow roots here, too. It doesn't necessarily have to be in the country, right?* These doubts were a plague, and when they showed up, she consoled herself by thinking of southern hospitality and charming cottages with yards she would plant a garden in. Slow was what she craved. Slow would be better.

A car alarm outside her apartment made Elle flinch. She glanced at her bed with longing but knew it was no good despite the early hour. Elle reopened her laptop and propped it on the treadmill's console. She typed 'how to garden' into the Google search field as she increased her pace.

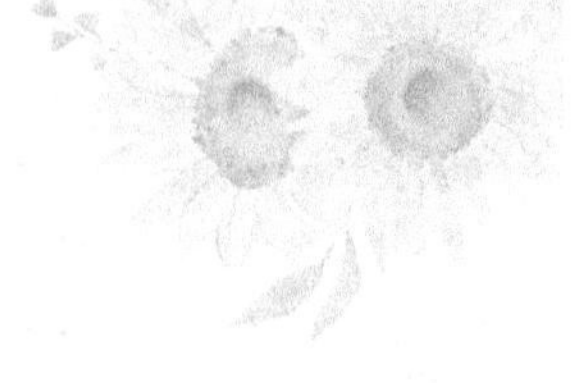

Two

SOME OF THE MOST COMMON MUSIC
EDUCATION PHILOSOPHIES ARE UTILITARIAN,
AESTHETIC, AND PRAXIAL.

Over the next few weeks, things slowed down for Elle, making her doubts about rejecting the job at Allentown fester. After applying for dozens of small-town positions across the states, she expected a couple callbacks but received none. In times like these, she wished she had someone to talk to. Her apartment lease would be up soon, and the thing about wanting to settle down in the country was that she needed a hint about which country to move toward. That was what her so-far-imagined job offers would provide: some direction.

Nights were the worst. Elle's brain created a mantra she fell asleep to. *I won't beg Allentown to reconsider me. Driving for Uber is always an option. Getting a job after graduation is hard for everyone.* It didn't help much.

She had been dreaming about her phone being broken and unable to receive calls when a loud buzzing roused her. In her waking stupor, she knocked the phone off her nightstand and had to dive from beneath the covers to retrieve it in time to answer.

"Hello?" Her greeting was croaky with sleep.

A man's voice replied, "Hello, this is Steve Colton. I'm the principal at Everest Middle School, calling for Elle Foster?"

Elle scrambled to an upright position. "Hi, yes, this is she!"

"Well, it's nice to meet you, Elle," Steve spoke with a slight drawl that Elle found enchanting. "I'm calling regarding your application to the band director position. I was so happy to see someone apply. I was worried we'd have to stick a sub in there. If you're still interested, I'd love to interview you."

Elle cocked her head to the side in silent question. *I applied for this position at least a month ago. Maybe their offices were closed, and Steve is only seeing the applications now?* "I am, yes. I'm definitely interested."

"That's great news. We could interview right now if you're available?"

Elle stumbled over her words, "Right... right now? Um, wow, I don't feel very prepared, I guess. Could we schedule a call for later? Even later today would be fine."

Steve clucked his tongue, "Of course we can. No problem at all; I just wanted to offer. Can I call you back at 1:30?"

Several things about the call struck Elle as strange, but she brushed them aside to prepare for the interview. The rest of her morning and afternoon was spent learning as much as she could about Everest Middle, the town of Everest, Alabama, reviewing common interview questions, and thinking about how she wanted to present herself as a Music Educator. Although the interview was over the phone, Elle also put on makeup, tied her curly hair up in a bun, and donned the interview outfit she had invested in, a rusty-colored wide-leg slack, cream-colored satin top, and a funky cardigan with colorful puffballs sewn onto it. She even changed out her nose ring to a golden hoop with pastel orbs on the side to match.

When Steve called her back, the conversation was still not

one she had prepared for. It was unlike any interview she'd ever heard of. Steve did ask about basic classroom management techniques and set expectations that the band would need a performance each semester. However, there was no inquiry about her teaching philosophies or music-related questions. Most of the interaction focused on the additional steps required to teach in Alabama since her certification was for Pennsylvania. Paperwork, nothing too bad.

Elle was surprised at his line of questioning, but the interview progressed decently all the same. When Steve opened the conversation to her, she asked about the band room (standard), what instruments they had on hand (only standard percussion for the classroom, no loaners), and the size of each grade level's band (Steve guessed around 20).

She was ready for Steve to tell her to expect a callback and let her know about next steps, but instead, he asked, "When can you start?"

Fluent speech once again became a struggle. "Oh! I am... so flattered. Wow. I mean, I'd want to be there to start the school year. I do have to figure out moving. When does pre-planning begin?"

"Pre-planning starts in two and a half weeks. I'll tell you what, I know a family trying to rent out a little space, if you want to call them. It's nothing fancy, but they're good people."

Almost everything she owned fit into 10 medium-sized boxes, which she filled carefully and taped up. It only took two days for Elle to arrange everything for the move. The ease of it was unpleasant, but she reminded herself that Everest was where she would grow roots. She bribed two college neighbors with the last remaining beer in her refrigerator to load her mattress and treadmill onto the U-Haul and mentally prepared for the 14-hour drive ahead.

Elle sat at the steering wheel for several minutes before turning the key in the ignition. She felt high up in the seat of the truck despite it being the smallest model U-Haul offered. An unexpected sadness settled over her, blanketing her excitement. This had always been her plan. Her dreams were coming true! Yet State College was where she had lived the longest, so perhaps melancholia was called for.

Steve's lead for somewhere to stay had panned out. Elle was moving into a small house on the edge of a farm. Her knowledge of the place ended there, however. The Smith family owned the property and tried several methods to give her a virtual walk-through. No matter what they attempted, the video was fuzzy and dropped connection frequently. They were kind and emailed her photos, but she still didn't quite understand what she was headed to. She glanced up toward her studio one final time. *My nights will be quiet, I will live slower, I will have the Stars Hollow life of Gilmore Girls.*

The trip did not take 14 hours. Driving a large vehicle was harrowing. Elle was somewhere in Virginia when the first storm began. The rain set her nerves off, but the wind was worse. The U-Haul caught each gust, acting like a sail, and veered the truck to the side of the road. She did her best not to overcorrect and drove as fast as she dared, but it still put her amongst the slowest travelers on the road. She intended to sleep in the truck overnight to save money, but this, too, did not go as expected. Her compromised pace necessitated a rest before the mid-point of the journey. When she finally located a rest stop that seemed safe enough, the sounds and lights outside made sleeping difficult. The second day was more of the same. Elle was so exhausted by dinner she was forced to try napping again and nodded off in a Wendy's parking lot.

Banging on her window jolted her awake several hours

later. A police officer aimed a flashlight at her until she cracked the window an inch.

A gruff voice floated through, "Everything okay, ma'am?"

Elle swallowed to clear her throat. "Yes, I'm fine, thanks. Driving a long way and needed a rest is all."

"Where you headed?"

"Everest, it's west of Montgomery."

"You're getting close. Look, I do apologize, but I have to ask you to clear out."

She couldn't have gone back to sleep anyway, not after her heart rate so suddenly took flight. "No problem, I'll get going now. Thanks."

It was one in the morning on a dark two-lane road in the middle of nowhere when she rolled past the Welcome to Everest sign. The sight was a cue for adrenaline, and Elle started taking in every possible detail. The deserted road gave way to sparse homes before giving way to a small downtown area. There were no lights on or signs of life, but this didn't curb her fascination. The storefronts included a Salvation Army, a jeweler, Tiny's Cafe, a Christian bookstore, and a florist. Several empty storefronts spotted the street also, including an abandoned old theater building and a sandwich shop. The street became residential after the couple of town blocks and was marked with a historic district sign. These were older homes but obviously cared for, most of them two stories.

The residences also lasted only a couple blocks before they were relieved with a commercial area. Elle saw what she assumed was a grocery store called Green's, a clothing outlet, and a Subway before she had to make a left, leaving it out of sight. She was a few short miles from her new home now. Anticipation swelled in her chest. There were no streetlights off the main drag, nor were there sidewalks as she drove further into the country. The houses along the road sat alone, spaced far from each other. At her next turn, the truck started to jitter and shake. She worried the U-Haul had broken down for a split second before realizing she had turned onto a bumpy dirt road. Her whole body shook from the vibrations, and the occasional large pothole caused the truck and her stomach to lurch.

The silhouette of a small yellow house emerged on the other side of a large field. It was vaguely familiar. *This is it, my new home!* Proud to have recognized it and her excitement peaking, she parked the truck in the drive and hopped down to the grass. There was some sort of large tree in her front yard, along with some smaller shrubs and plants growing around the little white porch. Down the road were more fields, but she could see some lights in the distance that must be other homes- one of them would be the Smith's house.

Elle stepped toward the porch but stopped when she saw the stars. The sky above was glittering, winking as if alive. She had never seen a night so full of stars. It was like sunlight sparkling off the ocean but on a canvas of the deepest velvety blue. Her mouth fell open in a silent 'wow.' This was some-thing she could get used to.

The house did not hold the same splendor as the heavens. The walls were stained, with aged paint peeling in some areas. The floors and all the surfaces were covered in dust and other filth that Elle chose not to consider for any length of time. The Smiths had told her it was furnished, and there was some furniture, albeit sparse. A table and chairs in the kitchen dining area, an ancient green upholstered chair in the living room, and an armoire in the bedroom, all of which appeared to be in poor condition.

Exhaustion returned in full force. Elle found a box of clothes that was easily accessible toward the back of the truck, spread them out on the warped hardwood floor, and fell asleep. She awoke the following day to golden light streaming in through the window. Dust particles floated lazily above her.

A cacophony of unfamiliar sounds played. There was a buzzing hum in the distance, occasional dog barks, a rooster crow, and a scraping sound outside the window.

The understanding she was actually here broke over her. This was momentous! And there was so much to do! *I've got to get the truck unloaded and set this place up.* Two priorities could not wait: stopping the persistent scratching sound and taking a shower. She dressed in clothes from the palette she'd slept on and stepped outside. Now the sun was up, she could appreciate the plants around the house. There were a variety of different flowers, all unkept and wild. Quite unlike the manicured appearance she was accustomed to on campus, but she liked it. Elle rounded the corner of the house to discover two trash cans and no hint of scratching. She shrugged and tried to recall where her toiletries were packed when the sound returned. The trash can nearest her shuddered. Heart racing, she approached the bin and lifted the lid. A brownish-tan animal was inside. It looked like a rat, but it was far too large, and as soon as its beady eyes found Elle, it let out a sizzling hiss. Elle screamed, slammed the lid back on, and ran to the porch. Whatever the creature was, if it wanted to live in her trash can, it could have it.

The manageable boxes were unloaded and stacked in the front room within minutes. Without the accessibility of frat boys, moving the treadmill and mattress would have to be a problem for future Elle. Current Elle found a towel and bathing essentials and brought them to the tiny bathroom. If you could call it that, even the bathroom in her old studio apartment was twice as large. She fiddled with the faucets in the shower stall, figuring out how they worked, then washed off the griminess of travel like a ritual. Each bubble carried away doubt and made room for determination. *The house won't feel neglected once I put love into it.*

She was drying her hair when someone knocked on the

door. Taken aback, she hurried to dress and called out, "Be right there!"

A woman in an oversized t-shirt and jeans with mud boots coming up to her knees stood on the porch. Her dark hair was pulled back into a low ponytail, and a streak of dirt was on her cheek. She said, "You must be Elle Foster! We saw the truck this morning and figured we'd give you some time to yourself before coming to say hi."

Elle smiled, recognizing the voice. "It's good to meet you! Mrs. Smith, right?" She stepped through the screen door and extended her hand.

"Yes! I'm sorry, yes. You can call me Darla." She shook Elle's hand. "How was your trip down?"

Elle smirked. "Let's just say it was long, and now it's over." They both laughed.

"I noticed you have some big stuff still in the truck. You need help with that?"

Elle nodded, "Oh my gosh, yes, I had no idea how I would get those last things out."

Darla turned toward the road, lifted her hands around her mouth, and yelled, "BOYS! GET OVER HERE!" Despite her slight frame, Darla could project. She turned back to Elle, "The boys will be here in a sec. Jed and Noah are happy to help."

In the distance, Elle could see two teenagers, high school age, she guessed, walking toward them. "Thank you so much, Darla. And it is really nice to meet you. I can't wait to get to know the area."

"I'm sure. Is there anything else you need? Everything okay with the house?"

"Yes, umm... There are two things I wanted to ask about, though. First, this is weird, I know, but there's something in the trash can, and it seemed pretty angry."

Darla laughed sweetly. "It's either a coon or a possum.

Don't have those up north, I bet! Keep the trash lid on real tight, or they'll get in there." She turned to the young men who had reached the porch. "Jed, go see what's in the trash, please."

"Yes'm." The older of the two boys jogged around the side of the house. They heard the lid scrape as he lifted it, and he called back, "Possum." There was a soft thud, and Jed reappeared on the porch. "I tossed him out back."

Elle started to thank him, but Darla spoke to her sons at the same time, "Thanks, Jed. I'd appreciate it if you two could help Ms. Foster unload the rest of her truck. I'm going to get back to the coop."

She started down the stairs, but Elle called after her, "Darla! Thank you again, and Jed and Noah, too. I was wondering, do you mind if I put some fresh paint on the walls?"

Darla made a shooing motion with her hands as if brushing the question aside. "Of course, I'm sure the house could use some sprucing up. Nobody has been in it for so long. Treat it like your own."

Elle's car, an old blue Honda Civic, was the only thing she had shipped separately. She'd been too nervous to drag it behind the U-Haul (a decision she didn't regret one bit on the other side of the drive). It wouldn't arrive for another couple of days, so she spent the time cleaning, unpacking, and setting up services. The limited cleaning supplies she found beneath the kitchen sink didn't make much of a dent in the accumulated filth. She started a list of improvement ideas on a refrigerator To-Do magnet, including other furniture she needed and paint color ideas for each room. There was a single internet provider in the area touting a service called DSL. They came to set her up on the second day, but the connection was oddly

slow. Even short videos would buffer and have trouble streaming. She added a line on her To-Do magnet to call them back.

On the third day, Elle awoke with the gnaw of cabin fever
in her gut. She'd pulled up a map to determine if it was
possible to jog from her house to downtown when her phone
rang. She recognized the number from the delivery company
and relaxed slightly as she answered the call.

"Mrs. Foster? We have your Honda, but I can't take this
thing on a dirt road. That was not in the description."

"Hmm, that makes sense. I didn't know about the road
when I made the arrangements. Where are you now?" The
driver had pulled over to the side of the road just before the
clay began. "I think I can be there in 10 minutes. Can you wait
while I come to you?" She was putting on her running shoes as
they reluctantly agreed. Elle ran along the country road as fast
as she could. The air was different here, humid, but the sheer
joy of running outside again was so intense that she giggled as
she navigated potholes and mounds. It was a shorter distance
than she recalled, and she made it to the semi in 8 minutes.

Once her car was back on the ground, the urge to be
anywhere but home demanded she make the drive into town.
Besides the change of scenery, she desperately needed to stock
her kitchen. Remembering the night of her arrival, she turned
her car away from the house and toward civilization.

Elle strolled through Green's Market, filling her cart with
staples. What staples were there, that is. She made several
passes through every aisle but concluded they simply did not
have what she was used to. Quinoa, couscous, and soba
noodles. Harissa and Chili Crisp. Micro-greens, broccolini,
jackfruit, pomegranate, and seitan. Almond flour and cashew
milk and cheeses. Many of the things she used weekly were
absent. Also unsettling was the feeling that other patrons were

talking about her. Several times, she caught someone observing her, and they turned their heads away a little too quickly, sometimes even commenting to the person they were with.

You're imagining things, Elle told herself. *You're self-conscious because you're in a new and different place.* It wasn't hard to believe her mind may be playing tricks on her. People had no reason to stare, much less talk about her.

Elle forgot the feeling of being a spectacle until exploring downtown the next day. It was a beautiful afternoon, and the sky had a crystalline quality to it where it wasn't dotted with puffy clouds. She had decided to jog the area. Exploring while she ran combined some of her favorite activities. She dressed in leggings and a patterned blue and purple sports bra and wore her favorite neon yellow Brooks shoes to mark the occasion.

Curiously, despite it being lunchtime on Friday, the town was almost as empty as it had been at 1am. She had plenty of room to run the sidewalk, at least. Another unusual thing were the shop hours. Many stores were only open 3-4 days a week or had restricted hours, operating half days. There were no artists or musicians on the corners. It was... quiet. Elle began to imagine the first scenes in a Zombie movie when she saw a family turn a corner toward her. She smiled and waved to the little girl between her parents. The girl waved back, but the Mother drew her closer to her side. As she passed them, she heard the woman hiss, "Did you see what she was wearing?" Elle inspected her clothes for stains or anything amiss, but nothing stood out. *Maybe she was talking about someone else?*

Though empty, the downtown was quaint. There were potted flower beds with vegetables spilling over their rims every few feet, the roads were pristine, and even the air smelled fresh. The area was distractingly small, however. Elle found herself coming to abrupt halts as the stretch of buildings simply ended. The main drag she had driven through accounted for most of downtown, and a second parallel street included a hair salon, a boutique clothing store with fashions she wasn't familiar with, and an animal feed store across the road on a corner.

She ran the streets three times each before deciding to drive around. Perhaps there were other developed areas somewhere else. If there were, Elle didn't find them.

Three

SUPERIOR - THE TOP RATING A BAND CAN
RECEIVE, REFLECTING THE FINEST
CONCEIVABLE PERFORMANCE FOR THE EVENT
AND CLASS OF PARTICIPANTS BEING
EVALUATED.

E lle walked through the doors of Everest Middle School, ignoring the heavy weight of anxiety pressing down on her. It was the first day of pre-planning before school opened to students, and all the middle and high school staff were slated for a kick-off meeting in the shared library.

The town of Everest had three functional schools but only two campuses. Everest Elementary handled kindergarten through fifth grades and had a campus across town. The middle school served grades six through eight, and the high school included grades nine through twelve, but they shared a single sprawling campus. Everest Middle classrooms were located on the east side of campus, while Everest High's were all on the west side. Each had small lunchrooms, administrative rooms, and gymnasiums but shared a library, auditorium, and courtyard.

The arrangement of the school grounds was a first for Elle. As she walked through the courtyard toward the library, she imagined the shared areas probably made for a cohesive student population and hoped the teachers would also convey a sense of community.

The library was large, clean, and organized. Elle navigated through the people milling around and chose a seat in the back of the room. She didn't quite know what to do, but her instinct was to take up as little space as possible. Other teachers didn't seem to share the feeling. They chatted animatedly, clearly catching up on their summer adventures. The cheerful faces were starting to help quell her intense desire to disappear when a voice made her jump.

"You must be the new middle school music teacher. I'm Mavis Worley." Mavis plopped into the seat next to Elle. She wore a floor-length black skirt, a black tank top beneath a lacy black shawl, and black combat boots. Her hair was short and bright pink. A silver hoop on the side of her highly arched left brow flashed in the light. You could say she stood out amongst the crowd.

"Correct. I'm Elle Foster. Nice to meet you, Mavis." She held out her hand to Mavis, who returned a placid handshake.

"How'd you know I was the music teacher?"

Mavis shrugged and said matter-of-factly, "Al was the one who retired last year." There was a beat of silence before she added, "Al Winters is the guy you're replacing."

Elle fiddled with the tote bag full of colorful wall hangings and supplies she'd stowed beneath her chair. "What do you teach?"

Mavis snickered. "They only let me dress this way because I'm the high school art teacher. I guess a certain amount of quirk is expected."

The response hit Elle awkwardly. "What does fashion have to do with anything?" Mavis shook her head and gestured toward the two men standing at the front of the room who were beginning the meeting. Elle recognized Steve Colton from his picture on the Everest Middle website. She assumed the other man must be the high school's principal.

Mavis confirmed this by leaning over and whispering,

"That's your principal, Steve, on the right. Mark is the high school principal on the left." Elle nodded.

The messaging was expected but dragged on and on. Steve and Mark talked about their excitement for the new year, the expectations and schedule for the rest of pre-planning, and legislative changes that affected what books were permissible in classroom libraries. They were about to dismiss for lunch, after which they would return to their classrooms to prepare individually when Steve started a drumroll with his hands against the nearest bookshelf. "Before we go to lunch, let me make the most exciting announcement of the day. Please welcome our new band director, Elle Foster. Elle, come on up here!"

Elle bit her lip and glanced at Mavis, who mouthed, "Good luck!" Then, she began to wind her way through the audience of teachers toward the front of the room. When she made it to the front, Steve said, "Now I know you all loved Al," someone coughed, "but Elle is going to do amazing things with our music program. Elle, why don't you tell us a little about yourself?"

The sea of teachers were silent and watchful. She waved to them. "Hello, I'm Elle. I'm a recent graduate of Penn State's Music School. I'm excited to be here in Everest. I'm passionate about music, but especially about teaching it in an accessible way. I have a few hobbies outside of work, but the major one is running. Let me know if anyone has a running group in the area!" She turned to Steve, hoping that was enough.

"Thanks, Elle. Derek, will you raise your hand, please?" There was movement on the right side of the room. Derek was pitched forward in his chair, his elbows resting on his legs, but straightened to raise his hand. His hair was dark and just long enough to look stylishly tousled. Even from a distance, Elle could tell he was among the younger teachers in the group, around her age and disarmingly handsome. Her breath caught in her chest, and she was suddenly grateful for the distance between them so he wouldn't know. "Derek Michaels over there is our high school director. He'll be showing you the ropes."

Mark dismissed them for lunch, and Elle returned to the back of the room to retrieve her bag before syncing up with Derek. Derek, however, must have had different plans because when she surveyed the room a short minute later, there was no sign of him. Momentary panic gave way to relief as a flash of pink caught her attention. She sped toward the color. "Hey, Mavis!" She stopped at her name. "Could you... show me where the music room is? It's my first time on campus, and I can't find Derek."

Mavis's face softened. "Of course. So this way exits out toward the high school side. If we head back to the library, we'll go the other way to the middle school. Follow me."

They exited the library to a covered sidewalk at the rear of the courtyard. Mavis explained the layout of the school as they went. "It's a big square. For the most part, each side is a mirror image of the other, like a Rorschach Test. The band rooms and the gyms are the two detached rooms. We'll take this sidewalk to go around the back." When they reached the other side of the building, Mavis pointed. "The first building is the band room, and the gym is the one beyond it towards the entrance. If you head further behind the school," they turned to the right, "those are the practice fields for football, track, and the marching band."

Elle thanked her for the tour, thinking they would part ways here, but Mavis accompanied her to the band room. She held her breath, wanting to commit this moment to memory, unlocked the door, and stepped in. All the chairs and music stands were pushed against the back wall along with a rough wooden platform. There was an amorphous vast black tarp covering something next to them. On the far left side were two doors; one was a small office with a window, and the other was a mystery. The dark brown carpet had long been defeated and was marred with copious stains. The walls were a drab eggshell, interrupted only by a zigzag pattern of square brown sound diffusers piled high with dust. It smelled of mildew.

Mavis scrunched her nose and retrieved a doorjamb to prop open the door. "That'll air it out a little."

Elle could feel her blood pumping through her. The room was dreary, but it was *her* room. She felt as if she could sense there had been music here. And she would continue that tradition! She almost skipped to the mysterious closed door. Opening it revealed a small area filled with filing cabinets of music. It was a mess. Scores were strewn on top of the cabinets, sheet music had fallen between them, and some even lay openly on the floor. She turned to Mavis, who was still standing by the door, and gestured for her to come over. "Do you want to eat lunch with me?"

They sat at the office desk and ate their packed meals. Mavis led the conversation. She had a knack for uncovering their shared similar interests. They learned they both enjoyed yoga and ramen. And though Mavis only read dark romance and Elle was dedicated to cozy romance, they both were fans of the genre at large.

They were laughing about Elle's move (now that it was behind her, driving the U-Haul struck her as much funnier) when Mavis asked, "Why did you want to move to Everest anyway? You could have gone anywhere."

Elle's smile faltered. Her country dream included finally making friendships, but she had long adopted the rule of not talking about her family. "It's been something I've wanted since I was a little kid. As long as I can remember." A half-truth.

Mavis seemed to detect there was more and said, "Maybe one day you'll tell me the whole story. I better get to my classroom. It was great to meet you." She got up and walked toward the door but paused and looked back. "Listen. It's tough to be new and… just… form your own opinions about things, okay? You know where to find me if you need anything." Her skirt swished out the door behind her.

If there was anything Elle knew how to do, it was how to be new. Still, it was good advice.

Derek hesitated, raising his hand to knock on the middle school band room door. He could tell Elle had been moving chairs and stands around, and the tarp had been taken off of the percussion instruments and folded up next to the timpani. He felt hot. Nervous. There was nothing to be done about it, however, so he rapped the knuckles of his still-raised hand against the open door.

He heard a fluttering paper sound, then a call, "Coming." The door to the music library opened wider, and Elle walked around the perimeter of the room toward him. The bouncy colored spiral ribbons clipped into her hair did nothing to ease his nerves. *Is she like this all the time? … Vibrant.* He stealthily wiped his clammy hands by putting them into his jeans pockets, then, as she approached, offered a handshake. "Hi, Ms. Foster, uh, Elle. I'm Derek Michaels, the high school director. I guess Steve said I should help you out. Um, you know that." He paused and broke the handshake. He could not remember giving a more awkward introduction. He swallowed and continued, "I'm sorry, I'm bad at this."

The admission made Elle smile, at least. One side of her mouth went higher than the other, and something fluttered in Derek's chest. She replied, "It's okay. Good to meet you, Derek. Welcome to my castle." She swept her hand behind her, indicating the room. "Do come in. I've been trying to organize the sheet music. There's a first question for you; I noticed we don't have anything in grade 3. Would the more challenging pieces be somewhere else?"

Derek had been walking behind her but stopped in his tracks. "You want grade 3 for middle school? Isn't that too advanced?"

Elle frowned. "The 8th-grade band could start to tackle grade 3 by the end of the year. Especially those wanting to continue into high school, don't you think? I mean, they won't be perfect, maybe, but it's something I hope to expose them to." Derek ran his hand through his hair, unsure how to answer. From what he had observed, that level of difficulty would only frustrate any fledgling musician. Elle continued, "We can talk about that later. What should I be working on? What can you tell me about the middle school band's history? I'd love to know how our bands work together."

This was the conversation he came hoping to have, and it was comfortable talking about things as they were. He sat in one of the student chairs, propping his right ankle on his left knee. "We're proud of our traditions. Everest High has been awarded superior ratings in marching and concert performances for the past 20 years straight. Your band is an important part of that equation, being the main feeder into the high school."

"Congratulations, that's quite the accomplishment." Elle had taken the seat next to him and was leaning in toward him. He could see the freckling across her cheeks and nose and dismissed the absurd idea of counting them.

"Thank you. We work hard for it. As for working together, we have been hosting our concerts together throughout the year. We have one before Christmas and another before we let out for summer."

Elle ticked off on her fingers as she spoke, "A holiday

concert and a summer celebration. Sounds amazing. Maybe we can come up with a fun theme together for them."

"Yeah. Besides that, you vet the band membership, so we have the best players coming over."

Elle cocked her head to the side, causing her curls and the spiraling ribbons to bounce. "What do you mean?"

"I can help you with it. It's no big deal. Basically, at the end of the year, you visit the elementary school and talk to the 5th graders. Make a little presentation about being in band and instruments, then give them a pitch test so you let in the people who are promising up-and-comers. Then you'll assess your 8th-grade bunch and recommend who should...." Derek pulled back at Elle's glowering expression. "What?"

She swallowed and focused on a stained bit of carpet before responding. "I can assure you I will be doing no such thing. Any child who wants to join my band will join. A pitch test? For untrained 5th graders?"

Derek pulled back further in his chair. "Whoa, whoa. This has been how we've always done it, and it's never been an issue."

Her eyes hardened as they met his. "It's an issue for me. And it should be an issue for you. You would deny a student who wanted to learn about music? Kids *need* band."

An unsettling memory emerged in Derek's mind, but he pushed it down. "I have to ensure the legacy of Everest High continues. I'm not sure you understand how important it is." The words coming from his mouth felt foreign, as if they weren't his own.

Elle jumped up from her seat, her face red. "Your legacy will take care of itself. Don't you believe in your ability to teach? What's your educational philosophy anyway?!"

Derek stood. He was much taller than Elle. This had all gone terribly wrong. "My philosophy is keeping our program funded! Besides, you have to have a way to weed out students;

you'd have too many. Not to mention, many of our families can't afford instruments around here in the first place! How will you manage a band without instruments?"

"I guess it's my job to figure it out, and that's no philosophy I've ever heard of. Utilitarian, Praxial, and Aesthetic. These philosophies are different, but they all agree music is for everyone who wants it. Maybe you should read about it."

Derek blinked, stunned, then started walking to the door. Guilt tethered him after a few steps, and he turned to see Elle wiping the corner of her eye. "This isn't how I wanted this to go."

Elle lifted her head. "Me either."

Derek intended to write his lesson plans before the school day ended but was getting nowhere. Now that he was back at his desk and relieved from the confrontation with Elle, it was his own recollections that continued the assault. Memories of his beginnings at Everest High kept thrusting themselves into the spotlight. Hadn't he questioned Al's onboarding practices? He distinctly recalled telling Al that he would take any incoming freshman interested in joining the band and how Al had tisked at him, waving a finger in the air, as if he was a toddler who didn't know better. Hadn't he gone into Music Education because he wanted to share the experience of music with others? And why couldn't he remember any of those damn philosophies?

He stood from his office chair in frustration, causing it to spin wildly behind him. He was uncomfortable by so many of his emotions today, and it was time to go home. He grabbed his bag when he heard the familiar swoosh sound of an incoming email. His face paled as he read through it.

. . .

Derek,

Thank you for our illuminating conversation today.

I will be outlining and deploying a more inclusive onboarding experience at Everest Middle beginning immediately. I'm letting you know this in the spirit of working together, which we will need to do despite any disagreement we may have.

Please rest assured that I, too, value the ability of our students to perform at a Superior level and will do my part to contribute toward that goal.

Regards,
Elle Foster

It was clear Elle thought he was a monster.

Elle sat at the wobbly kitchen table, staring at the long list of things needing to be done on the refrigerator. Considering how her first day had gone, she wasn't sure she would ever have time to get to those ideas for her home. Now she was faced with all the usual responsibilities of pre-planning but also the less typical needs to clean a carpet, organize a music library, research and apply for grants, create a new outreach and graduate system for her students, and (hopefully) find some way to open up spots to at least the incoming 6th graders this year.

Maybe if she acted early, she could pull in every student who had shown interest now instead of waiting until next year. That would benefit the students but also give her a chance to prove to Derek that her idea would work before she had to recruit. Ugh, and she had angry cried in front of him as their first interaction!

She sighed. For a brief moment in their morning kick-off meeting when she first laid eyes on Derek, images of Hallmark romances tickled her mind. She was the city girl who moved to the country, and he was the handsome gentleman who swept her off her feet. So much for that fantasy. She may be the misplaced city girl, but Derek was the obstinate villain for her to overcome.

Back to reality, Elle. She shook her head to clear it. It would have to be grants first. The number of loaner instruments would directly inform how many students she could support. Elle opened her laptop and started learning all she could about music grants and grant writing while jotting down her own ideas about how to open the doors to her classroom.

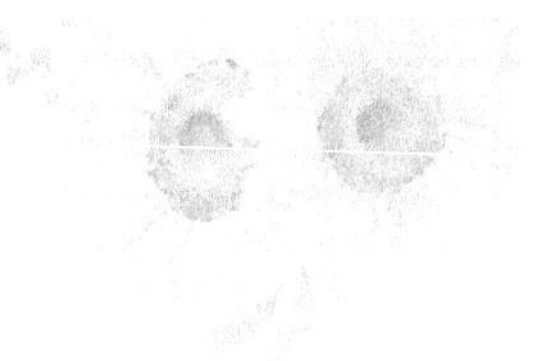

Four

DRILL - THE STEPS AND POSITIONS THAT MAKE
UP THE MARCHING BAND SHOW.

Elle was repulsed by the taste of her instant coffee. She hadn't been able to purchase a percolator yet, so it was instant or nothing for now, and she needed to be sharp after the late-night building of a slide deck. It outlined her most time-sensitive desire for an open-door policy. She took another sip of coffee, grimaced, and flipped through the slides. They were simple, yet she felt the visual guide strengthened the presentation she hoped to deliver to Steve. She gulped the dregs with a frown and placed the mug on the counter harder than intended before grabbing her tote and heading to school.

Steve was sitting behind the desk in his office when Elle knocked on the doorframe. He looked up with a smile and gestured at the seat across from him. "Good morning, my newest educator. How are you?"

Elle answered, "Good morning! I'm doing okay, but I do have some concerns I want to discuss with you about the band. I have a brief proposal, actually. Could I schedule some time with you?"

"A proposal! Oh my, so formal," He checked the clock, "We have some time now."

Elle sat and retrieved her laptop from the bag. She opened it to the presentation, arranging the computer screen so it mostly faced Steve. "It's come to my attention that our onboarding process involves testing untrained 5th graders and inviting only those who perform highly enough to join the band. This is incongruous with my mission as a Music Educator. Any child who wants to learn about music should be able to, and I want to make that possible."

Steve's expression was unreadable, but he nodded for her to continue.

She clicked to change the slide. "My plan is threefold. The first point is here," she indicated the screen, "Apply to grants. I understand we don't currently have instruments to loan, and not all families can afford the investment. I have already started research in this area and have located several grants I can apply to. If we are awarded a grant, this will ensure I can support more students. Some of my reading suggests that grants go unapplied for, so I'll be submitting to any I can find."

Steve remained silent but listened.

Elle moved the presentation forward. "The second point is the failsafe. Even if we're not awarded a grant for instruments, I am fully qualified to teach in the Kodály Method, which recognizes voice as 'The most natural instrument and one which every person possesses.' I could do this by forming a choir or even in combined classes. The strategy would depend on several things, but we have this to rely on."

She didn't wait for Steve's cue to progress but moved along on her own. "My real ask is the third point. I understand the headcount for my 6th-grade classes is already set. I would like to reopen the door to that grade to all interested people so we can start this method now instead of waiting until next year. I will do all the labor for this effort. I'll email the parents and collect responses. I'll even reprogram the student's schedules if someone can teach me how to do it in the system...."

Laughter halted Elle, and she reluctantly looked up at Steve. He held his fingers pressed together in front of his mouth, giggling to himself. "I'm sorry, I mean no disrespect. I just imagined how the other directors would react. Boy howdy. I can tell you're going to shake things up." His face became more serious, and he cleared his throat before continuing. "Elle. This is your band. You should run it how you see fit. Be sure you're keeping Derek informed and own your business. And please, *please,* don't mess with the student's schedules. Lettie will kill me."

Elle wasn't sure what she expected, but it hadn't been this. She got up to collect her laptop, muttering her thanks.

"And Elle?" She paused zipping her bag. "I haven't had a teacher write for a grant in a long time. Try to keep that spark." She turned with a shy smile and scurried to the library.

Mavis sat in the back of the room again, easy to spot by the bright shock of pink. Elle claimed the seat beside her, trying not to look too pleased. An attempt she must have failed at judging from Mavis's greeting. "You look like the cat who got the cream. Feeling good after day one?"

Elle strummed her fingers against each other in front of her face and put on her best evil villain look. "Steve agreed to let me invite any incoming 6th grader interested in joining the band. I didn't think he'd approve, but he said I should own the operations as long as I keep *Derek* informed." She spoke his name with venom.

Mavis was nodding appreciatively but stopped at the attitude. "Something happened with Derek?"

"Let's put it this way: Derek is more concerned about his band's performance ratings than about music education."

"I thought Derek would be the least of...." but whatever

Mavis was going to say was cut off by Steve's day two icebreaker.

Once again, the meeting seemed to drag on forever, and Elle's knee was bouncing up and down by the end. Her ever-growing list of to-dos making her impatient.

When they finally dismissed, Elle returned to the admin building. She had permission to contact parents but not a clue as to how.

An older woman with short, curly hair sat behind the front desk. "Uh, hello. I'm Elle Foster, the new band director. I think I may need some help."

The woman stood up and gave Elle her complete attention. She spoke with a wizened twang. "Elle, it's so good to meet you. New and needing help, bless your heart! I'm Lettie, and I know everybody. If I can't help you, I'll be able to point you to someone who can. I'm sure of it." Lettie gave off an aura of warmth, making a smile tug at Elle's lips as she spoke.

"Thank you so much, Lettie! I need to reach out to the parents of all the incoming 6th graders who aren't enrolled in band, but I don't have their contact information."

Lettie lowered herself back into her chair stiffly and rolled toward the computer. She began talking to herself, "Let's see here. I see the band students; let's eliminate them, then we'll grab the rest, and voila!" She turned toward Elle. "I'm emailing you the bunch. Good luck!"

"Thanks so much. You're a lifesaver!"

Elle exited the office and saw movement out of her left periphery. Someone tall was entering the high school admin door. She turned her head to see Derek. They both froze in their tracks, and time hung for a moment. Elle felt a savage pleasure that she was undermining his backward onboarding plans, and another grin crept up her face, this one smug. She had the slightest impression Derek reached his arm toward her as she walked away.

Elle left at the end of the day feeling proud about her productivity. She had emailed contacts for almost the entire class and called the rest asking about their child's interest in the band, completed the library cleanup, and started applying for grants. Yes, there was much left to do, but achieving so much was a relief. She hadn't spoken to Derek yet, as she intended to loop him in once her plan was complete. Or at least when she received numerous requests from all the new students who would be joining.

Derek settled into his stance, imagined the rhythm of the motion, and then swung his 7 iron. About 140 yards. Not bad, but Greg would take the piss out of him anyway.

"That's all you've got, Michaels? Let a real man show you how it's done." Greg rocked from one foot to another, took aim, and launched his golf ball with a fluid swing. The ball settled a few yards beyond Derek's. Greg celebrated by pumping a fist in the air. "Hope you're takin' notes, 'cause that's it." He high-fived the rest of the Band Misters.

The Band Misters was a self-assigned name that the directors in the area affectionately called themselves. Greg Howard and Matt Norris were the directors from the town of Darton, and Billy Thompson and Chuck Franklin were from Stoville. Derek and Al represented Everest, until Al retired. The group pre-dated Derek's arrival at Everest, and he suspected it had been going on for a long time. The six of them were the only music educators within a 50-mile radius. They met every other week at The Drive, a small driving range on the outskirts of Everest, to talk shop and blow off steam and occasionally went out on the greens for a full game. None of them were remarkably talented, but golf was an ideal sport for conversation.

"Got your marching drills set, Greg, Billy?" Derek asked.

The high school directors developed their drills during summer because Band Camp was held during pre-planning.

Billy answered, "Yep, going with a patriotic theme. I'm hoping to have at least one girl on rifle this year. They'll all want the flag, I know it." He shook his head.

Greg chuckled. "Simple. Tell the most talented one they have to do rifle. It's more challenging; it'll be a compliment to them." Billy frowned and moved his head back and forth, considering. Greg answered, "I'm doing Grease. What about you, D?"

"I'm doing Aliens as a theme. I've got some formations and one part for the color guard where the flags signify abduction that I'm excited about."

Greg sniffed. "I've never heard of an Alien theme," he elbowed Derek's rib, "You aren't afraid to send the wrong message about immigration, are ya?" Derek swallowed and waved him off while the rest of the men sniggered. Greg's company, these meetings, were entirely draining.

Matt took a swing with his pitching wedge but wasn't impressed with the outcome and spat on the ground. "I'm just gearing up to hear the squeaking and squawking from the 6th graders." Chuck pointed at him with an intense stare.

"Speaking of middle school. How's the new girl, Derek?" Greg questioned.

"She's... different."

Billy grinned. "I imagine she isn't like Al. Probably easier on the eyes, too."

Derek shrugged. "She's changing how we select for beginner band. I tried to teach her how we do it. Why we have this method, but she got upset...."

"Ah, let me guess!" Greg interrupted. "She wants to teach everyone the joy of music? Hah! You've got to recognize who has talent, and that ain't everyone."

"I don't see how I have much say in the matter. I've heard she's already contacted all the 6th-grade families to offer them a spot."

"You're gonna let her ruin your band? Roll over?" The other men watched them talk.

"No, I'll figure something out. It's just, the middle school is her band, you know?"

"Maybe she'll get abducted by aliens." Greg gave him a blank stare.

Derek cleared his throat. He needed to ask something he wasn't looking forward to. "I was thinking... I should invite her to join us?" It came out as a question, less assertive than he intended.

Greg laughed so loudly that other Drive patrons turned their attention to him. The rest of the men joined in, Derek last. When Greg caught his breath, he said, "That's a good one, Derek. Can you imagine?!"

"No, I guess not." It was true. Even from his one encounter with her, he couldn't imagine Elle getting along well with the men. It would be a kindness to keep her away from it, yet he felt guilty about excluding her from a group she should belong to.

Elle woke in a sweat, writhing to get out of her bedsheets. New places often disturbed her sleep, though she had hoped to skip this part of adjusting. She sat on the side of her bed, head in hands, willing her body to calm.

It's different this time. You're finally here, building something. Elle pushed herself out of bed and padded out to the porch. The screen door creaked as it swung forward to admit her, and the warm night air rushed upon her in a caress. It was quiet, but as she sat with the silence, her ears began picking up on smaller sounds. An owl hooted. There was rustling in the direction of the woods, some small animal moving, perhaps the owl's future meal. A truck trundled along the dirt road as it slowly drove by. She closed her eyes and let the sounds soothe her.

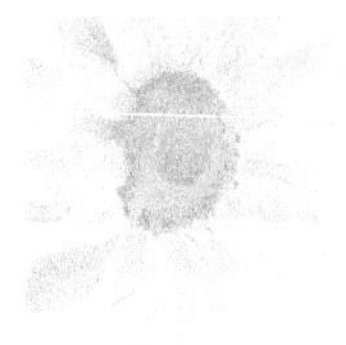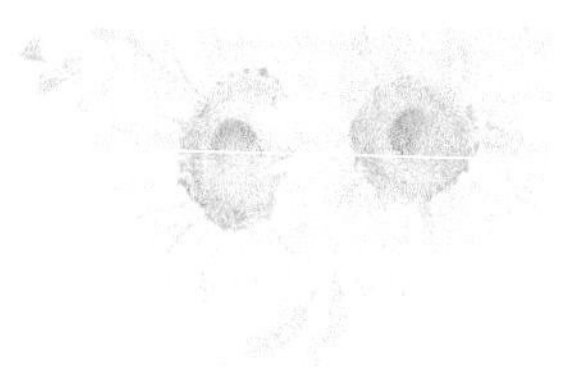

Five

AMERICAN BANDMASTERS ASSOCIATION - AN
ORGANIZATION FORMED IN 1929 TO PROMOTE
CONCERT BAND MUSIC.

Elle had run all the way from her house to downtown. Her hair was up in a messy bun, and she wore her favorite purple running shorts and matching sports bra. She had taken to running more than ever. It had always been her sport of choice, but now it was a daily event of greater and greater distances. She was vaguely aware it was problematic. Rest days were just as important as on ones, and she knew this was her go-to behavior when loneliness set in.

Today, Tiny's Cafe was Elle's destination, and it was right around the corner. She slowed to a walk and inspected herself for presentableness. Her hair felt heavy, so she took it down and flipped it over her head to air out the nape of her neck. When she flipped it back up to retie a ponytail, her vision fell on a man across the street leering at her. He put his hand to his mouth and cat-called. It wasn't in her head this time. Objectified and creeped out, she hastened into the cafe.

Jingling bells hanging from the door handle tinkled sweetly, announcing her entry. It was quiet except for the background music. Despite its low volume, Elle instantly followed the rhythms and progressions in her mind. It sounded like World music, yet it was also new; several different cultural instruments were used. A bubbly bleach blonde with two dimple piercings and heavy eyeliner popped her head up from behind the counter. "It's you! Elle, right?"

Elle shook off the momentary stun of being addressed by a stranger. "What? I mean, yes, but I'm sorry, have we met?"

"Oh no," she laughed, "I'm so sorry, what a weird way to meet someone. I knew it must be you because of the nose. I love your ring, by the way. I'm Sunny, but everyone calls me Tiny."

"This is your cafe, then? Nice to meet you. Um, how did my nose ring give me away?"

"Ah, there are only three people in Everest with a facial piercing. Word gets around, I guess."

"Word about... piercings?"

Tiny nodded emphatically. "And how you dress, and where you're from, and how you invited all the students to join the band. You're my hero!" Elle stared ahead, not knowing how to react. Tiny must have detected it and said, "Don't feel bad. This town talks about anything even the slightest bit different or new. You should have been here for the drama of summer 2010!... Anyway, what can I get you?"

Elle's eyes cast to the chalkboard menu on the wall. "A coconut latte, please."

Tiny bustled about making the drink. Elle couldn't decide if taking a seat or waiting at the counter was more polite since she was the only customer. After glancing around, she decided staying was best. "Hey, what is this music playing?"

A toothy smile stretched across Tiny's face. "It's Balkan Beat Box. They're one of my favorite bands. Good, isn't it?"

"I love it. I can't stop listening. Thanks, I'll definitely be looking them up."

Tiny set the cup she was using into a saucer and balanced it over to Elle. "Here you go. I hope you like it."

"Thank you." Elle took the saucer and chose a table in the corner. She closed her eyes and focused on the syncopated rhythms and instrumentation. Strangers knew who she was based on her nose ring and wardrobe. It was a little disturbing. In the city she was part of the crowd, as anonymous and inconsequential as anyone else. It was a comfort compared to this new reality of being known without knowing anyone else. She didn't prefer the spotlight feeling. Even more worrying, it was because she had a dainty nose piercing and she-didn't-know-what about her clothes. True, she enjoyed a little flair but wasn't too far down the rabbit hole.

Elle thanked Tiny on the way out and ran back to her house. She didn't encounter another person enjoying the downtown and hated that she was grateful for it. Imagined or not, she was tired of the stares.

By the last Thursday of pre-planning, Elle had received signups from 10 additional students interested in 6th-grade band! It was a huge accomplishment; she was flying high even through the mundane task of opening mail. She ripped open a heavy brown envelope and leapt from her chair. This couldn't be real, yet reading and re-reading the opening line didn't cause the words to change. *The American Country Music Lifting Lives grant is pleased to award Everest Middle School a gift of $10,000 to apply toward the purchase of musical instruments.*

Elle felt as if she was out of her body. She never expected to hear back so soon and hadn't counted on actually being awarded anything! A manic sound escaped her as she realized that restructuring her lesson plans for the year would be necessary. More work, but worth it. She flipped through the rest of the information packet, noting what actions to take. With

$10,000, she could secure loaner instruments for multiple grade levels. Her throat constricted at the idea.

Itching to share the good news with someone, she thought of Mavis and began the trek toward the High School. The sound of music caught her attention, however, and curiosity led her up the hill behind the school to the practice field.

Derek had his band in a block formation and stood beside the drum major, a student conductor. They were playing simple scales to warm up. Still, Elle was immediately impressed with the richness of their sound and how crisply they began and ended notes together.

"Get in formation, Toby. You're late!" Derek gave a genial shout without turning around. When Toby didn't emerge, he looked over his shoulder to find Elle standing stock still. It was strangely quiet since the band had stopped playing. "You're not Toby." Elle shook her head, embarrassed to have been caught watching.

Derek turned to the band, still at attention in their block, "Everyone, meet Ms. Foster. She's our new Middle School director." Nobody moved. "At ease." Motion waved through the block as instruments dropped to their sides and feet spread apart. "Do I need to conduct a greeting or what?" Derek lifted his hand as if to cue them, causing some laughter and a disorganized smattering of heys and hellos.

Elle waved. "It's nice to meet you, too! I didn't mean to interrupt your practice. I'm sorry, I must say you sound great. I'll let you get back to it." She turned to walk back down the hill, but Derek's warm voice stopped her. "You can't come up here and expect us not to show off a little." He turned toward his students, "What do you think? Can we show her the first piece?" They cheered and nodded before scurrying to their positions on the field. Derek beckoned Elle to follow him as he climbed the five rungs to a small platform at the front of the 50-yard line.

As the drum major raised his hands, each person on the field snapped to attention. He cued their start, and Elle's mouth physically fell open when the small band began playing Mussorgsky's Night on Bald Mountain. This wasn't anything she would have expected to hear from a marching band. She glanced sideways at Derek, who caught the look and grinned. Elle figured it must have been about 18 measures of the classic piece before the drum and bass line led the transition into Intergalactic by the Beastie Boys. When the change occurred, a laugh erupted from Elle, and she turned to face Derek, who she already knew was staring at her, awaiting her reaction.

"This is brilliant. So unexpected!" She couldn't help but smile.

Derek nodded his thanks. "Wait until you see the choreography come together. We've got some places to sharpen up, but we're only five days in." He pointed out to the field, and Elle let her eyes follow. "Those are supposed to be Galaga-inspired aliens."

"I totally see it! Derek, this is an amazing show. I've never seen anything like it before. Who did the design?"

"I did." He had a way of letting emotion shine through his eyes. There was pure pride there.

"You did." Elle's stomach twisted. A few minutes before, she had been excited about her grant acceptance. *Mainly* because it meant a wealth of opportunities for her students, but there was another small part defiantly delighted to prove Derek wrong. Seeing him lead his students felt incongruous with the Derek in her mind. These kids were great musicians and clearly loved and respected him. If he was exclusively concerned with ratings, would he also be able to build this culture?

The piece ended. Derek stepped to the platform's edge and called out, "That was the best run yet. I can tell you wanted to impress Ms. Foster." Even from a distance, Elle saw a few smirks on the field. She thanked Derek, waved at the band, and hastily returned to the school as he continued to give them feedback.

The unexpected detour had taken so long that instead of seeking out Mavis during the day, she emailed asking if they might meet up later. The reply came back almost immediately, suggesting a drink at a place called County Line.

Elle assumed County Line would be somewhere in the commercial area of town, where most of the other restaurants were. Instead, she found herself pulling into a singular building well away from anything else. She worried it wasn't the right location until spying the small, worn sign bearing the name. It appeared to be hand-painted and was so weathered the blue color used for the lettering was barely apparent.

The inside was dark, and Elle let her eyes adjust to the conditions briefly before taking in the scene. There was a bar, a small stage for performers, and various tables across the room, only two of which were occupied. Mavis waved from the first table and Elle walked over to join her, noting her shoes seemed to stick to the floor.

"You found it!" Mavis said in greeting, "I've got us some sours coming. Hope you like it. This is the one place around with a full bar, and they have some more adventurous beers."

Elle squinted and cocked her head slightly to the side in question. "There are no other bars?"

"That's why it's called County Line. Everest is in a dry county. Nobody can sell liquor, and no beer or wine on Sundays. Everyone gets around it by driving to the next counties over to drink."

"Doesn't that lead to *more* drunk driving?" Elle asked.

Mavis snorted, her eyes crinkling at the corners. "Of course it does!" Her face became serious suddenly, and she added, "Sorry, I shouldn't laugh about it. It's just one of those absurd things. I have to laugh so I don't cry."

Elle shook her head. "No, I know that feeling." A waitress swept past and placed their bottles on the table. "Thanks for coming out with me. I got some exciting news and needed to share it with someone."

"Oh?" Mavis asked.

At that moment, a strange movement caught Elle's attention from the other occupied table. She leaned in closer to Mavis and lowered her voice. "Those people threw something on the ground. On purpose!"

Mavis smirked and wordlessly got up and walked to the bar. She returned with a small bowl of peanuts, set them on the table between them, and shelled one to eat, discarding the shell on the floor.

Elle scrunched her nose. "So this is some sort of local thing then, I take it? I never imagined there would be so much to learn!" She reached out to grab a peanut and hesitantly threw the shell on the floor. "It doesn't feel right."

Mavis ruffled a hand through her short pink hair. "I think it's cathartic. We try to keep things so clean and orderly all the time. Tossing things on the floor is rebellious and free," she tossed another shell. "But don't keep me waiting. What news?"

The story surged from Elle. She shared about the ten new students who had joined the beginner band, being awarded the grant for instruments, having to rewrite her lesson plans, and all the other things still on her agenda, including cleaning the carpet. The more she shared, the easier it was to keep going. It was also getting easier to toss the peanut shells on the floor. She was surprised when her fingers scraped the bottom of the bowl.

"Congratulations on everything. It's impressive you've been here for such a short period and made so much traction.

School hasn't even started yet! Have you had much time to do anything else? Probably not, I guess."

Elle sat her beer back on the table and spun it in her hands. "Not too much. I've been running a lot. I checked out Tiny's Cafe, and it's weird, but she knew me already, or of me, I guess."

Mavis sighed. "You'll get used to it, and honestly, it will die down. Something will happen, or another new person will move here, and people will want to discuss that instead of you. I confess, in the case of Tiny, it may have been because of me. She's my bestie."

"Did this happen to you too, when you moved here? Why is it breaking news about piercings and what's wrong with how I dress? I don't get any of this."

"Oh, it happened to me. When I came here, it was shocking to the locals that I always wear black." She leaned back and indicated her tank top and jeans. "The talk of the town was that I was some sort of cultist. I remember one of the churches called me out in a Sunday service, saying I was a 'pathway towards Satan' and that any child in my class was at risk. It was... challenging. I almost left."

"Geez, I'm so sorry, Mavis. I can't even imagine."

"It's okay. They didn't beat me. No matter where you are, there'll be people who love you and people who don't. It's no different here. Only smaller, so it can feel sharp sometimes. Hang out long enough to learn who is who and to find your people, and you've got it made. I remember when I met Tiny. It was friends at first sight."

"You're the third person with piercings! I can't believe I didn't put it together before!"

Mavis made an exaggerated shrug. "I mayyyy have been the person who told Tiny there was another teacher with a nose ring. I promise it was in a good way, though! How's it going with Derek?"

Elle huffed. "Honestly, I don't know. He made me so angry when I met him. Then I saw him with the marching band earlier today, and they're so good! I'm not saying they wouldn't be if he had an open acceptance policy, but they seem to have a great relationship."

"Hmm. I've long suspected that Derek is... no offense to him because it's hard, but kind of a victim of his circumstances? The BMs are ridiculous. I don't envy him or you."

"Hah!" Elle laughed. "The BMs? Time to rethink the name."

"Well, they don't call themselves that exactly. It's the Band Misters. All the local band directors have this sort of little group. I thought you'd know by now?"

"Wow. Okay." Elle swigged from her bottle, "After the Band Masters Association but gender exclusive. Amazing. Guess I know why I haven't been invited." Hot anger reached her face, and her eyes watered. Elle hated her body for its propensity to cry when angry. She spat, "I'll have to introduce myself."

Mavis began to speak, hesitated, then offered, "I get you should be a part of this group, but you aren't missing out. Trust me. It might be better to keep your distance."

Elle shook her head. "These are my peers. Even if I don't fit in, I need to have a working relationship with them. They'll have to tell me to my face if they don't want me around."

Mavis puffed her cheeks, resigned. "They meet at the driving range most Thursdays. Do with that what you will, but be careful."

"Today is Thursday!" Mavis looked wary, but Elle drove on, "I can go now and just be super chill and introduce myself. That's all."

. . .

They exchanged numbers. Mavis suggested they get together at Tiny's some time and wished her luck. Then Elle found herself following Google Maps directions to The Drive. To her dismay, it was a short distance away. Not much time to think about what she wanted to say.

The parking lot at The Drive was a simple field shorn down from vehicle activity. Elle parked on the farthest side of the lot and tried to imagine how to introduce herself. If it were anywhere else, she might've simply been there by happenstance, which would feel more natural, but Elle knew nothing about golf and didn't dare try to fake it. Doubts raced through her mind. *Will they think I'm desperate or childish if I do this? Maybe Mavis is right.* She exhaled and opened the car door, unsticking her legs from the pleather as she exited. Projecting confidence would be key. They would respect her for making the introduction, which would start a great relationship.

Elle ran through scenarios in her mind on the way to the range. Derek would be there, so maybe she could greet him and ask for an introduction. Or she could simply say, 'Hi, I'm Elle, the new director at Everest Middle. I heard you might be here and wanted to meet my fellow directors.' Yes. That was it. It was straightforward, confident, and friendly. An ideal opener. Things would be easier when they saw she was genuinely interested in being a part of their team. Plus, she was on a roll today!

The driving range was a stretch of stations with groups of people huddled around each one. Each station had a paved section covered by an awning and a slightly raised platform from which people were golfing in front. The field they swung into was nearly identical to all the golfing courses Elle had ever seen. Green grass, man-made hills, and a few sandy spaces were accounted for. Yard markers and targets scattered about were the only differences. There didn't appear to be a place to buy tickets or check in, so Elle continued walking behind the stations hoping to find Derek.

Derek stood in the shade of the shelter between Chuck and Greg. Billy restocked their golf balls, pouring a bucket of them into a hidden compartment next to the tee. Greg was talking across him to Matt, but Derek was hardly paying attention. He kept replaying the memory of Elle smiling her lopsided grin and saying, "You did," when he told her he had plotted his band's performance. She was impressed, and that face she made… He couldn't get it out of his head. Didn't want to.

He used his forearm to wipe his brow, and suddenly, Elle was in front of him. For a crazed half a second he thought he was hallucinating but acted anyway, reaching out to grab her elbow and pulling her hard toward him.

"OW! What are you doing?!" Elle pushed away from him, startled.

"You were too close to the green," He pointed behind her, "Billy was swinging. You nearly got hit!" His heart raced. It had been a near miss.

They were both flushed. Elle only broke her glare at him when Greg spoke, "Well, well, well, who do we have here? Someone, you know, Derek?"

Shit. Why was Elle here? "Yes, actually. This is Elle Foster. She's the new director at Everest Middle." The cat-like grin that stretched across Greg's lips left an ominous feeling in Derek.

"Ah! We've heard so much about you," Greg winked at Derek, "your *unique* style." Elle looked from Derek to Greg. Derek tried to shake his head imperceptibly at Elle, but she didn't see it.

Derek cleared his throat to bring the attention to him.

"Elle, let me introduce everyone. This is Greg; he's Darton's high school director and Matt over here is with Darton Middle. Billy and Chuck are the directors in Stoville."

Elle shook hands with each of them as Derek made the rounds. "It's nice to meet all of you. When I heard you all met up here, I thought I should come to introduce myself. I'd love to get to know you all more."

Matt and Billy were observing anything but Elle while Chuck stared at her silently. Greg replied, "Always a pleasure to meet such a beautiful little lady."

Elle stiffened and seemed to choose her words carefully. "Thanks. Um, I'd like to be included in some of your get-togethers. If you're talking about our bands, I mean, I could learn from you and share...." She sputtered to an end, watching Greg shake his head.

"Well, honey, I can tell you don't know how to golf. It'd be boring for you to join us and downright impossible out on the greens. You don't want to slow us down, do ya?"

Elle shot a glance at Derek before swallowing and responding, "Surely there's a way for us to collaborate that doesn't involve me holding you up."

"Sure. Let's see what you've got." Greg extended his club to her. "You're a *modern woman*; maybe you can keep up after all."

Derek glared at Greg, "No. Greg. This is too much." But Elle had taken the club and was rolling it over in her hands.

"Go ahead, darlin', you take the next tee."

Elle stepped up to the platform. It was painful to watch. She lifted the club awkwardly, swung, and missed.

"Whiff!" Cried Greg, "Try again. It's a mulligan."

Elle backed the club up again, swung, and hit the tip of the ball, causing it to bounce a few feet forward.

"Dribbler! Too bad." Greg stepped on the platform to reclaim his 3 iron. Without a word, he swung and connected with the ball in one polished motion. The ball soared through the air and landed shy of the 200-yard mark. He lifted his club in the air victoriously. "That's how it's done!" Elle had backed into the far corner of their station, arms crossed. Greg turned toward her. "Maybe we can talk some more when you reach 150 yards." Elle didn't reply but walked away. "Hey, where ya going?!"

Derek closed his eyes tight. *Greg is the epitome of toxic masculinity. I hate being around these guys.*

"What's that face for?" Greg questioned Derek. Derek opened his eyes and shook his head. "You're up."

Six

MI - THE THIRD TONE OF A MAJOR SCALE.

E lle felt a surge of pride and energy reflecting on her first week of school. True, she had stayed late nearly every day, didn't yet have the instruments she needed for the 6th-grade class, still hadn't cleaned that damned carpet, and her to-do list continued to grow at an alarming rate. Other highlights offset those concerns, though.

Her students were wonderful. Elle could tell! After setting expectations, she got them straight to work to establish their routine. In the 6th-grade class, she played examples of what each beginner instrument sounded like so students could gauge their interest in what they wanted to play and introduced solfeggio so they could get used to reading music and basic rhythms. Her 7th and 8th-grade classes, while musically rusty from the summer vacation (it was clear many of them forgot to practice), blew her away with their wit. In a particular 8th-grade class, a student named Willa confused Elle by asking her to put a fermata over an E note on the whiteboard. Elle drew the fermata over the E, turned to face Willa, and asked, "Like that?" Only to find Willa dramatically fainting in her chair, wrist to her forehead, whispering, "Hold mi!" The entire class was in hysterics.

While the instruments weren't delivered yet, Elle had ordered them late Thursday night. It took hours of careful consideration to build the cart with the most cost-effective solutions that fit the band's needs, had lasting power, and weren't back-ordered. She had never pulled the trigger on a more expensive order, and submitting the purchase was surreal.

The other event of note was related to the High School's marching band. Derek's band. Friday evening, as Elle departed, she saw a scrawny frame running up the hill, trombone glinting in the sunlight. Snagged again by curiosity about how the group progressed, she trudged up to the field.

"Toby! Let me know when you'll start getting here on time, will you? Actually, everyone give me 10 pushups. Let this be encouragement to Toby." Derek delivered the orders in a serious but jovial way. Again, Elle was impressed by his relationship with his students. All of them groaned but lowered themselves to the ground.

Recalling that hiding her presence had not worked out last time, Elle announced herself. "Hey, thought I'd check on how the show was coming along."

Derek turned to her briefly. "Hi." He chewed his lip while watching the band complete their pushups and return to their feet.

It was the first time she had seen him since fleeing The Drive. *This is awkward. Is he going to say anything else? Should I leave?*

"We have a guest with us! Can we show her our 2nd piece?" Derek called to the band instead of speaking to Elle. This time, the students seemed less confident. "Come on, gang, we can do it. First position for ET. Let's go!"

Derek finally broke his silence toward Elle as the students

scattered to their marks. He addressed her warmly, "I'm glad you came to check."

Elle followed Derek and the drum major onto the platform. The drum major gave the downbeat. For the second time, Elle was shocked at their rehearsal. The rhythm of Katy Perry's ET began, marching tenor drums leading and winds picking up the melody. The musicality was brilliant, and their marching was clean... until it wasn't.

Derek waved his hands. "Stop, stop! We still aren't getting to our marks in measure 35. Can we practice 30-35 again?"

The band replayed the segment but without improvement. The drill moved them from a small clustered group to a large arch. The people backing into the arch had to glide to their position, and they were struggling with the distance. On the third attempt, when it was clear they would still not reach the formation, Elle had an idea. "Hey, Derek. Not to intrude, but I think they just need to focus on their power muscles."

Derek nodded and stepped to his left, clearing space for Elle to move beside him. "Listen to Ms. Foster, please."

"Oh no, I didn't mean..."

"Elle, please help," There was a note of desperation in his voice, "We've been working on this all week."

She reluctantly stepped to the front of the platform. "Um. So, back row, the people who are gliding backward. You've got a long way to go; it's not easy. I think some of you aren't thinking about *how* you get there, and by that, I mean what muscles you have to use. So, I guess first, let's try this. We'll make the same move but try to go half the distance. No music. Um," She regarded the drum major, "What's your name?"

"Pete."

"Okay, Pete, can you count them in?"

"Yes, Mam."

Elle called back to the field, "When Pete counts you in,

you'll glide half the distance, give your full attention to your body. What muscles are bringing you there?"

Pete counted them in, and the back glided to a perfect but smaller arc.

As she spoke, her confidence grew. "Okay, where did you feel that? Someone describe what your body did." A student raised their hand, and Elle pointed at them to share.

"I felt my ankles raise first, and when I was moving back, I felt it mostly here." She pointed to her quadriceps.

Elle nodded enthusiastically. "Yes! Those are your quads. They're going to help you power this move. Next time, try to move back and up at the same time. Let's do it again, but try for the full distance. Don't forget to think about your quads."

Pete directed their start again, this time without music, and they reached their positions.

Elle beamed. "Great! Now with music!" She watched as the band nailed their marks. Detecting Derek's absence beside her, Elle turned. Derek had moved to the back corner of the platform. He leaned against the railing, his body language relaxed, his face... *Is that admiration?*

He returned to the front next to Elle. She thought he might say something as he leaned in toward her momentarily, but instead, he straightened and addressed the band, "That's by far the best we've ever done that. Thank you, Ms. Foster! I think we could use more of her advice if she's open to it. What do you think?" The band erupted in agreement.

The second week of school wasn't going as well. It began with a simple permission slip. Elle sent home a form with all her beginner band students explaining that instruments would be provided throughout the school year and how students were expected to care for and practice them. At the bottom, it had a list of instruments available. The students checked which one they were most interested in during their class. The parents were asked to sign that they understood the expectations.

When Elle opened her inbox Thursday morning, she found two concerning emails from parents. One wasn't even a band parent but a friend of the concerned parent.

Ms. Foster,

We are shocked you would encourage Robert to play the flute. We find this wholly unacceptable and unnatural. We are withdrawing Robert from band as we find your influence a safety issue.

Robert Brown

The color drained from her face as she read. Her mind was racing but getting nowhere and kept circling back to those words. *Safety issue?* Her office phone rang. "Hello?"

"Elle, it's Steve. Can you come to meet me at the office?"

"Of course. I'll be right there."

Elle gave a soft knock on the doorframe.

"Good morning, Elle. You come and have a seat. Shut the door behind you, please."

Steve's good-natured greeting did nothing to soothe her. Her senses were on high alert. The vibrations of pulling the chair back over the carpet shot up her arm. The sound of friction buzzed in her ears. She opened her mouth, couldn't find the words, and closed it again.

"I'm just going to say it how it is," Steve began, "I received an email from Mr. Robert Brown. I'm aware he also messaged you."

Elle's mind churned through all the possibilities that could occur. *Am I getting reprimanded? Did I do something wrong? Can I make this better somehow? God - can he fire me for this?*

"How are you doing?" He asked it gently.

Steve's question, the way he asked it, abruptly halted her doom spiral. She studied his expression for the first time. "I'm... horrified, and... I don't know, confused." *And hurt.*

Steve exhaled audibly and nodded. "Understandable. I can at least help with the confusion, so let me explain. Robert believes you're encouraging homosexuality by saying his son could play flute because it's a traditionally female instrument."

"Oh. Wait what? That's... I mean, instruments aren't gendered, but even if we were going to try to make the point, it's inaccurate."

"I'm listening.... Though other folks may not." There was something apologetic on his face.

"The flute is an ancient instrument. If we think about the modern-day flute, its predecessors were used in the military because its higher-pitched tones could be heard clearly on battlefields. After that, all professionally played instruments were played by men because women were not typically employed. Even today, if you consider any orchestra, both genders are represented in every section." She cast around for an example, "You know Jethro Tull, right? Their flautist is named Ian something, very much a man."

Steve sighed, his shoulders drooping. "Elle, I respect you, and I'm going to be as upfront as possible. This sort of thing is going to continue to happen. Everest, this whole area, has beliefs about right and wrong that may not make sense to you. Things like this are always a struggle for folks who move here from outside. Boys learning flute or girls learning tuba is the equivalent of boys being cheerleaders or girls playing on the football team." He shrugged, bemused, "I can tell from your expression you don't see the big deal about any of that, but gender norms are a societal expectation here."

Elle chewed her lip. How much room did she have to disagree if she had already overstepped? "Then what do you suggest I do?"

A chuckle from Steve, then, "I can't tell you what to do. That's for you to tell me. I wanted to talk to you before you decided because you should consider little Robert's experience. If you somehow convinced his dad he should be allowed to play, he might be made fun of for it, which is largely outside your control. And... I wanted to make sure you were okay." He put his hands on his desk and stood up. "Let me know what you're thinking by Friday evening. I want to support you." Elle thanked him and, thoroughly demoralized, trudged back to her room.

The weather mirrored Elle's mood. It had turned eerily dark by lunchtime, huge undulating clouds overhead. She used the break to text Mavis, which had become a habit over the past weeks, and they decided to meet at Tiny's after school. Elle had reservations about meeting Tiny as a friend for the first time and immediately launching into her life problems. Still, she needed perspective more than she feared being misinterpreted.

Sheets of rain pounded the sidewalk when she parked in front of the cafe. The door was only a few feet away, but even so, Elle was drenched by the time she pulled it open. The sweet sound of the tinkling bells was drowned out by the storm behind her, but when the door swung shut, the silence of the cafe was almost as deafening.

Tiny popped her head up from behind the counter. "Hey! I've been expecting you; Mavis said to get a table ready," She pointed to one that already had a steaming mug set on it, "I'm finishing up our drinks, and I'll be right over."

As Elle sat, Tiny brought over two mismatched cups and slid one toward Elle, causing the contents to slip over the rim slightly. "Oops, sorry about that!"

Elle waved her off, "No big deal, thanks so much! I'm excited to meet you properly, by the way."

Tiny pulled the chair out to her left and plopped into it, stacking her legs one over the other. "Me too!"

The silence of the cafe was interrupted by a gale of wind as Mavis opened the door. She, too, was drenched and shook her hands through her hair to dispel some of the water before joining the table.

The sudden volume change jogged Elle's memory, and she turned toward Tiny, "No Balkan Beat Box today?"

Tiny blew a raspberry and gave a thumbs down. "When it rains like this, the wifi cuts out."

Mavis poured herself into her seat and eagerly reached out for her cup. After some quick swallows, she asked, "Did I miss anything?"

Elle replied, "No, I got here a few minutes before you."

"Good. I'm eager to hear what Steve had to say."

Tiny raised her hands, "Wait, wait, catch me up!"

Mavis tapped her fingernails along the cup. "You won't be surprised. I'll let Elle tell it. It's her story."

Elle recounted the full events, from the email to her meeting with Steve. It was easy to tell them. They were a good audience, tisking and reacting at the appropriate moments. It wasn't until she came to the end that Elle found her emotions kicking, jumbling her thoughts. "I've been thinking about how to respond all day, but the problem seems impossibly huge! Like Steve said, even if I convince Robert's parents, I'll condemn him to bullying. There's no way to win!"

A sly look passed between Mavis and Tiny. Mavis sighed.

"There might not be an immediate way to win, and that sucks, but we can influence things more than you realize, even just through representation."

Now kneeling in the chair, Tiny added, "And you're already doing it! These kids have never seen a female band director before. Now they have. When Mavis moved here, they had never seen a haunted bat before."

"Hey!" Mavis laughed and shoved Tiny's leg.

"Okay, okay, I mean a teacher who confidently chose not to conform their style and uses it as an outlet for expression. This is hugely meaningful! Showing other people how they can embrace who they are is not something we come by easy here."

"I hear you," Elle examined the contents of her cup, "but I don't think Jethro Tull will come to Everest Middle for their next performance."

"Of course not, but it's an example! You mentioned there were more famous male flute players. What about that guy who does flute beatboxing on YouTube?"

"He is a great example- that's Greg Pattillo. He was a guest speaker at Penn when I was there, and I got to meet him! The kids would love that, and it's such a modern and unexpected technique."

Tiny finished sipping from her cup. "Shoot, I want to hear more about him, too!"

Elle nodded slowly. "Okay, so I can be purposeful about representation. We can even watch Greg on YouTube when we talk about the evolution of music or modern music or music and technology.... but this doesn't help Robert. He told me he wanted to play the flute. I didn't pressure him! He simply liked it best. Now, I have a student with a genuine interest in learning music who is being pulled from my class! I know I have to meet with Robert Sr., but what do I say? I could apologize, I could ask if he'd consider letting Robert stay enrolled if he played something else, or I could push against the ridiculous belief that flutes are for women…. I'm so scared the last one would ensure Robert never gets to learn music and simultaneously feel like I should be an advocate for him."

Mavis arched her brows. "You need to weigh the best and worst case outcomes. If Robert can stay in the band, he will learn on whatever instrument. He has his whole life to apply that knowledge to the flute. Think baby steps."

They jumped at the sound of splashing rain as the door opened. Greg entered, followed by Matt and Derek.

The expression on Greg's face when he saw the women across the room turned Derek's stomach. Pure predator. He looked like a hunter who had spotted their prey.

"Well, look here if it isn't a motley crew." Greg drawled. "Workin' on that," he made a clicking noise and mimed swinging a golf club, "swing, Ellie?"

"My name's not Ellie."

Derek noted the tension in her body. She was seated, but her back was perfectly erect.

"Maybe you should consider a change, darlin'. Ellie has a more feminine ring to it, don't you think?" He didn't wait for a reply but immediately faced Tiny and continued, "You going to serve us or what?"

Tiny seemed to have a short internal struggle but rose from her seat and walked behind the counter. She smiled widely, plastically. "What can I get you… gentlemen?"

Greg ordered first. "Coffee for me."

"Room for cream?"

"Black."

"I'll make it extra black, then," Tiny said, maintaining her mockery of a smile. She took Matt and Derek's order and started crafting the beverages.

Derek headed for an empty spot on the far side of the cafe but stopped when Matt and Greg didn't follow. When he turned around, Greg was pulling a chair out from the table immediately next to Elle and Mavis. Resigned, Derek joined them.

"Some storm, huh?" Matt broke the tense silence, surprising Derek. Greg was usually the instigator for, well, everything.

Latching onto the safe subject, Derek eagerly replied, "You're right. I haven't seen the wind like this in years. Does anyone know when it's supposed to let up?"

Greg leaned back in his chair so it balanced on two legs. "Not sure. Shame, though, we know Ellie won't get in any practice today."

Derek glanced at the women. They appeared to have decided on ignoring Greg as the go-to strategy. Mavis said, a bit too loudly to Elle, "What were we talking about? Right, how you've gotten the largest group of incoming students in memory and instruments to support them all. Hell of a start!"

The legs of Greg's chair thumped onto the ground. He pronounced her name with a purposeful drawl, "Mayyyvis. One of my favorite females. There's no need for lyin' amongst friends. We all know how this ends. I heard you lost one already, only two weeks in. How long until they all quit?"

Elle's face was incredulous. "How..."

"I'm connected, Ellie. I know the entirety of what happens around here. Now you better listen to me because I'm not kidding about all of 'em going. You lost the Brown's kid, and that's just the beginnin'. Their family is a staple around here, and when you lose them, you lose 'em all."

Mavis fully turned her body to face Greg as if she were

acting as a shield. "Don't listen to him, Elle. Shut up, Greg. What is your game here?"

Tiny arrived carrying the three coffees and placed them in the center of their table.

Greg put his hands in the air, palms out. "No game! I'm merely concerned for our sweet newcomer. I wonder if you'll still get to keep a job if you have no members in the band? Funding the way it is, I'd wager not."

The sick feeling in Derek's stomach was getting worse. He was acutely aware of his powerlessness but had to do something. "Come on, Greg, that seems pretty farfetched. Plus, Elle is... talented. She helped my band figure out a tough drill last week."

"Al was always afraid the whole operation would go down when he left. Don't get yourself into trouble, too, now." Derek recognized the threat. Matt's dark eyes were wide and glued on the table.

Tiny watched them from her chair with interest. "Speaking as the non-teacher here, I'd guess you'd all be on the same side, right? Educators? Trying to teach the next generations?"

"That's always my concern. Teaching these kids. But you can't teach them if they aren't there, and when you have a teacher who's a *"safety concern,"* we'll be hard-pressed to have anyone to share our knowledge with."

At the words safety concern, Matt lifted his gaze from the coffee cup before him and narrowed his eyes at Greg. Before Derek could wonder about this, Elle was on her feet.

She quickly gathered her things. "You know what, I don't have to take this from you. I'm going."

Greg cackled. "That's where you're wrong. There are so many things for you to learn yet. Don't worry about leaving through. We'll head out."

The men stood at once, leaving their untouched drinks on

the table. Derek hung back and tried to give Elle an apologetic look before following Greg and Matt.

Friday was a blur. It seemed to leap forward quickly and then slow to a crawl, leaving Elle with a sense of whiplash. Despite Mavis and Tiny's insistence on not letting it get to her, she found it impossible to shake Greg's words. They had abused Greg soundly after the men left and boggled about his influence over the BMs. *Why do they follow his lead, and how did he know what was in that email?* Mavis had been impressed with Derek, claiming she had never seen anyone attempt to stand up to Greg. Elle didn't share the sentiment. Sure, Derek claimed she helped his band, but he was too willing to be steamrolled and had to dive deep for the word he used, "talented." At the same time, she hadn't been able to defend herself either and felt terrible for it. Why was it so hard to speak up for herself with him? Probably because she used all her energy repressing furious tears. The thought of Greg seeing her cry was repulsive. It could not happen.

Elle had been attending the high school's marching practice after school but decided to skip. Besides not knowing what to say to Derek, she still had to write to Steve about her plans, and the carpet cleaner she rented was scheduled to arrive at 3pm.

The letter to Steve was drafted, and the send button just waiting to be clicked. Elle re-read it one last time.

Steve,

Regarding the email we received from Robert Brown Sr., I would like to reply by offering to meet with him. In-person communication will go smoother and hold less room for misinterpretation, so I'm hoping he will accept.

My goals going into our meeting would be threefold:

- *Show I am a trustworthy person and teacher*
- *Share my curriculum for the 6th-grade year so my expectations are open and transparent, and I can address any questions*
- *Invite Robert to rejoin the band in any capacity, not pressing for any instrument, instead highlighting the benefits of music education in general*

Overall, I hope Robert gets to study music with me. He would be welcome to rejoin any time. It is never too late to learn.
Please let me know if this seems like a good approach. I am open to your input and experience.

Elle

She sighed and pressed send. Her knee-jerk reaction was to research every male flautist and the entire history of instruments to show they were for all people, but that would only drive the wedge deeper. Elle's ultimate goal of teaching music to any child interested had to stay true.

There was a loud knock on the door. Elle sped to it and opened it all the way out, putting a door jamb underneath the frame. The delivery man stood out front with a dolly. "Good afternoon, ma'am. I've got your carpet cleaner here." He gestured toward the dolly.

The cleaner was smaller than Elle remembered from the ad. It had been the size of a ride-on mower in her head, but this didn't even necessitate the dolly. "Ah, is this it?" She raised an eyebrow.

"Yes, ma'am. I can show you how to use it if you like?" He pushed the dolly over the threshold and steered it to an outlet. "You've got some different heads to choose from. For a space this size, I'd use the biggest." He affixed the largest head to the hose. "Now you do like this." He kneeled on the carpet, turned the machine on, and pulled the cleaning head across it, starting at a far reach and drawing it into himself.

Elle was doing the math. This was going to take approximately 500 years. "Is there, I don't know, some larger option?"

The man scanned the room. "I'm sorry, ma'am, this is our biggest one. I can let you have it overnight and pick it up tomorrow instead of the 3-hour window. Nobody else is renting it today anyway."

"Thanks." But she didn't feel entirely grateful.

He walked out of the room with a wave. Elle examined the space, game-planning for how she could clean it with maximum efficiency. A swoosh sounded from her office. Probably Steve replying to her email. Elle sprinted to her computer, but the email wasn't from Steve.

Ms. Foster,

We are withdrawing Michael effective immediately.

. . .

Regards,
  Mrs. Smith

Elle sobbed, not from anger. It was hard to breathe, and she gulped for air. Greg was right. He may be the biggest asshole she'd ever met, but that didn't change the accuracy of his prediction. She was going to lose all these kids. She walked over to the carpet cleaner and began cleaning as the tears rolled down her face. It seemed a pointless task, but one still with a deadline, and she didn't know what else to do.

"Elle?" She heard her name over the racket of the cleaner and turned her head to find Derek standing in the doorway.

"Elle!" He rushed to her and kneeled on the floor beside her, hand on her back. "What's wrong? What's happened?"

She sat back onto her heels and dropped the nozzle. Derek's presence caused her crying to intensify, but she tried to explain through it, "I can't tt. They're all leave... leavinggg." She wailed the last word.

Derek's expression was confused. He reached out to turn off the cleaner and swept her into a kneeling embrace. His hands pressed gently against the back of her head and her shoulder. His warmth and the pressure of him soothed her. She realized he was speaking softly, "It'll be okay. It's all going to be fine." It was like hearing the refrain of her favorite song. All of it composed her.

Elle could have stayed there forever, but she pulled back. "Wait, how are you here? You have practice." She hiccuped and saw Derek's lip quirk up on one side.

He replied, "You didn't show up, and I was worried about you. Pete's got practice under control." They stared at each other for a moment. "What happened?"

Elle looked down. "Oh no, we're all wet!" They'd sat on a cleaned portion of the carpet. Derek rose first and extended his hand to help Elle up. She brushed herself off and started to explain, eyes still fixed on her feet. "Another student withdrew just like Greg said. I don't belong here. I'm trying so hard, but everything I do blows up. I don't fit in, and if I can't make it here... there's no place for me anywhere."

Derek remained silent. Elle raised her gaze. His throat bobbed before he spoke. "I think you belong here."

"How can you say that when you, you know, when you...."

"When I meet you and immediately ask you to maintain the status quo and manage your band in a way you strongly oppose?" His face was tortured.

"Well. Yes."

Derek grabbed the back of his neck with both hands and then threw them up in frustration. "God, I don't know whether to explain how you make me remember and how much we need you here or tell you to run like hell because there's nothing we can do. Can we... Can we start over? Please?" Elle observed Derek, his eyes pleading, before nodding. He gave a brief nod back in acceptance and asked, "Do you like Chinese? It's the only place that does delivery." He had his phone out before she could reply, pulling up the menu.

Derek ordered food to be delivered to the school, met with Pete quickly, and then returned to Elle's room. They took turns with the carpet cleaner and ate spring rolls and vegetable fried rice. They mainly talked when they changed out the water and traded turns so they didn't have to shout over the cleaner's sound. It was 8pm before they finished.

Elle flipped the switch on the machine and wound the cable up at its side. Though her head was still underwater, she felt much better for Derek's help. They walked to the door together. Before he walked away, she said, "Derek. Thank you. Really."

He put his hands in his pocket and smiled weakly. "Any time. Listen. No pressure, but if you want to learn to golf, I could help." His face flushed. "I'm not great or anything."

A smile blinked at Elle's lips. "I would like that."

Seven

PRESTO - AN EXTREMELY FAST TEMPO, USUALLY
BETWEEN 168-177 BEATS PER MINUTE.

Elle regained some confidence over the next few weeks.
The Brown and Smith families declined to meet with
her, which stung, but nobody else had withdrawn, and she
was starting to enjoy her routine. Her classes were learning
rapidly, their tonality and articulation improving daily. After
school, she started helping the marching band on Mondays
and Fridays. Weekends were spent hanging out with Mavis
and Tiny. The two were determined to take her on a tour of all
the best things in the area. So far, her favorite spot was Crystal
Springs. They only told her they were going hiking, so when
the narrow trail opened to a clear pool sparkling enough to
please any merfolk, it was a surprise that took her breath away.

Friday afternoon was sweltering. Elle was halfway up the
now-familiar hill to practice when the first drops of perspiration gathered on her brow. She held her hands behind her
back to conceal what she was holding as she crested the hill,
and the band came into view. The students waved in greeting
from their block formation, causing Derek to about-face in
welcome. He'd changed from his usual school outfit of slim-
fitting pants and polo into grey athletic shorts that landed

right above his knees and a simple blue v-neck that hugged his shoulders and arms. She had never noticed Derek was built so nicely. Handsome, yes. Tall, yes. But he was also surprisingly muscular, a fact that was disguised in his usual attire.

Derek looked happy to see her. "Whatcha got back there?" He pointed to the hand behind her back.

"Hmm, I don't know. Can you guess?" She gave a theatrical head nod to the students.

A fair amount of eye-rolling ensued while several of the band answered in a groan, "An Arnold Palmer." Giggling erupted as she revealed the beverage and handed it to Derek. It had only been a couple of weeks, but her bringing a drink to Derek each practice had become a tradition.

"Thank you!" He reached out to grab the concoction. "Phew, gonna need this today."

"Yeah, I didn't realize I should've brought a change of clothes."

Derek nodded, hands on his hips, a finger looped around the bottle lid. "I can't imagine those jeans are comfortable right now. There's all this anticipation for wearing them on casual Fridays, but out here, it's gotta be shorts." He peeked at the band behind him, still at attention in formation. "Let's run the entire show from field march on. We're one week away from the first performance! Drums can give us the cadence once we're lined up." He jogged to the platform, tapping Elle on the shoulder playfully as he passed.

They watched as the band marched to their starting mark on the sideline. The drum line played a complicated break, signifying the band should begin marching to their starting positions on the field. Derek took a swig from the bottle Elle had given him and tilted his head toward her, "Are you free tomorrow sometime?"

The question caught Elle off guard. "Uhhh..."

He quickly clarified, "I was thinking, if you still wanted to, we could go to The Drive."

The band started Intergalactic. Both Derek and Elle gave their complete focus to the field. There was a minor clustering issue with the flutes in their last position, but they were able to course correct during their first move in ET. The finale was Elton John's Rocket Man, which wasn't as clean a performance. Derek let the band finish before addressing it. "We're having the same problems with Rocket Man from before. Don't be lazy! We're not completing our phrases. We must hold these notes at full length to get them clean and lyrical. The end front arch is also too subtle. What did you think, Elle? Was that an arch or a messy line?"

"I'm afraid to say it could have been either. Who is at the peak of the arch? Raise your hand. Great, Jessica is at the peak. Let her be the peak!"

Derek moved his finger in a circle in the air. "Let's rerun Rocket Man. Give those notes their full durations!"

Elle lowered her voice to a normal talking volume. "I still think Rocket Man is too slow to be the final work. I'm telling you to switch it with ET. They won't be as tired, which will fix the phrasing, plus ET is an exciting way to end."

Derek shook his head. "No way. I hear you, but Rocket Man is what saves this show. It's an oldie, so it will play better with the audience than the other two. I need to leave the crowd on a happy note."

Elle sang, "Whatever you say." Derek laughed out of the side of his mouth.

Rehearsal ended, and students walked down the hill, talking and joking. Elle and Derek followed together behind them. Elle's jeans stuck to her legs. "I'm free tomorrow. What time is good for you?"

They both stopped walking and faced each other. "Anytime. 10? I'll bring coffee."

"Sounds great. I'll see you there at 10."

The tempo of Derek's foot shaking was at least at a presto. He sat at the edge of a driving station, feeling nervous. Two coffees were at his right hand next to a canvas bag of various sweeteners and creamers. *I should have asked how she took her coffee.* His clubs were in their bag behind him, and he had snagged a few smaller public clubs that might fit Elle better and leaned them against it.

Derek lifted his head at the sound of a car. It was her. He scrambled to his feet, dusting his hands off on his shorts. Elle closed the car door, spotted Derek, and headed his way. His lips tugged up at her stride; she always seemed to have a little bounce in her step that set her curly hair to springing. She wore black leggings and an oversized crop top with large, brightly colored flowers. The neckline was wide, making her lilac sports bra strap visible on her left shoulder.

Elle trilled, "Good morning!" as she hopped onto the platform.

"Good morning." There was a beat of silence before Derek picked up the thermoses, "I brought coffee, but I don't know how you take it, so I tried to bring options." He tipped his head toward the bag.

Elle kneeled down to explore the bag. "Wow, okay, I see half and half and a 2% milk in here, heavy cream, sugar packs, fake sugar yuck, maple syrup, hmmm, and what is this?" She picked up a Tupperware and shook the white liquid within.

"That's for me. It's cashew cream. I make it myself. I'm lactose intolerant."

"You make cashew cream?"

"Yeah. Oat milk, too, but I ran out of it."

Elle looked up at him from where she crouched over the

bag. "Thank you for this. You didn't have to bring all this stuff, you can't even use most of it! I'd take it any way it came."

"I wanted to. I should have asked you."

"You didn't make yours?" She pointed at his thermos.

"No, I was waiting for you."

Elle pressed her lips together. A perplexed look crossed her face, but it was gone as fast as it came. "Do you mind if I try some of the cashew? It's actually my favorite creamer, but I haven't been able to find it at Greens. I guess I need to learn how to make it, too."

Derek groaned. "Yeah, you won't find it anywhere around here. Help yourself. I'll send you the recipe I use if you want." He watched as she poured the creamer and spun in a drizzle of maple syrup.

Sitting beside Elle, sipping their drinks, her presence anywhere felt good to Derek. Their conversation still had fiddly little pauses, but he noticed those were fewer and fewer. He found himself constantly seeking her- expecting her at marching rehearsals, searching for her walking in the court-yard of their shared campus. She was a comfort, and that made him anxious. "You sure you want to do this? You don't have anything to prove."

Elle wiggled upright, determined. "Yes, I do. I do have things to prove. I need my peers to take me seriously. I need them to respect me as their equal."

Derek grimaced. "I've been thinking about it. I worry this golfing challenge isn't how to do that. Things take time here. If you keep doing good work, the rest of them will see it, and it'll be proof enough. Golfing though.... it's just Greg being an idiot."

"Is it wrong that part of me wants to put him in his place? He makes me so angry, and it's like I freeze up and can't find the right words to say to him. I won't need words if I can over-come his stupid 150 yards."

Derek unfolded his legs and stood. He held out his hand to Elle. "Then let's start." Something like electricity sizzled through his arm when she accepted his hand. "Come stand right here," he indicated a spot right behind the green, "now watch me." He hopped on the platform and slowly drew his club back. Elle took several steps back. Instead of swinging, Derek carefully lowered the club and turned around. "The first lesson is safety. That spot was about where you stood when you met everyone last time. I'm sorry I grabbed you like that; it was pure reaction."

Color raised in Elle's cheeks, making the smattering of freckles on them stand out more. "Nothing about that inter-action went how I'd hoped. You kinda saved me." Derek's pulse raced at her words. "From the club, at least." *Ouch. Could a heart suffer contrecoup?*

He pressed on. "Let's see if any of these clubs fit you, and then we can talk about grip. Stand up straight and let your arms hang naturally." He held each of the three public clubs by her side, then handed her the middle one. "I think this one is the best bet."

"How do you know?"

"Honestly, there's some technical way to figure it out with your exact height and then adding or subtracting length to the standard club, but it also works pretty well to pick the club where the grip lines up with your hand."

Elle chuckled. "That makes a lot of sense."

"I thought so! Ha! Okay, now to grip the club. Your right hand will be just below your left, and you want to grip more with your fingers than having the club in your palm." She adjusted the club toward the base of her fingers. "Perfect. We're going to use the overlap grip," Derek reached out and gently placed her right pinky in the crook of her left hand's knuckles, "like that." He took a step back to appraise her. Elle studied the club in her hand, staring at it as if to memorize.

"You've got it. One thing to remember is not to grip too tightly."

Elle frowned slightly and glanced away from her hands to Derek before returning to her grip. "Okay, how do I swing it?"

"I think about the swing in three parts. The backswing, the downswing, and the follow through. It's like a rhythm that moves through your body." Derek stepped up to the green and pressed the button to load the tee. He spoke through the movements with his eyes closed, seeing them in his mind's eye. "It starts with your hip twisting your body back, your arms arc back, and you bend your wrists to increase the arc at the top. The downswing starts, and your weight shifts to your front foot. Your hips start to turn your body forward. It's like you're unwinding the backswing. Then, the follow through comes. Once you hit the ball, you don't stop. Your hips twist even more toward the front, and the club ends over your front shoulder." He stepped up to the tee and swung, making a satisfying connection with the ball. "Your turn."

Elle's eyes widened. "Uhh. Okay. But you covered so many things, and it was over in a second when you did them!"

"Fair. You kind of have to. Let me do it in slow motion." Derek repeated the directions but, this time, moved his body as he said each one. "Now it's your turn?" He asked, eyebrows up.

"I'm going to go slow first, too." Derek watched as Elle tried to recall all the motions he had described. It was jerky, and she forgot to bend her wrists at the top. On the downswing, her weight didn't transfer into her front foot as much as it should have, which prevented adequate follow through. When she finished, she arched her eyebrow questioningly at Derek.

"How'd that feel?" He asked.

"Bad! And unnatural."

Derek laughed. "It kinda looked that way, too." She put

on an over-the-top pout, causing him to laugh more, which made her join in. "This is how we all begin, don't worry." He gave her one piece to focus on at a time, and she continued to slowly swing, focusing on just her hips, then just her hips and arms. Adding on actions one by one.

After a few minutes, her motions were smoother, but Elle voiced a complaint. "I can't feel it. I want to feel it the right way."

Derek took a hesitant step forward. "Is it okay if I guide you?" Elle nodded, and Derek positioned himself immediately behind her. He had hugged her one day, weeks ago, when she was crying. This was the closest they'd been to each other since then. He adjusted her grip, then put his own hands over hers. Her hair tickled his face; it smelled herbal and citrus. His chest lightly pressed against her back. He whispered into her ear, "Let's take a slow swing first. I'll count the sections. One." Their hips twisted back, and he led their wrists to bend. "Two." They unraveled the arc they made, and Derek made sure to lean her weight into the front foot. "Three." He continued the swing until the club was behind them.

Time hung for a moment, and Derek found it hard to step away from her as if she were magnetic. He pulled back, overcoming the force. Elle gaped at him in surprise. "Where'd you go? We have to do a fast one now." She settled back into her stance. Derek rejoined her and said, "Okay, no counting this time. We're just going to try for a smooth motion." They repeated the swing three times together, becoming more fluid and confident each time. The way her hips fit his, the warmth of her... He peeled away from her again. "Do you feel it now?"

Elle smiled fully, the right corner of her mouth hitching slightly higher than the left. "I think so."

"Hit that ball, then."

Elle positioned herself on the green, swung, and sent the ball flying at a sharp right angle. It landed around the 50-yard marker. She dropped the club as she jumped and cheered. "I did it! YES!" Her eyes sparkled with excitement. "Did you see?!"

Her energy was contagious. "I did. Great first real drive!"

They kept practicing, Derek making modifications to her form and giving pointers. Elle trying to replicate his advice. By noon, Elle indicated she was tired and thanked him for the lesson. "Same time next week?" She asked.

"Definitely. Do you want to grab lunch at Katie's Deli?" It slipped out of his mouth before he could second guess himself.

To his relief, Elle replied in the affirmative, "Sure. I don't know that place; I'll follow you."

Derek sat in his car briefly before putting it in reverse. He was in trouble.

No wonder I never noticed this place before. Katie's Deli was a two-story house in an apparent residential area that had been converted into a small sandwich shop. Easily overlooked as just another home. The inside was dressed up how Elle imagined an English Teashop would look. Lace and doilies were dripping from surfaces. The walls were pastel blues, pinks, and greens. Floral bouquets were on each table, the counter, and all the shelves. There were even pictures of flowers hanging throughout the restaurant.

Elle grinned across the small table at Derek. "So, what's your instrument?" She couldn't believe she didn't know already. How had this never come up?

Derek strummed his fingers across the table. He tapped with his fingernails and then experimented with the sound of his knuckles on the chair seat. Elle narrowed her eyes, watching. "What are you...." Then he unleashed a rhythm using every part of his hands and coaxing sounds out of the mundane wood around them that envied any drum line.

He stopped abruptly; a smile crossed his face, lighting his eyes. "Percussion. What about you?"

"I can't believe you made that riff up right here. I do not have that talent. I was even uninvited from a jazz band once because I'm a total failure at improvisation."

"Uninvited? That sounds like a nice way to say kicked out."

Elle swallowed her iced tea and laughed at the same time, nearly causing her to spew. "That's correct. They were quite polite about it."

Derek shot his eyes up and pressed his lips together in concentration. "You were *in* a jazz band. However momentary. So that must mean you play some sort of wind instrument."

"Oh, I like this. Yes, please take a guess." She relaxed against the back of her chair and silently challenged him.

Derek leaned forward, elbows on the table, observing Elle. His eyes darted across her, assessing, before meeting her gaze. He grinned slyly and said, "Saxophone."

Elle exclaimed in disbelief. "How did you know that?!" Her reaction caused Derek to toss his head back in deep laughter.

"A little bit of luck. I saw the callous on your right thumb, which made me think sax or clarinet, and the saxophone is so much heavier," He shrugged, "That was the lucky part, but I just thought you're strong, you know?"

"Alright, Mr. Holmes." He let out another chuckle, and Elle noticed all his actions were rhythmic. His laugh and his golf swing. All his movements had a percussive and musical quality. *I bet he's a great dancer.*

Derek took a bite of his sandwich and asked, "So, why did you move here?"

Internal panic rose in Elle. She offered the partial truth she had given Mavis, but as her vision narrowed to Derek's kind expression, she found the words kept coming. "I've always dreamed of living in the country, even when I was a kid. Southern charm, right? Knowing everyone and having a close-knit community and relationships. The bustling of a farmer's market on the weekend. It's always seemed so enviable. Stable." Derek's eyes were soft on her, welcoming her to continue. "That's not something I had growing up. My parents," she sighed, "we moved a lot. I don't blame them. They never wanted kids. They had these big dreams of traveling the world, and then I showed up. At first, they took me with them. I was too young to remember, but apparently, I've been to Greece and the French countryside and New Zealand. When I started school, it made international travel difficult, and they decided to stay in the States, but we still traveled so much. I never started and ended a school year in the same place."

Derek narrowed his eyes. She could tell he was working through something. "That sounds... really hard."

"After a while, it was. It was normal to me at first- all I ever knew. It finally struck home in 3rd grade that not everyone is moving every year. I had made this friend, Jules. My first real friend. We did everything together, but then we moved again, and losing her was painful. Too painful."

"Did you ever ask them to stay somewhere?"

"That year, and probably 4th grade too. But it was out of the question for them. I was already a... well, a nuisance."

Derek shook his head. "No, come on. That's... To your parents?"

"I know. I stopped talking to people about my parents and childhood a long time ago. It's hard to believe. But I'm okay. They didn't know how to parent, and I got in the way of their desires. They had conviction for their goals. As soon as I went to college, they moved overseas. We talk at Christmas."

Derek chewed the inside of his cheeks. He looked... angry. Elle's prior attempts to explain her childhood had been met with disbelief or sympathy but never anger. "It must have been lonely."

Elle huffed a laugh, visibly shocking Derek. "I didn't even try to make friends. After Jules, I figured out it wasn't worth it. It was lonely. Yes, that's fair. You see why I always dreamed of settling down in the country?"

His anger faded, morphing into something like sadness. A slow, purposeful breath later, he said, "You can't know until you try it, I guess. Is it everything you've wanted so far?"

Elle sat back against her chair again. "Honestly? No. Well, some of it is wonderful, but the people are not as welcoming as the movies would have you believe, and I haven't seen any community events that make the town come alive yet."

The inexplicable sadness hung in Derek's eyes. "I can show you the events, and the people will come around- though I know what you mean. You don't miss having access to things? Cashew cream at your fingertips?"

"That's a good question. Mostly, it is the groceries!" The corner of Derek's mouth twitched up, and he nodded. "Maybe you could teach me some about that too, Mr. I-Make-My-Own-Non-Dairy-Creamers!"

"Hah! Okay. Give me a list of what you miss, and I'll figure it out. What about events?"

"I used to go to concerts and the symphony occasionally, but I figure those are only a drive away." This had the effect of setting Derek at ease. His shoulders relaxed.

"Thank you. For sharing with me. You mentioned you don't usually talk about your history. It means a lot that you'd let me in."

Sharing with Derek was a weight being relieved that she didn't know was there. Elle felt light enough to float away.

Eight

SIGHT-READING - READ AND PERFORM MUSIC AT SIGHT, WITHOUT PREPARATION.

It was the first football game of the season for Everest High, and Elle felt like she was in the twilight zone. She had come to see the band perform at halftime but wasn't aware the high school football game would be such a crowd-drawing event! Though early, she needed to park at the back of the stadium lot and join queues of people moving toward the ticket booths for entry. Since moving to Everest, Elle hadn't experienced being around such a throng of people. The surprises continued as she entered the stadium and noticed the home side of the stands was packed, and the visiting stands were almost as full. They were playing a school she wasn't familiar with and understood to be over an hour away. All these people made the rather long drive to be here. She stood directly behind the field goal to watch and listen to the crowd. Her heart seemed to expand slightly, a sense of sonder taking hold. This was a good thing. These communities were invested in their students and schools.

The sound of scales led Elle behind the bleachers, where she found the band in a circle. Looks of concentration were on every face as they tried to listen to each other over the noisy mob. They wore crisp uniforms of blue and white, a gold sequined sash across the front. Polished black hats with an iridescent black plume were at their feet. Many of the students noticed her presence. At the center of the circle, Derek cut them off with a small flourish and turned to see what had their attention. The sun was setting, so his face lighting up when he saw her was probably a trick of the light.

"Fancy seeing you here!" Derek exclaimed. He turned to the band. "It's her first time, you know?" There were some snickers amongst the group.

A clarinet player, Andrea, raised her hand. "Ms. Elle - I mean Ms. Foster, you're going to sit with us, right?"

Elle had not considered where she would sit. *Is it even allowed that I sit with the band?* She looked to Derek, who nodded and shrugged, which she understood meant she was welcome but didn't have to. Her "I'd love to" was met by some celebration.

"Are we ready?" Derek called out. "You know the order. Let's make our way to the stands." The percussionist led the group, followed by the woodwinds, then brass. Elle watched as the line snaked through the crowd and set up in a reserved portion of the stands. Derek and Elle took up the rear. As they followed, he told her, "This is my favorite thing, the football games. There's so much energy here; the kids come alive and get so into it, and it's the perfect practice for our competition."

"Yeah. I can't believe how many people are here! It's like the whole town."

"Wait until homecoming. Now that's a turnout."

"Plus, you get to spy on neighboring bands!"

Derek furrowed his brows. "Dang, Elle. Straight to spying? You down for sabotage, too?"

She winked. "I do have a competitive streak. But we don't need to sabotage; we're too good for that."

"Well, thank you. And I've noticed." Elle shot him a devious grin, and he chuckled.

Elle quickly learned, for her, football games were almost entirely about the band. They responded to what was happening in the game- playing their fight song when they scored, occasionally joining forces with the cheerleaders, but their joy was not necessarily related to what happened on the field. She got the impression it could have been any game, and the band would be equally invested in supporting them. They had their own cheers and dances for each of the songs. It was much more fun than Elle anticipated.

Halftime came quickly, and the band returned to their spot behind the stands. Elle waved goodbye as they filed out, then climbed to the top seats for the best view of the field. The visiting band was already marching to their original starting positions. Their band was larger than Everest High's but didn't sound that way. Their entries and cut-offs weren't as clean. There was at least one person out of step consistently. She found herself thinking Everest had this in the bag but then felt bad for such a harsh comparison. It was their first show at the onset of the season. Montford would improve, as would Everest, and it wasn't like they had done poorly. The crowd was entertained, and it had been a good show.

Still, as they marched off and Elle heard the complicated drum cadence start that led Everest onto the field, a mixture of eagerness and nerves for them kicked in. When the first measures of Intergalactic started, the crowd was distracted, as if they hadn't noticed the show beginning. However, when the music broke to the Beastie Boys, the shift in interest was palpable. Intergalactic and ET went nicely, with the band achieving the more complex drills. Rocket Man was the roughest of the set. The band still struggled to hold all the notes for their entire duration in places, and a formation they usually nailed was misshapen. She couldn't tell how it happened; it seemed some members had forgotten their marks completely. As they marched off the field, Elle screamed and clapped as loud as she could for them, drawing sidelong glances from people sitting nearby.

During the second half, the Montford band challenged Everest to a round of "We've got spirit, yes we do!" Which ended in both bands blaring a random collection of notes as loud as they could, followed by everything from giggles to raucous laughter. *These are such great kids!*

The tires of Elle's car crunched over the gravel as she pulled into Mavis's driveway. It was Saturday evening. They had decided to have a game night instead of going out to explore this week, and Elle was cognizant this was the first time she had been invited to anyone's home since moving.

Mavis answered the door before Elle could knock. "Come on in." She turned and led the way to the kitchen and dining room. The house shared Mavis's style. The walls were dark greens, burgundies, and blacks. Most of the decor was gothic, but then there would be an occasional pop of color: A bright butterfly watercolor in the living room, fuzzy neon cotton balls strung in a garland and hung from the ceiling above the dinner table.

"I love the vibe of your house!" Elle said as she took a bottle of wine from its long paper bag and set it on the table. Tiny got up to fetch glasses, obviously familiar with the kitchen setup.

"Thanks. You know what's wild? I didn't paint when I bought the place. Everyone thinks I did, and I would have, but I didn't have to. One of the reasons I knew this house was the one was because it was already donning my favorite palette."

Tiny grimaced as she uncorked the wine. "You were lucky." She lifted her head toward Elle. "Now you've seen this fine establishment; you can never come to my place. It's an embarrassment in comparison. No aesthetic at all."

Elle chuckled and suppressed a cringe. "I'm sure it isn't as bad as mine. I still barely have furniture. The house was uninhabited for years when I moved in and needs a lot of love. It's kind of a wreck."

Mavis placed a charcuterie in the center of the table. "Nosh first, then games?" They all sat in response and reached for the cheeses, meats, and nuts.

"This goat cheese is amazing." Elle spread some onto a second cracker. "Did you know Derek makes his own cashew cream?"

Tiny made an mmm of acknowledgment as she finished her bite. "I did, actually! Funny the things you learn about people as the only coffee place in town."

"How's business?" Mavis asked.

"Predictable." Tiny sighed. "I shouldn't complain. I love what I do, and predictability is getting me by. It's better than erratic. I just wish there was some way to get more regulars or mix it up somehow."

"How about you? How're classes going this year?"

Mavis put her hand over her heart. "It's honestly so good. I have some talented seniors this year who are invested in their craft and blow me away. One of them asked me about art schools! I've never had a student continue their art education after high school, and even having her consider it is such an energizer. It makes me remember my own college experience and things I learned that I haven't considered in years. I don't know; I'm refreshed this year. How about you, Elle?"

Elle's brain was in problem-solving mode since Tiny mentioned attracting new customers. She had been listening to Mavis too, but sitting on an idea which now burst forth from her. "Tiny, could you go mobile? I went to the football game last night, and there were so many people there. It was crazy! The visiting town even drove an hour to attend. I bet they would buy drinks from you there, and maybe that would turn into more regulars in the store."

Tiny blinked. Mavis whispered under her breath, "Ew, football."

"Okay, it was just a thought. There were a lot of people there. It was fun, and the band did so well."

Recovered, Tiny set down her plate. "No, it's a good idea. I don't know, though. I'm not sure how to do it. I'll have to investigate to see if it's even possible."

Mavis cut in. "Wait, wait, wait. You had fun at a football game? I don't even know you!" She scoffed dramatically, and they all laughed.

"I mean, I was surprised too, to be honest. You know I've been helping at practices, so it felt wrong to miss their first performance. Then I ended up sitting with the band, and Derek and those kids were the absolute best. You talked about feeling energized. Seeing them work together gives me the same feeling."

Mavis glanced at Elle and carefully said, "It seems like you and Derek are getting along now."

Elle leaned back and swirled her glass of red. "We are. When he's with his students at practice or at the game, or when we're together, he's this amazing person. Kind and thoughtful. But there's something that doesn't make sense...."

Tiny sat upright so quickly she hit the table, causing her and Mavis to steady their glasses. "Wait, when were you together?"

"Oh, he's teaching me how to golf."

Mavis's face fell. "Whoa. Does this have to do with the BMs?"

"Yeah, Greg said I could talk to them if I hit a 150-yard

drive. He doesn't think I'll do it, but I'm going to show him how wrong he is."

Mavis exchanged glances with Tiny. "I don't know, Elle. I would just stay away from Greg entirely. You don't want to be friends with someone like him."

"No, not friends, but I *have* to be his colleague as long as we're both around. And I want him to stop talking down to me. He's the type who'll stop if I show him I'm up to the task."

"He won't." Tiny had a faraway air about her. "Alarms go off about him every time I see him. He's not a run-of-the-mill misogynist. He scares me."

Mavis forcefully pointed at Tiny. "Yes. That's exactly it. He's always been unpleasant, but I've never spent significant time with him before. The look he had when we were at Tiny's.... It's like an intrusive thought that keeps invading my brain."

Elle nodded slowly. "He is the thing that doesn't make sense to me. Derek has been an amazing friend to me 90% of the time. But when he's with those guys, it's like he's a different person. Barely there. What is that?"

Board games remained stacked on a counter, forgotten, as the women continued to talk through the night. They didn't disperse until midnight when Tiny noticed the time and panicked about her early morning. As Elle and Tiny opened their car doors, Tiny called out, "You know, Derek is pretty hot."

Elle exhaled a laugh. "I guess that's true."

"Good! So you have noticed!"

Derek swallowed his beer and his rebukes all Saturday night. He wasn't sure which was making him feel worse. It vaguely occurred to him it was a dangerous game; drinking the Miller High Life cushioned him from Greg's presence, but with each acrid sip, it became harder to hold his tongue. He was seated at a round table in Matt's living room with Matt, Greg, Billy, and Chuck, and it was hour three of poker. Derek was desperate for the night to end.

So far, Greg had commented on one of his recently graduated students being stacked, kept trying to lead the group to high-stakes gambling, and managed to steer the conversation to Elle multiple times. "Didn't you say she helped the marching band? Not so much with Rocket Man, huh?" Derek let the jab go unanswered, card play filling the silence.

Being at Matt's place meant he was a little more talkative, but overall, the group dynamic didn't change. Billy passively agreed with everything, and Chuck was as silent as ever, relying on body language nearly exclusively.

"I'm good for one more hand, then I've got to roll out," Derek announced to the table.

Chuck grunted. Billy shuffled the deck. Matt handed him another brew, saying, "Beer for the road."

Derek accepted with a shrug, popped the cap, and downed half the bottle, grimacing.

"Why are you actin' different?" Greg stared intently at Derek from across the table.

"I don't know what you mean."

"You're quiet. Stewing on something. Thinking you're better than everyone again?"

Derek sighed. "I have never believed that, Greg."

"Have."

"If I haven't convinced you after all these years, I'm not sure I will. I'm not better than anyone. Never have been."

"Then why are you so quiet?"

Because I can't take much more of your shit but can't get on your bad side either. Derek's muscles tensed throughout his body.

Billy dealt the cards. Greg continued, not waiting for a reply from Derek. "You know what I've noticed? Whenever we talk about Ellie, you shut right up."

Derek focused on keeping his cool. He watched a bead of perspiration slide down the neck of his beer. "I have wondered why you bring her up so much?"

"Well, now you can't blame me for that! Fascinating business about a woman director. I'm worried about you, though. Your bands got a history to uphold. Maybe you disagree. She is mighty pretty." Greg hummed as if he'd just made a discovery. "Maybe she's influencing you with other methods?"

"I fold." Derek stood from the table. "Bad hand."

Greg laughed with apparent relish. The other men were silent, listening. "Looks like I struck a nerve. Don't get too attached."

Anger twisted inside Derek. "Just leave her alone, Greg. She hasn't done anything to you. Why torture her? Because she's a woman? The world is bigger than West Alabama."

Greg's eyes popped. "There it is; I told you! He's better than Alabama, too good for us." Derek turned to leave and heard Greg say, "Maybe a little of that pretty pussy will fix his attitude. She's at least good for that."

Derek whipped around. "This is going to be a problem. Don't talk about Elle. Don't do anything to her." His eyes roamed to each of the men at the table. "I'm going home. See you all later."

Lost in angry, worried thoughts, Derek navigated the tree roots in the yard by the light of his phone flashlight. He was nearly back to his car when a voice he didn't recognize sounded behind him.

"Can we talk for a minute?" Derek directed the beam of light behind him and recognized Chuck's black sneakers.

Chuck hissed, "Keep heading to your car. I don't want them to know we're talking. Meet at the park on Pecan Blvd and 12th."

Derek opened the GPS on his phone. He knew where the Band Misters lived but wasn't familiar with the rest of their respective towns. *What is happening right now?* These were more words out of Chuck than he'd ever heard, and he apparently wanted to talk more.

The little playground was dark. Despite being in a residential area of the town, the streetlights were sparse, and the ones that were lit made the large oak trees cast long shadows. Derek parked his car next to Chuck's. He was standing in front of the lot and gesturing for Derek to follow him. They walked silently until they reached the swings, and Chuck lowered himself into one. Derek took the one next to him. It was a bewildering experience. Two grown men on a swing set in the middle of the night. On top of that, Chuck appeared to have run out of words again.

Derek cleared his throat. "So, uh, you wanted to talk?"

Chuck kicked at the dirt with his shoe. "Yeah. I'm not very good at it, though. And I'm out of practice now, so probably even worse. You know I've been here the longest? I mean, apart from Al, but now he's gone, it's me. Matt came next. He replaced Ron, Greg came when Joe retired, then Billy, then you."

"I didn't know that."

"Now you do. I don't know why it matters except to say things haven't always been like this."

Derek hesitated. It occurred to him he didn't really know Chuck at all. "Like what?"

This question made Chuck lift his head and look at Derek as if he was an idiot. "Like what?! Like you know what." He paused, several sighs escaping him before continuing. "Before Greg was here, we barely participated in the Alabama Bandmasters Association. Our bands were smaller then, and the competitions and things were not on our radar. Don't think we didn't do anything; we still had performances and marched in our parades and all. We were all members of the ABA; we just didn't participate. It was like they were far off somehow. Anyway, when Greg came, he was a natural leader. Outspoken. He started taking his kids to these competitions and festivals and encouraged us to do the same. It was a good change. We thought we were doing the right thing."

Chuck took another long pause, but Derek didn't interrupt him. He suspected Chuck was collecting his thoughts and wanted to give him the space to do so. After a couple minutes, he did go on. "Greg got to be in leadership positions more and more. You know about his roles in the ABA, but I mean even here, amongst our group. He started to be... controlling. He would threaten us, jokingly at first, about giving us poor performance scores. Then, as he started gaining more power, I think, he started making comments that made me real uncomfortable. Sexist mostly but sometimes racist. Al ate it up, and they got to be the main voices. You know how Al is. And I just... Lately, I've been thinking I'm a coward. I decided to stop talking, run my band how I run it, and not argue. Our group slowly became so *strange*. By the time Billy joined, we weren't genuine friends anymore, but we always hung out like we were. Matt and I used to get along. I think he might be a good guy. Hell, same with you and Billy, but I don't rightly know any of you."

"I... Wow, Chuck, I've always been under the impression you were all close. Yeah, Greg is the loudest, but I guess I interpreted everyone else as kind of supporting him."

"That's why I knew I had to talk to you. I also assumed the rest of the group was fine. Then, the last couple times we were together, you seemed like maybe you didn't think so. Tonight, you said he was a problem. He's been a problem for a long time for me, but I never had the guts to say it." Chuck's head hung low.

Derek struggled to organize all this new information and history. It felt like he was sight-reading and trying to keep up. "What if we're all feeling this way? You said Billy got here before me. He could easily be reading the group the same. You think Matt might be a good guy, and you got along before Greg came. He could be acquiescing to maintain the group, too."

"It could be. Even so, what could we do? You've heard him. He's the chairperson for Adjudication, our District chair, and he's related to the President. Always talking about seeing Ira at family gatherings."

"I don't know. I remember when I started, Al was plain with me. Greg could 'take care of me' if I didn't fall in line by ensuring we got poor ratings. Then I'd either be replaced or worse, they'd consider shutting down the music program altogether."

Both men sat silently, swings moving slightly as they shuffled their feet. Derek almost whispered, "Elle is excellent. Passionate about teaching and determined."

Chuck gave Derek a solemn expression. "She probably won't stay. With Greg trying to run her off, making her life hard, and his ability to bomb her band, who could blame her? Even if we could somehow alleviate that, you know how it is. People move here for a couple years tops and then leave for the faster life."

The last sentence was like a knife in his chest. Derek clenched his eyes shut against the memories rising up in him. The most painful memories. "I do know. Even so, there has to be something we can do." Chuck shrugged. "I have to think about all this more. Can we talk later?" Chuck nodded, his face forlorn. "You aren't a coward, Chuck. You're a peace-keeper. I know for me, dealing with Greg has been difficult, but it was more important to me that our students continue to have a music program than it was to fight. Now that I know I'm not alone... We can do something, I'm sure of it."

A reluctant smile crept up Chuck's face. "Thanks, kid. I'm not as sure, but I thank you all the same."

Nine

DISSONANCE - LACK OF HARMONY AMONG MUSICAL NOTES.

Elle, Mavis, and Derek stood in front of the school awaiting delivery of a large portion of the new Everest Middle loaner instruments.

Mavis updated Elle, "Tiny has been doing all kinds of research for how to offer mobile lattes. It turns out it must be possible because there are whole latte catering companies. There are challenges, though. She would need at least two power outlets for the espresso and steaming machines, plus a place to keep fresh cold dairy, and it has to be portable enough to manage."

Derek piped in, "She'd need a way to track sales, too. Preferably an App so people could pay with cards, I'd imagine, but at least some way to track the numbers and monies."

"True. I don't think she's gotten that far yet, but good point."

Elle was pleasantly surprised at Mavis and Derek. She anticipated they might be stiff or not get along, but the opposite was true. They all chatted genially as they waited. *Now I think of it, Mavis has only ever said positive things about Derek. Why was I anxious about them getting along?* Elle frowned. "I didn't think about how complicated it might be for her to sell at an event. It seemed like such an easy idea at the time."

Derek moved his arm as if reaching out to touch Elle but drew it back in quickly. "Even if it's more involved, it's a great idea! Go where the people are. I guarantee they'll want a coffee. It's going to be cooler weather soon, too."

Elle actually did reach out and grab Derek's forearm in her excitement. "Oh my God! Is that the truck?!" She bounced on the balls of her feet. Derek looked down at his arm and smiled. Mavis suppressed a grin and quickly aimed her vision toward the approaching white box truck.

The driver parked at the curb and climbed down from his seat. "Ms. Elle Foster?"

She nodded. "That's me!"

"I've got quite a lot of boxes for you. Good thing you brought friends." He unlocked and lifted the truck door, revealing a Tetris of carefully stacked and secured boxes. "I can help you unload these here, but I can't help carry them onto the property. Regulation. Sorry about that."

Mavis replied, "We understand," and the team went to work.

Small boxes were unloaded first, making the job deceptively easy. That changed by the time they were on their third trip carrying the medium and large brass instruments. "How many more?" Mavis asked with a put-on whine.

Elle pulled the packing slip from her pocket as they returned to the curb. Once they got to the band room, she quickly opened each box, inspected for damage, and checked the instruments off the list. "We're close to the end, but the rest will be heavy."

The driver rested his arm against the final unloaded packages; they were almost as tall as he was. "This is it. Alright if I head out?"

"Can you wait just a sec while I peek in?" He stepped back

from the parcels, and Elle brought out a box cutter. She carefully peered into each one and made a check on her sheet. "Okay, thank you!" He climbed back into the truck and drove off.

Derek eyed the boxes suspiciously. "What are these ones?"

"I'm thinking you'll like these the best."

"You got percussion?!"

"Yep!" Elle clapped and put her hands up in a cheer. "They can't borrow these, but I got some things for the classroom."

Mavis scratched her head. "That sounds great and all, but how will we move them?"

Derek said matter of factly, "I'll go get the dolly. We have one for away games."

Mavis's voice became increasingly higher pitched as she asked, "You've had a dolly this entire time?!"

"Eeeee.... I guess I didn't think of it until now.... I'll be right back!" He jogged toward the high school.

As soon as he was out of earshot, Mavis widened her eyes at Elle. "You two are getting along *really well.*"

"I don't know what you're talking about."

"You do."

"Whatever could you mean?" Elle shot back coyly.

"Alright. Alright. If you don't want to admit it, that's fine." Mavis watched her closely. "He likes you." Elle's smile betrayed her, and Mavis celebrated. "I knew it!"

Elle padded out to the kitchen for a glass of water before bed. The light in the refrigerator blew as she pulled out the filtered pitcher. She sighed, grabbed the expo marker, and added "fix fridge light" to the bottom of the to-do list.

As she walked back to the bedroom, her mind strayed to Derek. *Mavis said he likes me.*

Elle placed the water on her nightstand and laid back against her pillow. She replayed a memory of him unpacking the percussion boxes. He was so excited at each unboxing and had even carefully assembled and tuned the snare and bass drums. Elle was grateful for his assistance and charmed by his genuine love for percussion, but now her mind was focused on how his arm muscles had strained against his shirt sleeves.

Did he get those from playing drums? She imagined him centered in a percussion pit and what he'd look like playing each instrument. *He's strong but also so gentle.* Elle remembered the light touches of his skin on hers during their first golf lesson. A tingling began between her legs. It made her feel alive; she couldn't remember the last time she was turned on. Elle closed her eyes and slipped a hand under the waistband of her pajama bottoms.

She was in her office after school. Derek leaned into the door, hands on the doorframe, arms tensed. His eyes bored into hers. It was clear what he wanted.

Elle beckoned him inside, and the door closed behind him with a click. Elle stood. The tension between them seemed to make even the particles of air hum.

Derek's voice was low and gravelly. "You sure you want to do this here?" Elle nodded, and he took his shirt off with one smooth motion. Her eyes followed his sculpted chest down his abs until she reached the button of his jeans.

Elle sat on the lip of her desk and pulled him closer. She ran her hands across those broad shoulders and down his torso. He unbuttoned her blouse. His crotch grazed against her inner thigh, and she gasped at the hardness beneath his jeans.

As she imagined the scene in her mind, her fingers swirled around her clit faster and faster. She saw herself unzipping his pants. His erection straining against his briefs. She reached for his cock, and... Release flooded her body.

Elle stilled. She didn't want to open her eyes. *Let me enjoy this for a minute.*

It was her first orgasm in months. She hadn't been cognizant of the fact, but now it occurred to her as a positive omen. Things were becoming more settled. There was a lot that needed doing, but her focus was in the right places. Her students, her classroom, her career, and forging relationships.

Since his conversation with Chuck, Derek had been preoccupied with what they could do to improve the situation. One of the problems was not knowing what their goal should be. He wanted Elle to be treated as an equal, but he also wanted Greg's bullying and uncouth comments to end. He considered the possibility of withdrawing from the Band Misters; he'd rather hang out with Elle anyway, but that left him and Elle open to Greg's influence. Ultimately, that meant Greg's power in the ABA would have to be neutralized, but doing so would be treacherous to pursue given his relationship with the President. He circled these thoughts, got frustrated, and daydreamed about Greg getting fired. That would solve everything, but did he really want him to lose his job? As far as Derek knew, Greg was a fine director despite his personal issues with him. He always reached the same conclusion. He would have to start small and gauge where Billy and Matt were. If the entire group was uncomfortable with his behavior, maybe they could have an intervention of sorts. *Not that I think it would work, but I don't know what else to do.*

If those lines of thought were stymying, it was nothing compared to figuring out how to talk to Billy and Matt. He believed Billy would be the safest to approach first since he didn't work as closely with Greg, but when they were together, Greg was always there. If he could get Billy alone, what would he say? It would have to be carefully worded in case they did have a genuine friendship. Plus, Derek didn't know how to ask without divulging his own feelings. Chuck was not much help when he tried to chat with him.

Derek Michaels

Any thoughts on how we might approach B? 3:36pm

Chuck Franklin

No 9:08pm

Derek Michaels

Me either 9:10pm

Days passed, and Derek felt caught in the problem alone. When his phone buzzed in his pocket while cooking dinner, he assumed it was his Mom and fetched it out to FaceTime with her. He was surprised to see Chuck's name flash across the screen.

Chuck Franklin

> I talked to you because you gave me a
> clear sign. 5:55pm

Derek lowered the heat on the pan and thought back on the message. It was a fact, but was it enough to inform what they should do now? What if they never gave any indication? Was it safe then to assume they shared Greg's perspectives? The stir-fry sizzled and popped, breaking him from his reverie. *At least this is somewhere to start.*

Derek Michaels

> Fair point. Let's observe for an opportunity.
> 6:00pm

Elle's swing was progressing nicely. Derek sipped his coffee and watched her land a ball beyond the 100-yard marker. "Nice!"

"Thanks!" She stepped off the platform and grabbed her own brew. Drinks had become their signature move. Elle always brought a cold refreshing something for them to band practices (usually an Arnold Palmer, but she mixed it up occasionally). Derek always brought coffee to The Drive (though he now brought them prepared coffee with cashew cream and a splash of maple or agave instead of an entire spread of fixings).

The morning light glanced off Elle's curly hair, giving her an ethereal glow. She wore what Derek now identified as her uniform: leggings and an eccentric oversized top. It was light green leggings with yellow stitching and a pink checkered shirt today. The tone of her quadriceps and calves noticeable beneath the nylon. " Earth to Derek! You're up!"

"Hmm? Zoned out there." It was a struggle not to whenever she was around. Derek grabbed his club and aimed. "Going for the target to the left by the 130." The ball landed well to the right of the target. He blew a raspberry. "Remember, I told you up front I'm mediocre at this."

Elle smirked. "Still better than me!"

"You'll be kicking my ass in no time. Come show me up." Derek stepped aside and swept his arm toward the tee in a low bow. Elle hopped onto the platform, curls bouncing on her shoulders. She was so buoyant. Derek enjoyed her turns because his eyes could wander over her without feeling like he was gawking. He saw small things he adored. Her clavicle was pronounced when she raised her club. She had a slim frame, but she was strong. Her triceps flexed during her downswing. Her freckles weren't limited to those dotting her face but appeared down her arms and even on her right ring finger.

"Did you see that?!" Elle was excited, but Derek hadn't exactly been watching the outcome of her swing.

"Uhhh."

"I almost got to 150!" She twirled on her toes, making her shirt flare out, then leapt from the platform and kissed him on the cheek. Derek's face went hot, and he raised his hand to touch the place her lips had been. Before he could respond, Elle apologized. "Oh my God, I'm so sorry. I don't know what came over me."

Ugh, don't apologize for something I want so much! "No, you're fine. I wish I were a better tutor; what would I earn then?" He winked at her.

"I don't know... I think the look on Greg's face will be sweet for both of us."

Derek's face fell. They hadn't spoken about Greg in depth before, and spending time with Elle made it easy to forget their goal of rising to his inane challenge. It happened in a moment. He had the intense urge to tell her everything he knew about the Band Misters, couldn't bring himself to do it, and then felt consumed with guilt.

"What's wrong?" Elle asked.

Each of his thoughts was dissonant with the one before. Showing up Greg at anything was dangerous for Elle, and he could explain it to her, but what good would it do? He didn't know where the rest of the group stood yet, and Chuck's words echoed in his head. "She probably won't stay." If she knew what she was up against, wouldn't it be even more likely for her to leave? *I can't tell her yet. When there's a solid plan, it'll be a better time.*

Derek shook his head. "Yeah. Sorry. I don't know what's wrong with me today."

"What are you thinking about?"

His stomach burned. "The football schedule. I can't remember when we're traveling to Stoville. Did you know we're playing Darton for our homecoming this year?"

"I didn't." Her eyes widened. "We *have* to do better than his band."

Hard determination lined her face, making Derek smile despite his unease. "I totally agree with you there! Though Greg will never admit it even if we did."

Elle rolled her eyes. "That tracks. I think I'm done for the day. Gonna end on a high. Do you want to do some more?"

Derek grabbed his clubs. "Nah, let's go."

They walked to their cars, deciding where to get lunch from. A look crossed Elle's face. *Furtive?* "I had a thought. Not for today's lunch, but, um, when is your school lunch break?"

"11:50 to 12:20. You?"

"12 to 12:30 for me. I guess if you ever wanted to meet up for lunch during the week, we have some overlap. It's okay if you don't want to."

"I have thoughts, too. First, I love your idea, and I definitely think we should. Second, why don't we go to my place today? I'll cook us up something."

Derek's house was a trove of discovery for Elle. From the moment they pulled into the drive, she either learned something new or saw something to pique her curiosity. His home was a near-perfect match of the one she had imagined all those months ago when she googled how to garden. The house was in a scantly populated area surrounded by woods on the outskirts of town. It was pale blue with white trim and had the air of being tidy and kept. Planters were hanging off the side of the porch railing; herbs like rosemary, basil, and oregano grew from them instead of flowers. There was a small garden bursting with life surrounded by a short picket fence on the right side of the house. Sunflowers were planted in a plot on the left side, and butterflies fluttered around them. A bee zipped in front of Elle's face as she climbed the steps to the porch.

"Is that a kayak?" Elle pointed to the porch's far corner, where two blue and yellow boats were.

"It is! I love kayaking. I'll have to show you my favorite thing about the property. I don't want to spoil it yet."

The mystery of the jacked arms is solved, then. The inside of Derek's home maintained the energy of being clean but still cozy and welcoming. Elle noted two bookshelves with photos and knickknacks displayed amongst the tomes in the living room. There was a couch and a dark blue squashy armchair, but no television. *Does he hate technology or something? Maybe he doesn't watch TV?*

The kitchen was stunning. There was a large window facing out onto the garden, and the wall was painted green, which gave the illusion of a connection between the garden and the room. The other walls were white except for the tile backsplash, which was patterned in a colorful fern mosaic. Several real ferns were in planters, and ivy varietals hung from glass orbs mounted to the wall. "Derek, your home is beautiful, but the kitchen is like a dream. You never told me you lived in a *Better Homes & Gardens.*"

"Hah! Thanks. It's been a work in progress, but I am especially proud of the kitchen. It's the most important room in the house."

"Why do you say that?"

Derek lifted his head, a thoughtful expression in his eyes. "First, I love cooking and baking, and just being in the kitchen. But also, we all need food. The kitchen is the place to congregate with family and friends." He started rifling through cabinets, the pantry, and the refrigerator. "What are you in the mood for? I've got a killer recipe for Chickpea Noodle Soup and some focaccia?"

"Let's do it!" Elle skipped next to him in front of a cutting board. "Knife me!"

Derek laughed and pointed to a knife block. "Help yourself." He began collecting the ingredients and piling them up next to the board.

"Are these onions.... Are these onions from your garden?!"

"They are! They came out great. I'll have some carrots soon, too. And for the next growing season, I've got some commissions. What was on your list? Micro-greens and broccolini?"

"You're going to grow things for me?!"

"I, um, have a recipe for seitan too." Derek looked down at the cutting board, but Elle caught his pleased expression.

They both began chopping onions, celery, carrots, and garlic. Elle's desire to learn about Derek overcame any qualms about asking too many questions. She felt giddy and strangely comfortable being in his space. "Are those your family in the photos?"

"Yeah, that's Mom and Dad and my brother John."

"You're close to them?" It was a sensitive thing to ask, but she had to know! She hoped to steer the conversation away from her own mess of a family and still learn about his.

His face lit up. "Yeah. They're great. They live in Atlanta, but we see each other as much as we can, and I talk to my folks about once a week on FaceTime."

Elle exhaled, "Thank goodness," under her breath.

Derek heard it. "What was that?"

She thought on her feet, "I was pretty concerned you were a technophobe when I didn't notice a TV."

"A technophobe!? Me!? Hey Siri, play 90's pop and turn on the lights in the kitchen." Man on the Moon by REM began playing from a hidden speaker, and a track of LEDs under the cabinets came on. Elle put her hands on her hips and cocked her head. "I just don't have a TV. I watch anything I want on my computer."

"Point proven."

They chatted about their favorite seasons and times of day (Autumn and evening for Elle and Spring and sunrise for Derek). They spent 30 minutes ranking their favorite music artists, eventually agreeing it was an impossible task after naming examples from Taylor Swift to Dr. Dre.

The soup was delicious, and Elle was impressed when the focaccia was just as tasty. "You weren't kidding about loving to be in the kitchen. This bread is everything! How do you have time to do all this?"

Derek sighed. "I'm afraid you now know the whole story about me. All I do is band, fix up the house, kitchen stuff, gardening, and kayaking. I'm boring, to be honest."

Elle chewed quickly to respond and swallowed. "I wouldn't say that."

After clearing the table and storing the remaining soup, Derek said, "Let me show you one more thing, my favorite thing."

Elle followed him out a back door. The backyard was shaded by the large trees at the edge of the wood behind the house. She stopped and looked around, expecting him to show her something in the yard, but Derek kept walking toward the forest, and she had to jog a few steps to catch back up to him. Derek led her to a small foot trail in the trees and continued their journey on the path.

"What is this?" Elle asked, thrilled. "This is the coolest thing. You have hiking right out your door!"

"It's even better. Wait 'til you see."

They hiked for 10 minutes, spotting different flowers and birds. Then Derek stopped. "Do you hear it?"

Elle listened. "You've got to be kidding!"

She ran further along the trail until she found the source of the babbling water. A slow-moving river, sunlight glistening off its ripples. Derek stopped behind her. "I bring the kayaks out here as much as I can. It's slow enough you can paddle both ways."

"I can see why it's your favorite. This is perfect." They stayed and listened to the river for a while before making the hike back.

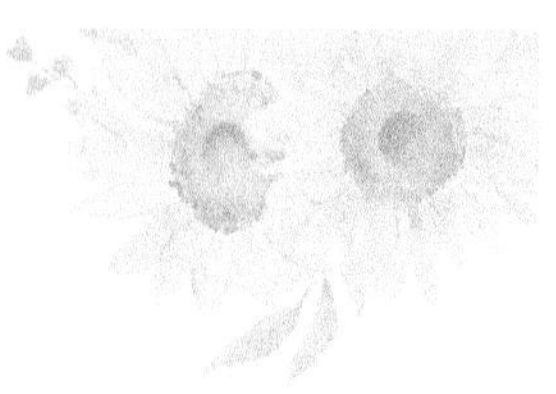

Ten

TIMBRE - THE CHARACTER OR QUALITY OF A
MUSICAL SOUND OR VOICE AS DISTINCT FROM
ITS PITCH AND INTENSITY.

Since their last lesson at The Drive, Elle and Derek met for lunch on their breaks every day. They alternated meetings in each other's rooms. Occasionally, Mavis popped in when they met at Derek's (her lunch was 11:35-12:05, making the trip across to Elle's side of campus impossible).

Today, it was Derek's turn to host. As noon approached, his eyes flitted to the door in anticipation. Elle's arrival was announced by sound instead of sight, however. At 12:03pm, a rhythm began playing from his door. Whoever was on the other side used a combination of taps, raps, and scrapes. His head tilted back in amusement as he jogged to the door and opened it to Elle, hands raised in mid-knock. She twirled into the room, causing her crayon-patterned dress to fan out around her.

"Nice beat. I love your dress, by the way."

Elle batted her eyes. "This old thing? Kidding, it's totally new, and thank you for saying so." She followed him to his office and took her usual seat across the desk. "I worked on that jam for a super long time."

Derek pressed his lips together. "Oh really? It sounded like it."

"That means a lot coming from you."

Derek gestured for Elle to follow and proceeded to the percussion area. Being the high school director, he had many more instruments in the section than Elle did. He grabbed a snare and sticks and started improvising a beat, keeping a keen eye on her expression. Then, he spun around, positioned himself in front of the marimba, grabbed 4 mallets into a modified Musser Grip, and began playing The Mario Bros theme. This took more concentration, but he managed to glance up to see Elle bopping along to the tune.

When she caught his eye, Elle stopped singing and said, "You're just showing off now."

Derek stopped playing. "Well, yeah. You laid down a challenge; I had to do something!" Elle's laughter was beautiful to Derek.

"Good show. I don't think I'm much of a threat to you on percussion. Next time we'll have to go head to head on sax."

Derek twisted his face into a show of horror. "I grant you the win outright. Here and now." Then, in a small voice, "Please don't make me." More of her musical laughter. This time it reminded him of the sound of water flowing over river rocks. Depending on the type of laugh, giggle, or guffaw, genuine or sarcastic, her timbre brought different things to mind.

The computer in the office made a familiar swoosh sound, and the two walked back to finish their food. Derek opened the Mail App after taking a bite of sandwich.

Greetings All,

Homecoming is right around the corner in two weeks! Homecoming Spirit Week events and activities are listed below.

The Homecoming Dance will take place after the game on Friday, September 26th, at the Ag Center until 11pm. **We are in desperate need of chaperones.** *If you can chaperone, please reply ASAP.*

The email went on, but Derek's ability to read further had screeched to a halt. He watched Elle across the desk. She was focused on scooping hummus onto a carrot, but even watching her do this mundane task made his insides roar for her. He thought about asking her out on a date every time he saw her but never found the courage to do it. *We're practically dating already. I see her all the time between lunches, rehearsals, and The Drive. Making it official will only make it hurt more when she leaves.* And there it was. The fear that festered within him. His thoughts always landed there, making him hang back, but the temptation to ask felt increasingly urgent. Maybe it would be worth it. He could ask her to the homecoming dance.

A new timid idea emerged. *What if she does stay?* It broke his heart and fortified him at once. Derek tried to capitalize on the seed of hope in him. "Would you go to the dance? To homecoming dance?" He let out a short, exasperated breath and tried again slower. "Would you like to go to the homecoming dance with me? They're asking for chaperones." *Fuuucccckkk me, 'they're asking for chaperones?' What the fuck is wrong with me?*

Elle lowered her carrot, an appreciable amount of hummus balanced on the end. "Sure. I could help chaperone."

"You know, Derek has been a big help getting me set up for this crazy experiment." Tiny affixed a sign bearing the "Tiny's Cafe" logo to the folding table.

Elle cut her eyes to her. It was increasingly clear her friends were looking for them to date. Elle knew how Derek had assisted but asked, "Is that so?"

Tiny nodded while plugging the equipment into the brick wall behind them. "It is! I guess his brother is an Accountant, and he got this ledger for me to track sales until I can join the 21st century and accept card payments. Plus, he connected me with the school to get permission to sell here."

"He's a pretty helpful guy."

They stood back and admired their work. It was a simple setup. Cashbox and ledger. Coffee with powdered cream and sugar.

Elle saw Tiny frown. "What are you thinking?"

She sighed. "I don't know. I wish it was more than brewed coffee. I couldn't figure out how to do the espresso drinks out here without buying different equipment."

"Well," Elle caught her eye, "I hope it's a big success, but even if it doesn't work out, I'm so proud of you for trying something new."

Tiny's frown turned into a smile. "Thank you for the idea and helping me set up, and just... Thanks."

The volume of the area was increasing as people lined up for entry to the game. Tiny's table was set up to the right of the gates, against the side wall of the concession area. Because the concessions didn't offer coffee, her request to sell at home games in exchange for donating 10% of her proceeds to the school was granted easily and met with delight.

"Wanna hear something weird?" Elle gazed absentmindedly toward the queuing people.

Tiny also took in the line, though she regarded them with heightened attention. "Hmm?"

"Derek invited me to the homecoming dance, but OW!"

Tiny slapped her arm. "You're just now telling me this?! Does Mavis know?! Why'd you sit on this information?!"

Elle shook her head, lips pursed. "It's not like that. I mean, I thought it was for a second, but then he said they needed chaperones. Which makes sense. Adults wouldn't go to a high school dance as a date. I don't know what I was thinking."

"Mmm. You were thinking you wanted him to ask you out. And I don't know, I'm not convinced it isn't a date. What did he say, exactly?"

Elle tried to recall his words, and the pair debated what Derek may have meant. All the while, more talking and jovial noises rose around them. Tiny could not convince Elle it was a date, and as the gates opened to let the first attendees in, she had to raise her voice to continue speaking. "You should still dress up for it anyway. And you know you could ask him out? Even in Everest, women can ask out men now."

Elle smirked and rolled her eyes. "I've got to go get my sax. Good luck!" As she departed, a small line formed in front of Tiny's table.

Elle hastily pulled on last year's band shirt, adjusted her neck strap, and took off the long way around the bleachers. A few of her students already sitting waved at her as she sped by, and she could've sworn a few other people pointed at her. *This is an improvement, and so what if they don't like my hair clips.* She waved back to the friendly faces and ignored the pointers. Mavis and Tiny had gently (finally) explained the pieces in her wardrobe that caused a reaction. There were her running clothes, "Because you show your midriff when you wear the sports bra." They also advised how some of her other outfits would qualify, "If it's too bright or different, it'll be considered 'out there.'" Elle supposed her butterfly barrettes with moving wings on springs might be in the 'out there' category.

Around the back of the bleachers, she slowed down slightly. This was the hard part of the plan. Elle crept along the stands until she could see the band clearly, then turned around so her saxophone wouldn't be obviously spotted. She waited, watching every few seconds to see what Derek was doing. Then the moment struck! Derek walked away toward the field. Elle squatted low and ran to join the saxophone players. The section parted for her to join between Amanda and Topher, who suppressed giggles.

Now, she just needed to blend in. See how long it took Derek to notice the additional band member.

Seconds. Or was it less?

He walked back toward them, saying, "I don't see her any...." Then stopped dead and raised an eyebrow, looking directly at Elle. Many of the students did let out a small laugh before regaining themselves. He was positively playful. Elle had the sensation of resisting going to him. It would be natural to skip over to Derek. Pinch his firm arm.

Derek slowly approached until he stood directly in front of Elle. "Ms. Foster. *Where* did you get that shirt?"

Topher wheezed to her right. "This is my shirt. You don't remember it? It's from last year."

Amanda pressed her lips tight to keep quiet and turned her head away. Derek ignored the students, keeping his focus entirely on Elle. "Oh yeah? And when did we last wear that shirt at a performance?"

Elle's eyes traveled left and right as she searched for an answer. "I believe it was Veterans Day?"

Derek bit his lower lip before bursting out laughing. "It may have been! I honestly can't remember. Good guess, though." He reached for her hand and pulled her out of the circle of students. "Get over here." The touch of his hand on hers seemed to linger far after he let go.

Elle spent the first half of the game alternating between playing with the saxophone section and talking to Derek at the front. The students taught her the choreography they made to some of their favorite stadium tunes. Derek complimented the band shirt and tried to guess who loaned it to her. After striking out several times, she put him out of his misery. "It's Jessica's. Her sister is in my band, and we ran into each other, and, I don't know, an idea formed."

"Jessica! Sweet little Jessica pranked me?"

"Yes, and all the saxophones, which I'm pretty sure told the rest of the band. So I'd say we all pranked you. Being fair." There was something about his stare then. *Maybe the dance is a date, after all?*

His gaze faltered suddenly, and he swore under his breath. "It's halftime! Let's go go go! We don't want to be late!"

Sure enough, when Elle looked to the field, the rival band was already marching to their positions. Elle helped raise the alarm and took her usual position at the top of the stands. Something felt different tonight. She considered it for a moment before it struck her. The bleachers were quieter than usual. She spun around and found far fewer spectators than there should be. *Where did they go?* She stood up and immediately saw a large crowd, not at the concessions but to the side.

Elle ran down the stands, pushing her way through the crowd and muttering "Excuse me" on repeat as she went at nobody in particular and everyone all at once. Tiny's face was drawn tight in concentration. Money changed hands so fast that it was hard to follow. Elle joined Tiny behind the table without waiting to ask permission and shouted, "I can help the next person!"

The throng of people split into two lines. Tiny took the

length of a heartbeat to catch Elle's eyes and mouth, "Thank you," between handing a cup to a customer and taking cash from the next.

The third quarter was well underway by the time the line dissipated. Elle exhaled loudly. She turned to check on Tiny, who was wide-eyed in disbelief. "That was… Phew. Thank you for rescuing me."

"No problem. Half the stands were down here! I don't think the cash box can fit any more in!"

Tiny sounded slightly manic. "Ha! It won't have to. We're out of everything. I can't believe it."

Elle smiled. "You've got this, and I'll help at all the games if that's what we need to do! Are you alright if I go back to the band for now? I'll come to help break down after the game."

Tiny caught her breath before agreeing, and Elle returned to the stands.

"There you are; I thought you were all trying to trick me again." Derek lowered his hand to Elle to help her up the large stadium steps. These innocent touches were becoming so commonplace. "How did we do?"

"I'm so sorry, I actually didn't see it. So many people were buying coffee from Tiny that it was like a giant traffic jam down there. I ran down to help her out."

"That is an acceptable reason. Hell yeah, go, Tiny!"

"Right?! I'm so excited for her!"

Between cheers and plays, they wondered what Tiny was thinking and dreamed about where she would take things given her initial success.

Meeting with the Band Misters was more stressful now that Derek needed to be hyper-attentive to his colleagues instead of zoning out. All their time together went the same. Greg inevitably made crude, infuriating comments. Matt and Billy gave no overt indication about where they stood through their reactions, and Chuck was silent.

Derek pressed his fingers against his eyes and then moved them out to rub his temples. He watched the color blobs shift and dissipate on the back of his eyelids before opening them. *Here we go. Pay attention, but keep your cool.* That was the problem. His heightened awareness of what Greg was spouting made it difficult not to punch him in the jaw. Then there was the disappointment that nobody else seemed to feel the same way and the sad recognition that he had acted as if he didn't care for years now. He felt ashamed for his past inaction and desperate to do something now.

Last weekend, he tried talking to his Mom about it on FaceTime. Derek grimaced at the memory. He didn't want her to worry, so he withheld information, describing having issues with a senior colleague. It wasn't a perfect analogy, and his Mom interpreted it as a disagreement between himself and his principal. She told him to try to see from Mark's perspective and, "I'm sure you'll figure it out; you've always gotten on well with everyone."

A loud rapping noise on his car door jerked him into the present. "You coming or what?" It was Greg. He turned to the others, "Doing his makeup in there, hah!"

Derek fought the urge to drive off, reluctantly retrieved his bag, and joined the group as they walked to their station at The Drive.

"You ready for next week? Big game. Rivals at homecoming, eh?" Greg elbowed Derek in the ribs.

Derek replied, "Should be a good one."

"You know I'm not talking about the teams. Is your *band* ready?"

He decided to try a new tactic. "That's what I meant too. My band is more than prepared. Good we're talking about this now; I wouldn't want you to be embarrassed Friday." Matt glanced at Derek. Billy's eyes widened in surprise, but he showed no other reaction.

"Oh ho, look who's finally showed up. It's about damn time." Greg howled. "You don't stand a chance, son."

Derek grinned as deviously as he could and said with an air he hoped was casual. "I've never been more confident in my group. We've got it down by heart... I guess we'll let the crowd decide."

A wildness sparked behind Greg's eyes. "I guess we fuckin' will let the crowd decide. You're actin' mighty big for some reason. Don't get to cock...."

Derek interrupted, "I'm not too cocky; we're just that good." He saw Billy make a silent whistle as he turned his head to the side, and he could have sworn Chuck laughed behind him.

"Boy. It might do you good to remember who you're talkin' to."

"Aw, Greg, come on. It's all respect. Don't tell me you can't take a little competition." Derek wasn't sure how long he could keep this banter up or how long Greg would tolerate it. Even his movement was erratic and bothered. *Alarming he's this easy to work up.*

Fortunately, he did calm slightly at Derek's last statement. "Respect, yeah. Friendly competition. Let's golf."

Derek's phone buzzed in his pocket, and his heart skipped a beat. Elle was nearly the only person who texted him. Checking the phone was tricky, though. He knew from experience if he did so in front of Greg, it would set his middle school teasing off, and if he found out it was Elle, it'd be worse. He waited until Greg was at the tee, then quickly checked.

Elle Foster

> What are you wearing to the dance?
> 4:39pm

Hope swelled in his chest like a balloon. Maybe he hadn't botched the invitation to her as badly as he feared!

Elle Foster

> I mean, is there a dress code for
> chaperones? 4:40pm

Or maybe he had. He swallowed a sigh and shoved the phone back away. He'd have to answer on Greg's next swing.

Derek Michaels

> No official dress code. Why don't we dress
> up a little and have some fun? 4:50pm

There, maybe that hinted at something.

· · ·

Elle Foster

Okay, let's have some fun :) 4:51pm

Derek's insides were a waltz, but he tried to maintain a neutral affect.

Greg wolf-whistled, bringing Derek out of his joy back to reality. He looked around and spotted a young woman at the next station. She wore her long dark hair in a sleek ponytail, jeans, and a tank top; a hoodie was tied around her slim waist. She turned at Greg's whistle, and Derek was struck by how young she was. She could have been in high school.

The party she was with was as fresh-faced and clearly there to let loose. She swung the club awkwardly, missing the ball completely, and collapsed into giggles. To Derek's horror, Greg approached the other station. "That actually wasn't too bad there, sweetheart. Do you want some tips from a pro?"

Derek quickly tipped his head at Billy and Matt. It was not discrete- there was no time for discretion! Billy's eyes were dead; his throat bobbed. Matt caught Greg's eye when he turned to wink at the Band Misters and made the cut-it-out motion with his hand, slicing the air in front of his neck. *What did that mean?!*

Greg ignored Matt's warning, turning back toward the girl. She was frozen as if she didn't know what to say. She turned several times to her friends, but they seemed as unsure as she was. "Um, I guess you can tell me some tips. We're just here to have fun."

"Well, sure, I can tell you. It's more effective to show, but I'll tell ya." Greg stepped onto their platform and explained as he demoed, but Derek focused on his peers. Matt exhaled and concentrated on his shoes. Was it out of relief, exasperation, or something else? Billy was the opposite. He couldn't seem to tear his eyes away. Derek suddenly recalled that Billy had a daughter and wondered if he imagined his pallor based on his own unease or if it was real.

Nervous giggling made Derek turn his head toward the neighboring station. The girl and one of her friends were now on the platform with Greg. Her friend gently tugged the girl back toward the others protectively. *Funny, it's her girlfriend pulling her back, and the two guys just stood there. They were on high alert, at least.*

"Greg, it's your go." Billy gestured at their green.

Greg eyed the girl. "It was mighty, mighty nice to meet you. I guess I gotta go." He pointed over his shoulder with his thumb.

Derek was left uncertain after the interaction. He had finally witnessed reactions from Matt and Billy, but Matt may have been looking out for a friend. Making sure he didn't get in trouble. Billy was subdued. It was hard to know whether he was imagining things or not. It didn't matter. This was enough to do something. It had to be! He could no longer stand the inaction and decided to approach Billy about the incident right then.

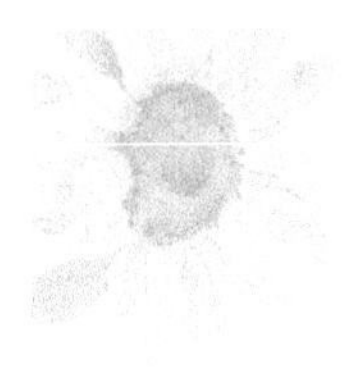

Eleven

COMPREHENSIVE MUSICIANSHIP THROUGH
PERFORMANCE (CMP) - A METHOD OF
TEACHING PERFORMING ENSEMBLES THAT
INVOLVES INSTRUCTION OF MUSICAL
CONCEPTS AND HISTORY IN ADDITION TO
TRADITIONAL PERFORMANCE TECHNIQUES.

Unlike the rest of the men, Billy cleaned his clubs at The Drive before heading out. If Derek lagged behind, he might find some alone time between them. He packed his clubs away as slowly as possible without raising suspicion. His hair was on end with anticipation, but the idea panned out. Greg, Matt, and Chuck left for their vehicles first, leaving Billy and Derek alone.

Billy finished polishing his clubs and waved at Derek. "Have a good one."

Derek didn't know what to say. "You too. I mean, hey..." Billy stopped. Derek searched for how to begin. "Umm. Did you see Greg and that girl?"

Billy let out a sharp exhale. "Yeah."

"That felt a little... I don't know, off. To me, I mean. I guess I just wondered if I was the only one? It totally could be just me."

Billy appraised him carefully before answering. "It," He paused and glanced toward the parking lot, "wasn't just you."

"Oh. Okay." Derek's courage swelled slightly. "I feel like sometimes... I guess sometimes I feel like he's a little sexist."

There were long seconds where Billy nodded his head silently before agreeing. "Yeah. I can see that."

He's as apprehensive as I am about talking about Greg. "Do you ever wonder about things being different, or...?"

Billy shuffled his feet and seemed to slowly deflate. "No. Things are the way they are. You're worried about your new middle school director?"

Derek saw the opportunity to lay everything out. It was a risk, and he felt constricted as he spoke, like his skin was too tight. "I am, but also, while we're being honest, it's more. I don't want to be threatened anymore, worried he'll punish my band if I get on his bad side."

"You already are on his bad side." Billy made a sad chuckle. "I understand what you're saying, but there's nothing for it."

"What if there were, though? Because right now, you, me, and Chuck are on the same page. We're the majority."

Billy's face brightened momentarily before flattening again. "That is something, but what are you suggesting? From what I know, he has the power to make all our lives hell."

"I don't know. Could he do anything if it were all of us? That's where I'm stuck. I thought about maybe even having a discussion with him? We could request a level of professionalism." Billy exuded skepticism, so Derek quickly added, "Maybe there isn't anything, but could I at least text you if I come up with something? And likewise, I'm not asking you to do anything, but if you have any ideas, let me know?"

"Greg cannot find out about any of this. They'll be filling positions for your middle and high school bands."

"I know it. And let that give you a little trust in me. I'm on the line; I won't say anything to him. In full transparency, I do want to try to talk to Matt. See where he is in everything, if possible."

Billy nodded. "You're crazy, man."

"Yeah. Maybe."

"It's going to keep falling down if you don't let the glue dry sufficiently first! Work on something else while it's drying, please!" Mavis shouted instructions left and right. Her clothes were the sole black items amidst a hurricane of colorful streamers, papers, and banners. The eye of the storm. "Jackson, let's tie that part up with the string instead. Paige, you need to alternate the gold and blue; there's a doubling up happening over there." She stood between two trailers being transformed into floats for the Homecoming Parade. Elle was impressed at how she simultaneously tracked every step for both projects. Mavis was so tuned into what was happening with the floats that she overlooked Elle's presence.

"Great job, wow, you've really got this!" Mavis jumped and turned wide eyes onto her friend. Elle laughed, "Sorry! I didn't mean to scare you. You were in the zone."

Mavis lowered her voice so only Elle would hear, "Thank God you're here. I'm losing my mind. Look at him." She sneered and barely nodded her head to the left.

Elle followed her nod. A rotund man sat atop a cooler, aiming a handheld misting fan at his face. Fall weather had begun, and it wasn't particularly hot outside, but the man was still sweating profusely. "Who is that?"

Mavis rolled her eyes maliciously. "Stewart. Mr. Greckle. You don't recognize him? He's the art teacher from Everest Middle."

Elle was shocked. "I... have somehow never seen this person. How does that work?"

"Pfft. I'm not surprised." Mavis sighed. "Nor am I at this," she gestured around, "I always help with the Everest High

Senior float, but last week Stewart asked if I'd help with his stinking float too. And I knew it; I knew I'd be doing all the work, but I couldn't bring myself to say no."

"Oof, the worst. You're doing great, though!"

Mavis toed at a clump of grass. "Doing them both at once was a mistake."

"I'm here to help, and Derek's on the way. Tag me in, coach!"

Mavis chuckled. "I hope I don't crush that enthusiasm. This one is supposed to be a tiger eating an eagle. The middle school's is a little easier, your basic platform, and they're going to have people in tiger suits ride on it."

Elle stuck out her lips and nodded. "So Darton are The Eagles. Got it. I have no idea how to make giant animals, but if you tell me what to do, I'll do it."

"Don't worry; the kids will want to do most of the work. We'll mainly supervise, but if you can help decorate the rim of the middle schools and then pile on the hay bales, I can focus on getting the papier-mâché going. Which *will* take forever, even under the best circumstances." They exchanged a smirk, and Elle took off toward the middle school float.

She knew some of the students decorating from her 8th-grade class. Willa, Rob, Martin, and Francesca introduced her to their classmates. Working with her students outside of the band room was novel. Elle admired how they came together as a team, particularly at Willa's leadership and willingness to get hay tangled in her hair.

They were stacking rectangular bales onto the trailer when Elle heard his voice. A waterfall of endorphins cascaded through her. Derek had arrived. She turned around, eventually finding the source of that familiar baritone over by Mr. Greckle. Derek spotted her at the same time, waved, and promptly abandoned Stewart, who made a flabbergasted expression at Derek's back.

"Greckle's as helpful as ever, I see," Derek said in way of greeting.

Elle subconsciously reached her arm out and embraced Derek in a side hug. He returned the squeeze with comfortable pressure.

The middle school float was completed in short order. Elle's students went home, and she and Derek joined forces with Mavis. It was tedious work. The wireframe animals were large. Mavis had arranged two long rows of painter trays filled with paste and three stacks of newspaper with scissors. Each person cut paper strips, dipped them into the paste, then took it to the wireframes to place it in a production line. It was not an ideal environment to talk due to all the constant movement necessary. Still, a game emerged between Elle and Derek.

It started with Elle staring in his direction. She loved to watch Derek work with students; he was so amiable with them! It didn't hurt that his smile amongst his evening stubble was so handsome it made her heart ache. She could see an outline of his pec when he turned the right way in the waning light and noted, as usual, that he worked in a way that betrayed his expertise. *There's his rhythm coming out again. He must be spectacular in bed.* At that moment, Derek caught her studying him and raised his eyebrows. Heat flooded her face, and she quickly got back to work. A few minutes passed, and she glanced at Derek to find his eyes fixed on her. She pursed her lips and narrowed her eyes, and he shrugged and mouthed something that may have been "not sorry." It went this way throughout the evening, their reactions at finding each other's gaze becoming more over the top each time, ending in full-out modeling poses.

What seemed like a comical amount of newspaper at the beginning of the project dwindled to barely enough by 9pm when they laid the last strip on the tiger's left ear.

Mavis pushed up her sleeve with the back of her opposite

hand to avoid soiling her shirt further. "Good job, all. We did a lot of work. We'll paint in a few days after this dries; I'll email you the details. That should be much more fun, thankfully." The small group of students who remained clapped and hooted.

Elle felt warm breath at her ear. Derek leaned toward her. "I'm starving. My place for a late snack?" She nodded, and they took off.

Elle wondered if it was strange that Derek's home felt more familiar than hers. Since her first visit, she had come more and more regularly, and while she technically spent more time at her own house, it still lacked the care it needed. It was foreign, whereas Derek's place was like a real home, comfortable and relaxing. Spending time there also made them closer as she slowly asked all the burning questions the surroundings brought about.

She knew he'd attended the Hugh Hodgson School of Music at the University of Georgia and that he had seriously considered focusing on Composition instead of Education. He'd inherited his love of gardening from his Mom, a Horticulturist at a botanical garden. His Dad was an engineer who worked for Lego (something Elle totally geeked out about). Derek wanted to get into beekeeping as one of his next projects, and his guilty pleasure was face masks. Elle had discovered this one day when he asked her to fetch headache medicine from his bathroom, and she opened a drawer containing at least a dozen different kinds of moisturizing masks.

"Grab the spinach outta there, too." Derek collected spices and honey from the pantry while Elle leaned into the refrigerator for jarred peppadews.

"Makes sense since we're making spinach dip and all," she

teased. Elle preheated the oven, grabbed a knife, and diced the peppers. She caught Derek looking at her. "What?"

"You know your way around the kitchen, is all." He smiled as if he treasured the fact.

Soon, they were standing around the island, dipping crackers and veggies into the sweet and tangy concoction. There was a lull in their conversation. Elle glanced up at Derek, mouth full of cracker. "Are we keeping on with the staring game tonight or what?"

"No, I was thinking... wondering. Can I ask you something personal?"

"You ask me personal things all the time," she laughed, "go ahead."

"I've been thinking about your parents. I'm sorry. I don't know them, and I'm struggling not to judge them. You know what, my question isn't even about them, not really."

Elle made a show of crunching into a cucumber slice, waiting. She had learned much about his family over the past months and shared more of her experiences. Derek usually became exasperated hearing about Elle's past but had only gone so far as to tell her that her parents were selfish. This had come when they compared Christmas traditions, and she shared that they didn't do Santa.

Derek swallowed. "It's just that I wonder, since you had this experience and aren't close to your parents... Do you want kids?"

Elle noted the tension in his jaw, his neck muscles feathered. She took another bite and bobbled her head back and forth to both find her words and relish Derek being on the edge of his seat.

His iPad on the counter rang before she could answer. It was Derek's Mom. He went to answer the video call, and Elle scooted out of view of the camera.

"Hey, Mom. It's late. Everything okay?"

A crisp female voice replied, "Of course, I missed you earlier. Are you busy?"

Elle recognized the woman's face from the pictures on the wall. Her skin had a permanently tanned quality, and she had the same dark wavy hair Derek did, albeit substantially longer, and with a few streaks of gray, it flowed down past the camera cut-off.

Derek turned in Elle's direction. "Sort of."

His mother's face lit up, "Oh my God, is she there?" She raised her voice, "Elle, are you back there?!"

Derek mouthed an apology to her and gestured for her to join the call. Elle stepped beside him. "Um, hi, Mrs. Michaels. Nice to meet you."

"Likewise, we've heard so much about you. You're shaking things up for the better at Everest." She paused, then cackled, "Wait until I tell your Dad I got to meet her first!"

Elle looked down, huffing a laugh. "Thank you, Mrs. Michaels, that's kind of you to say."

"It's a fact, and please call me anything else: Mom, Kelly, Hey You."

Derek shot his Mom a death stare, which she finally noticed. "I don't want to interrupt your night; you two kids have fun. Be safe."

The call dropped, and Elle said, "I love her. My new favorite person." Derek's shoulders relaxed. "But, *what* have you told her about me?"

"Oh, most things." She scrunched her face and punched his arm. He chuckled. "Come with me. I *think* it's cool enough the mosquitos have returned to hell."

Derek opened the front door and sat on the porch swing. Elle sat next to him. It was a small swing, and their legs touched. Derek pushed with his foot and set them to a gentle rock. The night was cooler and quieter than summer, frogs and crickets taking the season off.

Elle cleared her throat. "To answer your question. I definitely do. I love kids."

Derek put his arm around her, and the pressure of their legs together increased.

"Do you? Want kids, I mean?" Elle alarmed internally, realizing she assumed he did but didn't know.

When Derek answered, his voice was low. "At least two." He pushed the swing more and stroked her hair.

"Are we," Elle hesitated but quickly decided to plunge onward, "What are we?" She expected him to kiss her, to gently turn her head, lift her chin, and kiss her.

But Derek withdrew his arm, and chill air rushed to replace it. He walked to the porch rail, leaving Elle stung. "I subscribe to Comprehensive Musicianship through Performance, which I guess is not so much a philosophy but a teaching method." He turned toward Elle. "You once asked me what my teaching philosophy was."

"I, that was a long time ago. I'm sorry about...."

Derek shook his head, "Don't be sorry; you were right. I had forgotten what mattered. I read through all my old textbooks after that day. I reminded myself of all the theories and beliefs, but does it matter if music is for music's sake or if it serves a function?"

Elle tripped over her words, "I, I mean, I always believed music serves all purposes. They're all right, together."

"Exactly." His expression was fierce. *What is happening right now?* She crossed the few feet to stand by him at the rail, but when she was near enough, he grabbed her shoulders, positioning her directly in front of him. "You're my colleague who challenges me and makes me better. You're my friend who helps me and brings me joy. You're the person who I always look for, who I always want around. You're all those things, all right things."

The only thing keeping Elle from floating away were his

hands on her shoulders; her essence was hovering somewhere above them, even still. She inched toward him until they were firmly pressed against each other. His heart thumped loudly in her ear. "I want more." It came out a raspy whisper, but Derek heard her and stilled. She stared up at him and lifted onto her toes while he leaned into her, meeting for a kiss. The kiss. Elle wrapped her arms around him, running her hands up and down his back. The stubble on his cheeks scratched against hers, rough but pleasant. She pressed into his body, losing all awareness of time and space, yearning to be as close as possible to him. His cock hardened against her abdomen, and her body responded. They stayed intertwined, exploring each other with their hands and lips; she didn't know how long.

At some point, they returned inside and sat on the couch. Elle had been resisting stroking his hair, putting her hand on his arm, brushing against him for so long. Now they had crossed that bridge; the freedom to touch him was a relief. She sat sideways on the couch with her legs over his. He caressed her thighs absentmindedly as they talked into the night.

For Derek, the week of homecoming was a marathon. One he enjoyed for the most part, but after a week of daily dress-up themes, rowdy students, lunchtime pep rallies, and marching in the parade, he was ready to be on the other side. It didn't help that no small part of him was nervous about the game. He'd challenged Greg about the halftime performance, which could go badly. More than that, he was in a precarious position with Elle.

Something new and wonderful and scary was happening between them. It was the best thing, like living his most treasured dreams. Everything between them was so effortless. Even their first kiss had been instinctual, free from the awkwardness of learning how a partner moved. Greg could not find out about them. Not yet. And while he and Elle agreed to avoid public displays of affection as teachers, he worried what they had was so obvious it would be easily spotted. Once again, he suppressed the rising tide of guilt for not being completely transparent with Elle. If their being together was the most natural thing, keeping things from her was the most perverse.

Football games were always a hive of energy, but nothing compared to homecoming. The addition of alumni and the allure of the event brought hundreds more attendees. Even expecting this, Derek was taken aback by the crowd on both sides. He couldn't see Elle, but he could sense her where he knew she was. Unable to resist saying hi, he instructed Pete to take the band through the typical warmups, then picked his way through the people toward Tiny's stand.

A long line had already been formed before the table. Tiny, Elle, and Mavis were all smiles and hustle as they took cash, made change, and poured coffee like clockwork. Derek scooted behind Mavis and tapped Elle on the shoulder. She didn't slow her work but replied with a singsongy, "Hey, Derek! How's the band?"

Before he could answer, Tiny interjected, "More like are you ready to... what is it you're doing? Ah, *chaperoning*?" Elle smirked, and Mavis cackled.

"What I want to know is who will be chaperoning you two?" Mavis quipped.

Mavis and Tiny knew about their relationship and were enthusiastically supportive.

"If the band is as good at multitasking as you three, there will be no competition tonight." Derek savored the warmth unfurling in his chest as he watched Elle.

"There you are! That twiggy lil' guy said you went this way." Greg stood to his left, arms crossed and head tilted down, observing Derek through the tops of his eyes.

Derek quickly edged from behind the table, positioning himself between Greg and Elle, praying he wouldn't spot her. "Hey Greg, how are you?"

Greg ignored the question. "Big game today, and last I saw you, there was some big talk. Now we're facing the music; you probably wanna make nice."

He did not want to make nice.

Derek swallowed and steadied himself. This didn't need to escalate. "We talked about this. I was pulling your chain. Friendly competition, remember?"

"Look, you're the one who's going to feel stupid when Darton wipes the field with you!"

"Greg. I was smack-talking. I wish your band all the best, and mine too. Let's give everyone a great show." Greg was smoldering, his body tense and his hands in tight fists. It struck Derek as amusing. He wasn't trying to piss him off anymore, just get away from him, but apparently, what he set in motion was doomed to gain momentum. *He's reading my acquiescence as a further provocation. Fascinating. Not good.*

Greg spat on the ground, earning a disgusted glare from a passerby. "It's going to be a great show. Hopefully, that stick figure you have conducting doesn't get blown away."

"Maybe don't talk about the kids, man; come on."

"Look who's upset now!?" He put on a high-pitched, lilting voice, "Boohoo, don't talk about the kids. Let's give everyone a nice show. You sound more and more like a female all the time."

Derek burned. He felt dangerous. "*Don't* talk about my kids."

Greg clapped Derek on the arm. "Have a good game, Mama Bear." Derek watched him walk toward the visitor's side until the crowd blocked him from view. Someone squeezed his hand, and he turned to see Elle behind him. "I know we said we were too good to sabotage him, but I'm actually leaning toward foul play now." The angry flare in him receded. "I'm only part kidding; tell those kids to play their hearts out tonight."

Derek smiled. "They will. It's homecoming!"

Derek led the band behind the bleachers early under the guise that the stadium was so packed it would take longer for them to maneuver anywhere. The truth was that he needed a few minutes to talk to them. *Remember, this has nothing to do with Greg and everything to do with your seniors.*

Once they achieved their circular formation, Derek stepped into the middle. "I don't have to tell you this is a big night. We've been celebrating all week, but why don't some of you tell me why homecoming is important?" Hands shot in the air, and Derek pointed around the arch.

"There are lots of people here."

"Yeah, good for us to practice in front of a crowd, so we're ready for competition."

"I think it's important because we're coming together to celebrate our school."

Derek nodded along to all these, then asked, "Who are the people here?"

"Everyone."

"Alumni."

Derek agreed, "Yes, and yes! And who here, right now, are seniors? Can you step forward?" A large ripple occurred as 10 students stepped inward. "You're going to be alumni next year. Let that sink in." He waited a moment. Several students wiped at their eyes. "You've all worked incredibly hard to be the best musicians and team. Seniors, this is your last homecoming game as students. The last time you'll perform in front of a crowd like this one. Everyone else, appreciate that for them and you. Seniors, now think of this. How would you feel if you came to homecoming next year and the band sucked?"

They laughed and shook their heads. "Not possible, Mr. Michaels."

Derek smirked. "I don't think so either, but it would be awful, right? Like this thing that is so important and you put so much care toward was left to die." He started walking around the students. "Tonight, we will give the best performance ever to our town, our alumni, and ourselves. You deserve it. You've accomplished so much. And I..." He wiped at his own eye, "I am so damn proud of you." The buzzer sounded, and the band lined up.

Darton High's band filed past them to take the field first; they wore uniforms of Maroon and White with golden helmets, each with an arched white plume on top. Greg only offered a glare as he passed. Derek wished he could see them perform from the stands but wasn't comfortable leaving his band while they were still queued on the sidelines. The sounds of We Go Together began. It was no surprise, but Darton sounded fantastic. They were in tune, balanced, and played with precise articulation and dynamics. Summer Nights was next. Derek had heard Grease-themed shows countless times, but Darton was still exciting to listen to. Greased Lightnin' was the last piece and the crowning achievement. Toward the end of the show, Derek saw what appeared to be smoke trailing behind a formation. The audience clapped and whistled.

As the band exited, Greg was jogging up and down the line, having heated conversations with several students. *I wonder what that's about?* As he drew nearer, Derek shouted, "Hey, y'all sounded awesome!" but Greg made no response.

Everest marched to their positions, and Derek turned to see the stands. Elle was at the top of the bleachers, waving at him. He made a split-second decision and ran as best he could through the people crowding the path to join her at the top. "They sounded excellent."

Elle agreed, "They marched pretty well, too. I filmed them so you could see properly." She lifted her phone.

"Was there smoke?"

"Yeah, that was really cool, actually. They made a race car formation, and two of the color guard had this bottled smokey spray or something for the exhaust."

"Shit. That is cool."

Derek saw Elle reach for his hand but retract it to her pocket. "Don't worry, they weren't exactly perfect. Look! Here we go!"

The first note began in such unison Derek's forearms erupted in goosebumps. Even the crowd seemed more tuned into the field than usual as the volume swelled. At the drum transition to Intergalactic, people stopped talking to each other and gave the band their full attention. Someone yelled, "HELL YEAH!" then there was movement across the stadium as pockets of people stood and started doing robotic dances.

Elle looked at Derek in disbelief; tears shone in her eyes. "They're dancing!" The cheerleaders, who usually spent half-time resting, positioned themselves at an interval across the stands and began leading an impromptu choreography. An intense feeling of connectedness took root in Derek.

The highlight of ET was the perfect execution of the most complex formation of the show, where they formed a UFO that hovered to the top of the field, the color guard using golden flags as flashing lights.

By the time Rocket Man started, the cheerleaders had somehow acquired lighters. They waved them back and forth through the air, the crowd following suit. Both sides of the stadium sang. It was like being at a rock concert, but this was for his band. Derek felt a hard lump in his throat as he locked eyes with Elle, both of their faces wet. She only nodded, but he knew she understood exactly how he felt because she felt it, too. This was a moment they would never forget.

As the band began marching off the field, Derek ran down to meet them. He gave each person a high five and a hug to all his senior students as they reclaimed their seats in the bleachers.

Twelve

TRILL - A QUAVERING OR VIBRATORY SOUND,
ESPECIALLY A RAPID ALTERNATION OF SUNG OR
PLAYED NOTES.

Why am I nervous? This is ridiculous. You're an adult chaperoning a high school dance. Get ahold of yourself. Elle tried to walk gracefully along the road. Parking at the Ag Center was limited due to construction, which forced many cars into surrounding neighborhood streets. She found a free spot two blocks away and hoofed it alongside many happy and laughing students. Elle stumbled and cursed the uneven ground. She wore a fitted dress of shimmering blue material, the top a bold angle, exposing her right shoulder. She styled this with black peep toe stilettos and dangling star earrings. Her hair was swept up in a romantic twist, several strands of curls left down to frame her face.

A messy line of early students was formed at the front doors. Chaperones were to enter through a side door to meet before admission began, so Elle walked past the line. Except there wasn't a side door. Regretting her shoe choice more by the step, she continued around the building. Thankfully, she heard voices floating out of an open door in the back corner.

Elle stepped through the threshold into a room filled with teachers from the high school whom she recognized by sight but didn't have names for. Derek was having an animated conversation with the football coach and who she believed was the 12th-grade English teacher. He turned to see who had entered, and his face went slack. His eyes fixed on her and moved from soft to something wilder. The right side of Elle's mouth hitched up, and she joined the group.

"What were you saying, Derek?" The English teacher prompted. Elle swore she saw the coach chuckle silently.

Derek made a mental return to the conversation. "Uh, what were we talking about? Have you both met Elle?"

"We've seen each other at games, but I don't think we've been properly introduced." The coach nodded toward her, then extended his arm for a handshake. "I'm Wayne Williams. Everyone calls me Coach Williams."

"And I'm Liz Pine; I teach the 11th and 12th grade and the Honors English classes."

"It's so nice to meet you both. I'm Elle Foster, the band director at the middle school."

Liz gave her a knowing look. "I've heard a lot about you."

"I've heard that before," Elle tittered nervously, "Hopefully nothing too bad."

To Elle's surprise, Liz responded plainly, "Mmm, you *did* have some of the families at Darton First Baptist good and riled. That was a whole thing." She waved her hands as if indicating whatever "that" referenced.

"Chaperones, your attention, please!" A woman in high-waisted jeans and a sports jacket who had no problem projecting her voice addressed the room. She had the air of someone you didn't want to cross. "I'm Jennelle Banks, president of the PTA. I want to start by thanking you for volunteering as chaperones this evening. In your role, there are several things to watch out for. We won't be tolerating any drugs or alcohol. No drinks are allowed in the building, so if you see someone with a bottle, please confiscate it immediately. The kids will obviously be dancing, but we don't want them to grind or touch inappropriately."

Elle heard something behind her. She glanced over her shoulder to see Liz whispering in Wayne's ear, both snickering. Liz grabbed his ass, and Elle swiftly averted her gaze.

"Be on the lookout for any fighting, making out, or other sexual activity."

Elle heard a slap and a yelp behind her. Many of the teachers giggled.

Jennelle concluded in a forceful tone, "We all will be *examples* of good behavior."

The music pumped into the room at such a volume that Elle felt vibrations through her feet. Something Liz said needled at her, but she was in no mood to deal with it. She was elated. Tiny's experiment proved a runaway success; the Everest High band's performance trounced Darton, and they won the game. Then there was Derek. Derek looked delicious in his blue button-down with the sleeves rolled up and fitted slacks, and he couldn't keep his eyes off her. Elle relished the effervescent feeling of it all.

Elle, Derek, and the other chaperones idly circled the room. Elle didn't see any suspicious activity to curtail except for some dancing deemed "too close" by a few teachers towards the beginning of the night. A chaperone would sweep onto the dance floor, tap the students in question, and ask them to put some distance between them. Once, she was close enough to Jennelle to hear her advise to "leave room for Jesus." Some teachers joked with students they recognized as they passed or even got dragged onto the dance floor for parts of a song.

Elle and Derek kept close to each other, shouting commentary and conversation above the music. "I should have worn Converse. I'm the only chaperone in heels, and let me tell you, I won't make this mistake twice."

Derek laughed, barely audible. "You look... God, you look...."

"Huh?" Elle couldn't make out most of the sentence, but her insides twirled happily all the same.

Suddenly, Derek moved toward the dance floor. No, he was being pulled by Toby. Derek grabbed Elle's hand so they were both tugged through the horde of dancers. They stopped in a group of band students in the center of the floor. Toby, Pete, Sarah, Amanda, Michelle, and Caleb bopped along in a circle. "Dance with us! Please?! You have to!"

Derek shrugged at Elle and started to move. The students cheered their approval, and Elle joined in, swaying her hips and stepping from side to side. It became immediately apparent Derek outclassed them all. She focused on his feet first; he was shuffling but then seamlessly swapped styles to salsa and back. His hips and shoulders swiveled invitingly during the salsa. His arms formed more angular shapes during the shuffle, and he occasionally swept a hand back through his dark hair. His movements were perfectly timed. It was like seeing rhythm embodied. Elle struggled to decide what to watch: his body or face, which was beaming at her. *I knew it! I knew he would be a great dancer!*

The song ended with preternatural speed, and despite protests, Elle and Derek excused themselves. They made another round of the room, Elle wrapped up in the memory of the dance. "Where'd you learn how to do that?"

"Shuffling isn't hard; I watched some tutorials on YouTube during the pandemic for something to do."

Elle scoffed. "Take credit for your skills! You're amazing!"

Derek stopped his slow walk of the room's perimeter and turned around to face Elle. "Can I see the video of Darton?"

"For sure." Elle fished her phone out of the small, mostly decorative purse slung across her body.

"We'll need to go someplace quieter." It was still hard to hear, but Elle detected a rumbling quality in his words. They had agreed to avoid touching each other in public, but Derek grabbed her hand and led her behind a door she hadn't noticed.

The door shut behind them, muffling the music and leaving them in complete darkness. Elle lifted her phone to find the video. The light from it fell across Derek's face. He was close to her. So close. He purred, "Let's watch that later."

A thrill ran through Elle, and she fumbled to put the phone away, dropping it on the floor. The screen stayed on, illuminating Derek's muscular arms and shoulders as he leaned over her. He rolled his body into hers, pressing her against the wall. She ran her fingers through his hair and kissed him with abandon. He thrusted his hips against her. Elle was vaguely aware of his being in time with the thumping from the next room. Yearning for him rose in her body as his hand crept up her thigh.

A laugh rang out from down the hall, and they both straightened suddenly, arranging their hair and clothes. Elle picked up her phone. "What do we do?"

Derek chewed his lip, deciding. He called down the hall, "Who's there?"

The giggling stopped. They heard footsteps coming toward them after a moment of silence. Coach Williams sauntered into view. He scratched the back of his neck. "Hey, thought I saw some kids open the door and wanted to check it out." Even the dark couldn't hide the lipstick smudge on his chin.

"Find anyone down there?" Derek asked.

"Nah. Better get back out to the dance. Should be wrapping up soon." He walked back to the main room, beckoning for them to follow.

Elle and Derek exchanged a look. There was no way that laugh came from Coach Williams.

The DJ's amplified voice rang out, "We'll end the night with a slow song. You've been a great crowd, have fun and be safe!"

Derek cupped his hand over her ear. "Can I have this dance?"

She smiled but hesitated. "Are you sure?"

He took her hand. "I've never been more sure."

They swayed back and forth on the dance floor. Elle's arms wrapped around Derek's neck, his hands on her hips. Elle briefly noticed the other couples doing the same and felt as young and giddy as she suspected they must.

"Oh no!" Elle laughed. "Look!" She spun and inclined her head to the hallway door so Derek could see Liz creep out and rejoin the crowd.

Derek snickered, shaking his head. "A fine bunch of role models we have. What do you say we get outta here?"

"I like the sound of that. And out of these shoes!" Once through the door, Elle pointed to the neighborhood she parked in. "I had to park way back there. I'll meet you at your place."

"You parked where?"

"A couple blocks up this way." Elle pointed.

"Much too far for a lady in distress to traverse!" Derek eyed her feet.

Bemused, Elle asked, "And what would you suggest, kind sir?" Derek glanced around before picking her up and jogging around the back of the Ag Center. "Ah! What are you doing?" Elle's voice shook from the jostling of being carried. She held tight around his neck and giggled. Derek set her down gently next to his car, opened the door for her, and bowed as she slipped into the passenger seat. "I did not expect that," She got out between laughs.

"We have to take care of your feet, milady." He knelt on the ground before her and undid the clasp of each shoe.

Elle stole glances at him as they drove. The streetlights passing over the car made shadows fall beneath his Adam's, in the hollows of his cheeks. Though his eyes stayed on the road, his right hand lightly brushed her thigh.

They pulled into the drive, and Derek commanded, "Don't move." He ran around the car, opened the door, and again scooped her into his arms. He carried her up the steps, through the living room, around the corner to his bedroom, and laid her on his bed. Elle was ready to be with him. Her body recalled the pressure of him rolling against her in the hall, and an ache began between her legs. But Derek exited to the bathroom, returning with a bottle of lotion moments later. He lowered the lights in the room, warmed the lotion in his hands, and carefully massaged her feet.

Elle couldn't help it. She half whimpered, half moaned. Derek smirked. "I'll try to recreate that sound later." She relaxed into the bed. "I don't think you heard me before at the dance." His voice was sultry and deep. "You look ethereal. Too perfect for this world. You're a goddess; I know it. I can worship you... if you'll let me?" She didn't have words but dipped her chin in a nod. He tisked at her playfully, still rubbing her feet. "That won't do. I want to hear it. Tell me to worship you."

Her eyes flashed as her brain unjammed. "I'm an alter, then."

Derek dragged the back of his fingers up, up, up her legs, lifting her dress and pulling her panties down. "So you admit it. You are a deity."

Elle would have replied, but the only thing that escaped her lips as he slid his tongue up her center was a small "Oh" of surprise. Derek started slowly, licking and sucking at her labia like an explorer charting territory, carefully setting the shape of her to memory. He moved from bottom to top until he reached her clit where his mouth remained. His tongue swirled gracefully, giving more or less pressure in a pattern. Elle moaned, and he increased his pace, adding a flickering motion that reminded her of a trill or how rolled r's sounded. Heat rose in her body, and she unconsciously thrust her hips to meet his tempo. He growled in response to her movement, and the rumblings coursed through her being. The vibrations nearly sent her over the edge. She pressed a hand against his head, "Stop!"

Derek immediately pulled back. "Are you okay?"

She panted. "Yes! But I don't want to come yet."

Derek laughed. "You didn't want to come?! I would gladly lead you there again."

Elle sat up and scooted toward him. She unbuttoned his shirt, planting kisses and nipping along his toned chest and abdomen as she went. At the last button, she whispered, "Not yet." Derek giggled. *How can he be nervous after that master class?* She edged off the bed and unbuckled his belt. His erection pushed against his pants as she undid them and slid them onto the floor. Elle couldn't help but pause, taking in the view. He took her breath away. "You're... beautiful." She ran her hand along the muscles in his arm and chest, gently tugging the hair there.

"Me? Have you seen you?" Derek stood, his obliques flexing. He slowly unzipped the back of her dress and let it fall around her ankles. She was fully exposed but felt safe and something more. Powerful. He traced the line of her clavicle and pulled her into a kiss. They breathed passion back and forth between each other. Elle played with the waistband of his briefs, then broke their kiss so she could glide them off. His cock glistened with pre-cum. She grasped him, her fingers just able to meet around his girth. He was already hard, but she felt him stiffen further as she pumped her fist.

"I want you in me." Derek obediently embraced her and guided them back to lying on the bed. He slid on a condom, grabbed his cock, and rubbed it against her clit, teasing her.

"Mmm, you're so wet." He bit his lip, closed his eyes, and pushed into her.

Sparklers set off along her skin, skittering and sizzling pleasantly. Her awareness peaked, and she felt a connection between them on a cellular level. His legs against hers, his hair against her cheek when he whispered in her ear, every caress of his lips, where their stomachs touched, the sharpness of his pelvis, and their warm, electric overlapping.

They fell in sync, taking cues from each other about when to slow, maintain, or drive. Elle pushed against his left shoulder, and Derek wrapped an arm around her and rolled, flipping them so she was on top. "I wish you could see you... in this light." Derek struggled to form the sentence but smiled wide and admired Elle. He grabbed her hips hard and swiveled his own in an undulating motion. Elle gasped and sat up to ride him. He reached between her legs and massaged her bud. The combination of sensations was too much, somehow perfect. Heat rose in her again, from her feet up to her head, but she didn't stop it this time. She let the feeling crash over her and gasped in pleasure. Elle shuddered and let herself fall forward with the force of the orgasm. Derek increased his pace as she came. His cock engorged before he roared in satisfaction.

They lay next to each other, touching and giggling. Elle couldn't remember being this happy. "If I'm a goddess. You must be a god."

Derek toyed with her hair. "I can't remember being this

happy, maybe ever."

Is he reading my mind? "Me either."

Elle woke the following day snuggled under a soft white comforter. The first hints of sunlight streamed in through a sliding glass door. Derek slept beside her. She'd been in every room except this one, so she let her eyes roam. It was kept simple. A closet with bi-fold doors was closed on her right. There was a wood dresser opposite the bed with a picture and a fern, Derek's wallet and keys between them. A small night-stand was on the other side of the bed, along the wall with the glass doors. It had an open book on top of his laptop. The walls were beige- the only beige room in the house and the least decorated by far. It still shared the home's tidiness, yet the love that had gone into the other rooms wasn't quite present here.

Elle gazed out the doors. They faced the backyard and the trail to the small river beyond. She saw robins hopping around the grass before the woods, pecking at the ground. Derek caressed her arm, and she smiled at him. Even with a pattern of red lines from his pillowcase on one side of his face, he was striking. Elle tried to bottle up the serenity of the moment; she wanted to hold onto this memory, this feeling, forever.

"Breakfast?" Derek asked.

"Hmmm," Elle opened her eyes, "Why don't we go to my place? If you drop me at my car, I can drive it back home, and we can make some eggs?"

"Let's do it."

Derek pulled his car alongside Elle's in her yard. As they approached, she spoke in a small voice, "Ummm, it isn't much, but welcome to my home," she had to push hard to get the door to open, and it made a squelching sound when it finally unstuck. They stepped across the threshold.

He wasn't sure what to expect, but it wasn't this. Derek's eyes danced around the house, taking in unwanted sights. Peeling wallpaper. Beaten furniture. Warped floors. And no decoration, no pictures, no plants. *It's like nobody has lived here in years!* Panic pulled at his gut.

"I think I have some eggs. We can make some sunny side up on toast?" Elle smiled at him, but her face dropped when she saw him. "What's wrong?"

"Nothing. That sounds great." He forced warmth into his face, which he didn't feel. Derek walked to the refrigerator and pulled the eggs and margarine out while Elle grabbed a pan.

Derek pulled several drawers but without success. He finally asked, "Where are the butter knives?"

"Ah, they're at the end drawer over there. I know I need to move the cutlery, but these other drawers didn't open when I moved in. There's a lot to do here." She sighed and pointed at the to-do list. It had run out of room on the board itself, and she had pinned up another paper list with magnets beneath it.

"Wow, that is a long list." His panic twisted, and he felt nauseous.

They sat at a rickety two-person table that swayed threateningly when Derek leaned on it. He was aware of his silence and Elle attempting to engage him, but he could barely eat, much less hold a conversation.

Elle stood to take her plate to the sink. "Are you... done?" She pointed at his untouched plate.

"I have to go. I'm sorry." Derek stood, shaking his head.

"Wait, no. Derek. Please talk to me! What's wrong?"

His mind was racing with things he didn't dare say to Elle. The thoughts, so cruel to him, echoed in his brain. He needed to get out. "I just have to go."

Elle cried on her bed. Yesterday seemed so far away. *What could have gone so wrong?* She tried to logic her way to understanding. Something changed after they made love. In the light of day, maybe Derek had regrets. But hadn't they been close for months now? Had she imagined the tension between them this whole time? He had expressed his feelings about her, and his actions consistently supported his words. *Until now.*

The more she dwelled on his rush to leave, the less it made sense. She needed answers but wasn't quite sure what to do about it. They'd usually be meeting at The Drive for their Saturday practice. It might be a long shot, but she snatched her keys off the nightstand and headed to the range.

Derek wasn't there. He hadn't replied to her messages or picked up the phone when she called. Worries joined her confusion and hurt. She waited for 20 minutes, and as she decided to leave, his car pulled in. She didn't ask before sliding into the passenger side.

Elle wanted to rage at him, but now, being in his sad presence, she didn't know how to start, and they both sat silently, not looking at each other. She finally snapped her head around to see him; he had been crying. Instead of yelling, she whispered, "What the fuck, Derek?" Renewed tears welled in his eyes. He mumbled something she couldn't make out. "What? Please talk to me."

Derek shouted, "I said you're going to leave!" He seemed surprised at his own volume; lowering it, he continued, "I thought... I thought maybe you wouldn't, and I'm so stupid. I knew it was a long shot. I knew I would get hurt if I fell for you."

Elle listened, confounded. "Why would I leave?"

"People who move here always leave. It's too slow. They miss having access to things. Then, with Greg... it felt inevitable. But then you were different. You're doing so much work at the school and building relationships. I started thinking maybe... Maybe, despite it all, you would stay."

She actually laughed in relief. Elle grabbed his hand. "This is crazy! Derek, I'm not leaving." Instead of reassuring him, his face became more pained.

"No. You aren't trying to stay. The evidence is there. You haven't done anything to make a home, and you can't possibly stay if you don't have a job."

"Ouch. Okay, I know my house is terrible, but I didn't know you'd read so much into it. Listen, please, I've been so focused on the band room and just starting teaching it's taken up most of my time... but why wouldn't I have a job?"

His throat bobbed with a hard swallow. "It's not all in your control. You don't understand Greg's influence."

She yanked her hand back and folded her arms across her chest. "Then explain it to me."

Derek swallowed. "He's in charge of Adjudication for the ABA, and it's no secret he can sway performance scoring however he wants. He's also related to the President. He's... he's untouchable and has all this power. He's already implied you won't be here long."

Elle sucked her teeth. All her emotions vacated to make room for outrage. "And you weren't ever going to tell me?" Derek stuttered a reply, but Elle didn't let him finish. "We've been together almost every day. You've been teaching me how to golf to put him in his place! And you never told me this. Any of it!?" Her only solace was that no angry tears welled in her eyes. She was all cried out. She got out of the car and slammed the door.

She heard Derek close his door, but she was already speeding toward her car. "I was trying! I was trying to figure out what to do!" Elle ignored him and drove away.

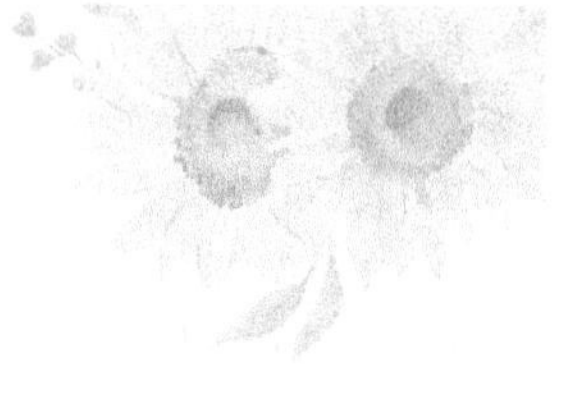

Thirteen

GLISSANDO - A CONTINUOUS SLIDE UPWARD OR DOWNWARD BETWEEN TWO NOTES.

Elle didn't know where she was going. She was barely aware of driving at all. Derek had lied to her and made assumptions. *Why is he so convinced I'd leave? How could he think I'd let Greg bully me into going? If Greg is this dangerous, why would he keep that information from me this entire time?* She couldn't understand any of it. Hadn't she been vulnerable with him? She had shared her whole painful family story with him; didn't that deserve trust and honesty in return?

Elle's phone announced a message from Mavis. 'How are the lovebirds this morning?'

The question stung. Last night was an eternity ago. Elle relived flashes of Derek dancing, laughing, stealing kisses, and making love. *No, not love. I only thought it was.* She did want to talk to Mavis, though. She craved somewhere to unload. "Hey, Siri. Text Mavis things fell apart comma can we talk question mark."

It took seconds for Mavis to reply. "Can you come here? Tiny's here."

· · ·

Mavis was on the porch waiting for her when she pulled up. She wore black sweatpants with a pink stripe down the leg and a shabby black tank top. "Coffee's already poured. Tiny may have already spiked yours. I told her to ask you."

When they entered the kitchen, Tiny shook a bottle of Bailey's. "Seemed like you could use something stronger than coffee?"

Elle sighed. "Go ahead." Her eyes widened as the pour lingered.

Tiny slid her the mug and gently asked, "What happened?"

Elle told them everything from the high of the halftime show to the sweetness of their night. "Then this morning, it was like he totally freaked out. We went to my place for breakfast, and he changed in an instant. Wouldn't talk to me, and then said he had to go and left! I was shaken up; what do you do after something like that? We usually go to The Drive on Saturday mornings, so I took a chance to see if he would show up. He did." Elle paused to take a big swallow of the mostly-Bailey's in her mug.

Mavis and Tiny were immersed in the retelling. "What did he say?"

"He is totally convinced I'm going to leave Everest. He said he knew I would move because my house is still a disaster." She stopped at the looks exchanged by Mavis and Tiny. "What was that?"

Mavis became suddenly interested in her shoes and cleared her throat, but Tiny answered. "Listen, we're not advocating for how he behaved. It sounds like he could have done a much better job communicating with you. I'm surprised you don't know..."

"Know what?" Elle searched their faces.

Mavis picked up, "Well... When Derek moved here, he didn't come alone. He and..."

She searched for a name that Tiny provided, "Sarah."

Mavis pointed at Tiny in confirmation. "He and Sarah moved here together. They were College sweethearts. He was totally over the moon for her."

Tiny took over, "She made it a year, and I don't know her personal reasons, but she decided to go. He didn't want to; he did everything possible to convince her to stay. There was a public incident one day. They were at a little outdoor concert, and he proposed to her, and she declined. She left the same weekend."

Mavis nodded, adding, "I don't think there are words to describe how brutal her rejection was on Derek. It was heartbreaking to watch; I still remember him just... crumpling." After a brief pause, she continued, "It's like Tiny said; he should've talked to you, but I understand why he might be afraid of you leaving."

"Why wouldn't he have told me any of this?" There was a pang in her heart for him, but she was still angry. "He also didn't tell me Greg is trying to have me fired, and apparently, he can achieve that!"

This time, her friend's expressions were confused. Mavis asked, "How could he? Obviously, he's an idiot, but he doesn't even work at our school."

"Apparently, he has some title at the state Bandmaster's Association and is related to the current president? I don't really understand it, to be honest. Bandmaster's Associations are a normal organization in every state, but the people in them don't have any sort of ultimate power. They help organize different things at that level: competitions, Honor Band, et cetera."

"This is a whole different thing!" Tiny strummed her fingers on the table in thought. "We have to figure out if that's true. Regardless of what happens with you and Derek, you need to know if your job is safe."

Mavis observed Elle. "She's right. The BMs together are an unpleasant bunch, Derek aside, but Greg? I'd believe anything about him. If there's some twisted situation where he found a way to get power, I'm sure he would take it."

Elle wasn't responding to his messages. Since she had driven away, Derek sent three. The first apologized, the second asked for time to explain, the third a force he couldn't stop. He understood her silence. He was frustrated with himself, too. Primal, unexpected fear overtook him when he'd seen her home. He let it get the best of him, his mind replaying Sarah's noncommittal behavior along with Chuck's voiceover, "She probably won't stay."

Derek had regained control of his emotions now. Elle's explanation about where her energy had been spent made him realize he was jumping to conclusions. Instead of dread, he felt guilt and a renewed need to take action. He should have told her the whole scope of things up front. He'd known that. Elle didn't need his protection, and she didn't deserve to have the truth withheld from her. And Derek should have been working harder at neutralizing Greg's threats. At this point, did his own security even matter? He picked up his phone again and waffled about what to say and how to say it. *Just be as straightforward as possible.*

Derek Michaels

> Hey. Are you guys open to meeting with me and Elle? 10:43am

Chuck Franklin

> Shit. Okay. 10:52am

It took Billy far longer to reply, but Derek didn't dare try to press him. He remained jumpy, on high alert whenever his phone buzzed, waiting for his response. *It's a good sign Chuck agreed so readily. Take that win. Maybe it'll help Billy get there.*

Billy Thompson

> For what purpose? 11:31am

Because she deserves to understand our position. Because we should have explained Greg right away. Because we've been kowtowing to this idiot for years, and it has to stop. Because we're her colleagues. Derek considered what the most compelling reply for Billy would be before sending.

Derek Michaels

> It doesn't feel like it yet, but she is our colleague and that gives us more numbers. Besides, we all know it's the right thing to do. 11:33am

Billy Thompson

Shit Okay it is, then. 11:40am

Derek Michaels

Thanks guys. I'll let you know. 11:40am

It was a huge win, but now he needed to fill Elle in and hope she was still interested in meeting any of them. The desire to find her or keep calling until she answered was unshakeable, but he didn't give in. She would talk to him when she was ready, and he would respect her space, even if it felt like he couldn't breathe.

When his doorbell rang at 5pm, Derek froze. It could only be her. He opened the door, and Elle stood before him, arms crossed, an unreadable expression on her face. She could have hit him or sobbed. "Why didn't you tell me?"

"I was trying to fix it. I wanted to protect you from him. I know I shouldn't...."

He stopped when she held up a finger. "Why didn't you tell me about Sarah?"

Derek squeezed his eyes shut. "Sarah," his voice rasped at her name, "Her leaving was the most painful thing I've ever had to go through. But it's nothing compared to what you've endured."

"You should have told me. I shared all the horrible things I don't talk to anyone else about with you! And it was easy; you made it easy to talk about! It should be easy for you to talk to me, too."

Elle *was* easy to talk to. Everything with Elle was effortless. "I'll tell it all." And he did. They stood on opposite sides of the door, and he told her how they met, fell in love, and how they'd been happy. They'd moved here with dreams of a charming community, but Sarah had felt like an outcast. "She was never at home here. Thinking back on it now, I can see she tried, and I tried everything to make her feel better. But I wasn't enough. I didn't figure out for a long time that she wasn't enough for me to leave here either."

Elle dropped her crossed arms, and Derek reached for her. She let herself be pulled into him, and her head found the familiar space on his chest. The smell of her hair was a relief. He closed the door, and they sat on the couch while he explained what he'd uncovered about the Band Misters.

This is going to be awkward. Elle couldn't imagine what the meeting with Chuck and Billy would be like. After talking to Derek, she tried to go in with an open mind, but part of her was skeptical. Derek offered to meet them in Stoville, the idea to make it as easy as possible for them. However, Stoville was even smaller than Everest, so their meeting place was decided for them. Subway was the one restaurant in town. Derek pulled the car into the parking lot, the Eat Fresh neon insignia blazing from the window. "Are you ready?"

Elle sighed. "Ready as I'll ever be."

They were the first to arrive, so they ordered (Elle getting a veggie sub and Derek the turkey on rye), found a corner table, and waited. Several customers came through, but they remained the only patrons at a table. Everyone else ordering to go or picking up.

Chuck and Billy walked in together. They waved their

acknowledgment toward the occupied table and made their orders before taking the seats opposite Elle and Derek.

Derek started the conversation. "Hey guys, thanks for coming. You've met Elle before."

The men were stoic. They seemed incapable of speech. After a minute of silence, Elle longed to break the tension. "Let's agree that the first meeting doesn't count." She reached across the table to shake their hands. "It's nice to meet you both."

Chuck cracked a smile. "It's nice to meet you, too. Listen, me and Billy have been talking at school, and well, how much do you already know?"

Elle inhaled deeply and looked to Derek, who nodded at her. "Derek's caught me up. I understand the need for discretion and appreciate you meeting with me."

Chuck replied, "We understand your position too, and I'm awful sorry about everything. But... and this is hard to say, but we just don't see a way out of this. If we talk to him, we're putting ourselves at risk."

She and Derek expected this, but it still left a sour taste in her mouth. "I can show you one potential lead." Elle opened the web browser on her phone; it was already on the page for the Bandmaster's Constitution. "If you read this, chairpersons have clear term limits." She passed her phone across the table. "I'm not sure why he'd be able to serve for so long. I'm guessing it's some sort of loophole if nobody else from our region volunteers. I don't know for sure; I didn't want to ask in case it raised attention."

Billy's eyebrows shot up to his hairline as he read the screen. "Interesting. I've never seen anything come through regarding the ABA besides information about participating in the concerts and events."

Elle nodded. "They should be soliciting for volunteers to serve every two years."

Chuck shifted in his seat. "It could be his relationship with what's his name? Ira?"

"Ira Birch, he's the current president. It is possible."

Chuck added, "That's still a problem then. Even if something is going on with his term limits, if it's approved, there's not much we can do."

Derek shook his head. "One of us could volunteer." The men stiffened and began talking over each other, but Derek interrupted them, "I know what you're thinking, and you may be right. It is a risk, but showing interest in helping the ABA is normal, right? It would be good and encouraged under usual circumstances. It would be hard for Greg to talk down about interest in volunteering even if he felt threatened."

"Man, anything could go wrong with that! He could still be the chair! He could find out and make things difficult before a decision's even made! His influence, even with the community here, is... pervasive." Chuck sputtered out.

Elle said softly, "But if *I* volunteered... I don't have anything to lose, and it makes sense as a narrative for me to want to be involved as a new director; I can feign ignorance, and I'm outside of his sphere since he doesn't want me to hang around with you all. You'd be safe." The men stared at her. "I'd only ask that you continue to act like things are normal. If it works, he won't have the position anymore; I have to think his power against our jobs would be limited. I'm sure he'd still be a world-class asshole, but after he's out of the position, you could all decide if you still wanted to be around him or not."

She could feel Derek beaming beside her. "I vote not, personally.... so, will you help us?"

Later that evening, Elle cleaned on her hands and knees next to a friend for the second time since moving to Everest. This time, the friend helping her was Mavis, and they were at her house scrubbing every surface while Elle recounted the events of the meeting.

"How can you be sure they won't tell Greg? I don't understand why you shared the plan when you could've executed it with you and Derek, not told them at all, and gotten the same results."

Elle scrubbed a foul patch of baseboard. "We did consider leaving them out, and you're right; it's a little precarious. Ultimately, I thought including them was a way to bond and show an extension of trust. Maybe that's worth something."

Mavis shrugged. "If it works."

"It'll work." Elle nodded her head to herself. "It's gonna work."

"Impressive motivational speech," Mavis jibed with a laugh, "I'll do anything I can to help. It's frustrating I'm so outside of this."

"You are helping! Look at where you are right now! In this ramshackle cottage, sponging down the walls. This is a huge help, and I'm so grateful."

Mavis tossed her sponge into the sudsy bucket. The water beneath the foam had turned a murky brown color. "We're painting next? I think that will go a long way."

"Yep! And I've already ordered some new furniture. What a relief to get tables, chairs, and bookshelves delivered to your door. I do have another small favor to ask... I don't want Derek to know we're doing this. I kinda imagine showing him as like a Christmas present. Is that cheesy?"

Mavis pressed her lips together, suppressing a grin. "Oh, it's the cheesiest, but it's perfect for you two!" Her voice became more sincere, "And it will mean a lot to him. I bet he'll never forget this. Do you... Never mind."

Elle opened her eyes wide. "You can't do that. You can't start a question and never mind your way out of it. What is it?"

"Gah, it's none of my business, and it doesn't even really matter." Elle circled her hand, waiting for Mavis to out with it. "Do you love him?"

Elle's eyes softened. Derek had texted her those words the day everything happened, but she hadn't brought it up yet. As for her, it was a phrase that kept occurring to her randomly. He would do something, and she'd think *Gah, I love this man!* or they'd be parting ways, and she'd have to hold her tongue, carefully controlling herself to not blurt it out. "Yeah. I do."

Mavis let out a glissando-like squeal of joy and danced over to Elle, pulling her into a hug.

Fourteen

DOWNBEAT - AN ACCENTED BEAT, USUALLY THE
FIRST OF THE BAR.

Derek could feel the tension and nerves of his band as their performance time grew closer. They were at the District Marching Performance Assessment in Montgomery, as were near all the other local High School bands, including Darton and Stoville. The stadium was packed with students, parents, directors, and ABA officials who would be judging each performance and awarding ratings at the end of the day.

Everest High was set to take the field in 40 minutes, so they had retreated from their seats in the stadium where they were watching and cheering for other bands, back to their buses to get into their uniforms and warm up. This was the big show. The moment they worked all season for. *And the kids know it.* He could see it in every face as he looked around the bus; a seriousness held around their eyes and mouths. *Good. We'll do well, then... As long as they don't forget to have fun, too.*

"Hurry up, gang! Get your instruments ready and meet me in front of the buses." Derek joined Elle and waited for them to circle up. Elle had requested to come to the competition. Derek knew she was just as invested in their performance as he was. Thinking of it gave something in his chest fluttery wings.

"How are they holding up?" Elle asked as he approached.

"They understand today is the day. I just hope they don't take themselves too seriously." Students began flooding off the bus and taking positions around Derek and Elle.

"Can I do something with them? If you don't mind, I have an idea."

"Of course, you can. Shoot, I think they like you better than me at this point." Derek chuckled.

"We do!" Someone shouted from the circle, eliciting giggles from the group.

Derek turned his head toward the direction of the shout. "I do, too!" He stepped back from the arc and gestured to give Elle the floor.

Elle let her eyes roam the circle of students, her shoulders back, exuding pride. "First, I want to thank you all for including me this year. It has been an honor. Second..." She paused and smiled wickedly, "You put your left hand in, you put your left hand out, you put your left hand in, and you shake it all about. You do the hokey pokey, and you turn yourself around; that's what it's all about. Take it, Derek!"

The entire band, fully dressed in their pressed uniforms, instruments hanging from neck straps or grasped in hands, did the Hokey Pokey together. By the last verse, they were shouting the lyrics, and band members from other schools were regarding them curiously.

After the song concluded, Derek stepped into the center of the students and spun around, finding eye contact with each of them. "You're such a special group of people. It's not every year I see such dedication down to each person. We all know that this moment, this performance, is what we've been working for. This is the last time we'll perform this routine. So do your best, have fun together, and leave it on the field."

Derek started leading their line to the field. Elle didn't follow. "Are you coming or what?" He called to her. She frowned in surprise and scurried to join him. They walked ahead of the band, leading the line around the back entrance of the field. The band marched in perfect step from the back left corner, around the front, and to their position on the sidelines. Derek and Elle stopped at the turn as the students marched past. Once the last person had taken the left turn, they jogged to the front of the field next to the Drum Major platform.

Despite his conviction that they were ready and would do themselves proud, Derek's heart took on a rapid tattoo. Anything could happen during the competition. In the last performance they saw before exiting, a color guard member made a lousy catch in the first song, almost certainly breaking her nose. She kept performing the routine, blood streaming down her face and onto her uniform. He didn't have to see what happened when they marched off the field to know she'd be crying, not from the pain, but from not doing her best when it counted most and the fear she had let her team down. Aside from that, he truly wondered about Greg's influence over the judges for the first time. Was he angry enough at Derek to pull strings?

Elle sidestepped closer to Derek. They weren't touching, but she was so close he could sense the heat from her arm on his. He knew she was trying to comfort him without showing their professional sphere. It was hard for him not to grab her hand and squeeze.

They began in perfect unison on the downbeat. It was difficult to see the formation from the ground. Still, Derek knew this vantage point from all his time walking around the practice field, making minor adjustments to placement. Aside from one slightly wobbly formation, they were all in step and meeting their marks.

The crowd, composed primarily of musicians, reacted strongly to the shock of classical music on a marching field. At the transition to Beastie Boys, they erupted in cheers. Derek bounced on his toes and tried to contain his growing excitement. They were doing it, and the recognition from the knowledgeable audience above sent him soaring. During E.T., when his color guard simulated the UFO in flight, someone from the crowd shouted, "Take me with you!" Which led to a shared chant of "Abduct me! Abduct me!" The band played Rocket Man as beautifully as they had ever performed it. The intonation was impeccable, and the articulation crisp.

The longer they played, the more emotion built up within Derek. He felt pride and admiration at his students' accomplishments as a reel of memories from the season played in his mind. They were a completely different group during those first days of Band Camp. Elle spying on them and how it had morphed into her spending countless hours at rehearsal helping them get to where they were now, the relationships forming amongst them, their silliness in the stands at football games. And the whole time, Elle. She was in nearly all those memories. Smiling and laughing but leading and directing.

It happened at once. The band cut off the final note with such precision it echoed in the stadium. Derek leapt into the air, pumping his fists as his students marched off the field. He saw recognition of their achievement in each of their faces as they filed out, and as the last student joined the queue, he turned to Elle. The tension of all his feelings gave way, and he swept her into a kiss. The tears streaming down her cheeks were now wetting his own, and for a moment, everything stilled. Time and sound and the stadium itself faded to nothing, leaving only Derek and Elle and their embrace.

When they broke apart, the noise and light flooded back in, and because he felt it with his entire being, Derek said those words. "I love you, Elle."

Elle looked at him fiercely. "I love you, too." He hadn't expected her to say it back, but the words set his insides roaring when she did. He was invincible. Derek picked her up and twirled her around before realizing the next band was making their entry. He took her hand, and they jogged to catch up with Everest High.

They made it out of the field and shut the gate behind them, but before Derek could address the band, they were clapping and whistling at him and Elle. "It's about damn time!" Someone yelled from the back. Elle blushed beside him, but then she shrugged and called back, "I can't disagree."

Elle was light as air. Having their relationship out in the open was more freeing and reassuring than she could have anticipated, and though they hadn't discussed it, she understood. They were together now, and the whole world would know. Derek's home had been like home from the first time she visited, but it wasn't actually his house; it was him. He was home.

There were a couple hours left of competition before the awards would be given out, and the band had returned to their section in the stands. They were infectiously happy. Talking and joking, eating boiled peanuts and popcorn, and analyzing and cheering for other bands who took the field. Elle and Derek spent their time sitting with different sections of the students, joining their fun. Billy waved at them and shouted his congratulations as Stoville High exited to prepare for their show.

While walking to a lower row in the bleachers, Derek nudged Elle and pointed to the bottom walkway of the stands to the left of where they were. Greg was talking to a tall, slim man with coifed blonde hair. He wore a brown suit and bow tie, unusually formal for the occasion. Elle didn't recognize him, but Derek whispered, "That's Ira."

They were too far away to hear what was exchanged, but they both watched the interaction as if mesmerized. Greg was smiling too much, a truly shit-eating grin. Ira maintained a neutral composure. He attempted to excuse himself several times, but Greg clung to him, keeping a mostly one-sided conversation going. When the men did break apart, Greg turned toward the right, and Ira rolled his eyes.

Elle inhaled sharply. "Did you see that?" Derek nodded but put his finger to his lips in a hushing gesture.

"There ya are!" Greg climbed the stands toward them. He seemed in high spirits. "I was waiting for ya. Wanted to say congratulations. You put on a great show this year."

"Thanks for saying so, Greg. That means a lot." Elle was impressed at how natural Derek replied. She was shocked at how polite Greg was, which threw her off. "Darton also did great. We saw you go on earlier. Job well done for us all."

"Well, thank you. Between you and me, I won't be sad to see some of my people go next year. Tough season for quality, but we pulled it together by the end." There it was. Elle turned away to hide her disgust. "I better get back to the band. Supposed to be taking a piss."

Once Greg rounded the corner, Derek looked at her, brows knit. "That was weird. He's acting weird. He complimented me and totally ignored you."

Elle laughed. "Those are improvements!" Derek's face was still etched with worry. "Even if he's up to something... You saw Ira's expression, right? I don't think he's close to Greg at all. I bet Greg is just claiming they are! Even if they are technically related, there is clearly some distance there."

· · ·

Everest High received straight Superior ratings for the 21st year in a row. The band maintained professional composure until they were back at the buses, then shouted their elation to the skies. They went to the local mall to grab dinner at the food court and relax for a couple hours before the long bus ride home, but the night wasn't over for Elle.

Since seeing Greg and Ira's interaction, she was confident there was some way for her to apply pressure there. By the time they arrived back in Everest, she had decided. "I'm going to email Ira. Now is the time; I know it!"

Derek slowly nodded. "I can't think of an advantage to waiting for another time."

"Great! Then help me write!" She weaved her fingers through his, and they walked to her classroom.

Dear President Birch,

We haven't had the pleasure of meeting in person yet, but I'm Elle Foster, the new Everest Middle School director in District 6. I've been thinking about serving on the ABA for some time now, and today's D6 Marching Performance Assessment was so exciting I couldn't wait another day to inquire!

I see newly elected chairpersons start their tenure in August each year and typically serve for two years, but I don't know how to volunteer for positions. Could you please point me in the right direction?

Sincerely,
Elle Foster

· · ·

"This is good, right? Unassuming, genuine, clear?" Elle searched Derek's face.

He was paler than usual but gave her a peck on the cheek and agreed, "I think it's exactly what we're going for."

They both re-read it one final time, and Elle pressed send.

Fifteen

CONCERT BAND - A RELATIVELY LARGE GROUP
OF BRASS, WOODWIND, AND PERCUSSION
PLAYERS WHO PERFORM IN A CONCERT HALL.

"Now that marching season is over, it's time for our first official collab." Derek tried to keep a straight face. He was lying on his side under the down cover of his bed, facing Elle.

Elle closed her eyes as if searching for patience. "Our... *first* collab?" She grabbed the pillow from underneath her head and swatted him with it.

"Ouch! Remember at the start of the year, you asked me how our bands work together? We'll both be working on our Concert Band performances next semester. We usually put together a holiday concert with both bands for the rest of this one."

"I guess if this is supposed to be our first collaboration, the year has taken some surprising turns," Elle smirked.

Derek gazed dreamily at the ceiling. "It really has. I can't imagine waking up next to Al, that's for sure." She swung the pillow at him again.

Over breakfast, Derek told her how the holiday concerts had gone in the past. It was nothing too shocking. "Any chance you'd like to change it up?" Elle asked.

Derek arched a brow. "I think the one thing I've learned this year is change is good." She smiled and continued, but Derek spoke simultaneously, "Speaking of something a little different. Thanksgiving is right around the corner, and, uh, it's my turn to host. My parents are coming and... No pressure, because I want you to be comfortable and have a great holiday, but I would love for you to be here, too."

He was nervous. Derek always held tension in those broad shoulders. Elle felt nerves bloom within her stomach as well. Yet, she couldn't imagine not being with Derek on any holiday, especially when he wanted her there. "And meet your parents in person?"

Derek unclenched his jaw, relaxing slightly. "Yeah. They're eager to meet you. If you aren't ready, though, I understand."

Elle sat back in her chair. Part of her rejoiced at the invitation, and another part was afraid she didn't know how to act and might not make a good impression. "I want to be here," His shoulders instantly relaxed, "but I'm worried. Deep down, I've always wanted a close family... like other people have. Like you have. But I'm scared I don't know how to do that."

Derek's mouth pressed into a flat line. Elle could tell he was choosing what he wanted to say carefully. "Elle. Your parent's behavior had nothing... Nothing to do with you. You are easy to love and know, and my parents... they already adore you." He reached across the table to squeeze her hand.

"How do you celebrate?"

Derek's smile was warm, and he daydreamed aloud for Elle. "I imagine we'll have a kitchen day the day before. Prep what we can: cranberry sauce, bread, pies, get the stuffing ready, and brine the turkey. We'll do a little more on Thanksgiving morning: get the bird in the oven, listen to Christmas music, and sneak tastes of everything. Mom and Dad will probably get here late in the morning or noon. Mom will want to critique the garden, so we'll walk around there. If it's nice, we could hike the trail. They'll be curious to talk to you and ask you some questions, but not overly personal. They aren't like that for the most part. We can make a little cocktail before dinner when we're back from hiking. The meal will be incredible, of course, then maybe we play Scrabble."

Elle took a deep, slow inhale. "That sounds... incredible." She paused. "Can we make a peach cobbler?"

"Best idea I've heard all day." Derek's warm laugh settled the last butterfly in her stomach.

One side of Elle's mouth quirked up, "Ready for another? Let's go for a hike right now."

Derek stood up and offered his hand to her. "Let's go."

When they'd returned from the trek, Elle opened the email on her phone. She leaned over the screen as new messages began to display.

Derek asked, "Anything?" She shook her head. It had been a week since she'd emailed Ira, and while she didn't expect him to reply over the weekend, it was hard to resist checking.

Elle fidgeted with the phone. "You haven't heard anything from Greg yet either?"

"Nothing." After the marching competition, Greg canceled the next Band Misters meeting and acted noncommittal about the next one. It was an extreme aberration in behavior. Since Derek started at Everest High, he could only recall Greg not making one of their meetings, and it was because there was a death in his family he had to travel for. Even then, he had reinforced their next get-together. This was utterly different.

Instead of messaging in their group text, Greg messaged each of the men individually that he couldn't make it to The Drive next week and that they should cancel. It was normal for Greg to recommend a cancelation instead of wishing the other men a fun time. He hated the idea of them meeting without him and had dissuaded it numerous times before. What stood out as fishy was the individual messaging campaign. Derek thought it best to reply neutrally. "Hope all is well. See you week after next then." The response from Greg was simply, "We'll see."

Derek immediately scrolled down to his group text with Chuck and Billy and asked if they had received the same communication, but as he typed to them, a text from Billy came through.

Billy Thompson

> Did everyone get the message from Greg?
> 9:45am

Derek Michaels

> I was just going to ask you. Mine said, "I can't make next Thursday, let's cancel."
> 9:45am

Billy Thompson

> Mine was the exact same thing. 9:45am

Billy Thompson

Why did he message us separately?
9:46am

Chuck Franklin

Why was it so short? You know he usually
goes on and on, and he didn't even give a
reason? 9:46am

Derek Michaels

I told him I'd see him week after next and
he said, "We'll see." 9:46am

Chuck Franklin

This is some sort of test. He's trying to
figure out if we're talking to each other
without him, or if we'll meet without him.
Something is up. 9:47am

Billy Thompson

Yeah. I don't like it. 9:47am

Billy Thompson

> Could Ira have said something to him about
> Elle emailing? 9:48am

It was the elephant in the room. Derek had updated them on
what he and Elle had seen and the email as soon as they'd sent
it. Chuck and Billy received the news admirably, but they were
all anxious.

Derek Michaels

> It's possible. We still haven't gotten a reply
> back for the record. 9:49am

Derek Michaels

> Is there a way we can find out if Matt got
> the text too? 9:50am

Billy Thompson

> I'll message him. You should stay out of it
> Derek 9:50am

Billy messaged back a few hours later, confirming Matt did receive the same info from Greg. Elle half-heartedly suggested he might have simply deleted the group thread, and all this speculation could be for nothing. Derek still felt uneasy. Why wouldn't he simply make another shared message? Chuck's suspicion felt right; Greg was trying to see if they would meet without him or were otherwise communicating. He was at least testing them, but why now?

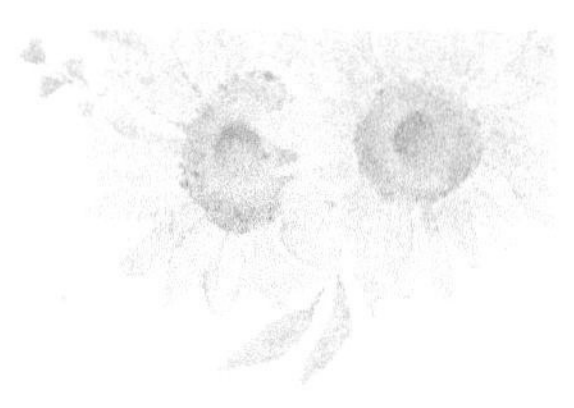

Sixteen

IMPERIOSO - A MUSICAL MARKING INDICATING
TO PLAY IN AN IMPERIOUS OR OVERBEARING
MANNER.

Tiny was up to something. She wasn't especially good at hiding it. Elle and Mavis received a message from her begging them to come to the cafe on Tuesday after school. Strange, since they stopped by at least once a week after school as is.

At 3:30pm Tuesday, Elle and Mavis walked to their cars in the staff parking lot, keys jingling. Elle asked, "What do you think the surprise will be."

Mavis shrugged. "I'm not sure I've ever not known what she had going on before, but today... No clue."

When they entered Tiny's Cafe, nothing appeared different. It was still the dimly lit room with mismatched tables and chairs and low music pumping in the background. Even the chalkboard menu contained the same items. Elle happily noted that several tables were occupied. Tiny, however, was nowhere to be found.

They approached the counter and waited until one of the customers said, "I think she's out back. She needed to take a delivery." Mavis looked perplexed and led Elle down a hallway through a door with an Employee Only sign and to a back door of the cafe Elle hadn't known existed. The bright light from outside blinded them as the door opened onto a parking lot.

She heard Tiny before her eyes adjusted, "Ah! You're here!"

Mavis exclaimed, "Holy shit! Is that what I think it is?"

Tiny was nearly shaking with excitement. "Come see!"

As they approached the food truck, she flattened slightly, saying, "It's not much, and there's some work it needs."

Mavis stopped walking and grabbed Elle's hand to stop her, too. "We aren't going any closer until you stop that right now. This is huge. You get to be happy and nothing else."

Tiny shook herself out. "Thank you. Okay, let's go!"

The outside of the truck was worn down, like it may have been through several hurricanes. The paint reminded Elle of what some of her walls looked like, stained and peeling. *But not for long.* She expected the inside to be as rough as the outside, but when they stepped in, it was polished and functional. Plain, yes. But the stainless steel on both sides sparkled, and even the floors were in good condition and clean. It was like being in a small, elongated kitchen.

Elle let out a low whistle. "This is amazing, Tiny! Life changing! Holy wow!"

"I really owe it to you," Tiny's eyes sparkled, "You challenged me to try something new that I would've never considered, and now...." She gestured broadly. "It's got more kitchen tools than I have in the cafe. I do need to get another espresso machine and inventory I can store here. Of course, the outside needs to be repainted. After that, though, I can take this to all the football games. Any other sporting event I want to, parades, events, parties, concerts, the possibilities are endless!" Mavis mumbled something under her voice, causing Tiny to ask, "What?"

"I said I'll paint it. If you want me to."

Tiny's voice went high as she cried, "Of course, I want you to if you want to!" They hugged. In a flash, a hand reached out and brought Elle into the embrace.

"I'm just so fucking proud of you," Mavis said between sniffs.

Elle brushed a curly strand of hair from her face and admired the bright yellow living room walls. This room was done. She'd rolled out a pink, white, and black statement rug in the middle of the floor in front of a deep blue loveseat and coffee table. A bookshelf was on the opposite wall. Or would be, all the furniture was towards the middle of the room now so the paint could dry. And it looked... *Like somewhere I'd live.* She smiled at the thought.

The other rooms were coming along, too. A small desk was in Elle's bedroom, and she'd ordered a new table and chairs for the dining area, but they wouldn't be delivered until next week. Buckets of lavender, white, and sage green paint were waiting to be used on the rest of the house and the porch. After painting, the finishing touches would be getting some potted plants in each room. She'd even bought some pots and soil out of a clearance bin outside Tractor Supply.

The sound of buzzing broke her reverie, and she turned to see her phone skittering on the floor. Carefully picking it up to avoid getting paint on it, she answered the unknown number. "Hello?"

A man's voice, deep and gravelly but pleasant, answered. "Hello, this is Ira Birch calling for Ms. Foster?" Elle's heart was somewhere around her larynx. She wished Derek was here and briefly examined the phone to see if she could figure out how to record the conversation. "Hello?"

She gave up the search. "Hi, President Birch; this is Ms. Foster. You can call me Elle."

He chuckled. "You can call me Ira, too. I promise there are no imperioso markings on my score." He felt approachable and kind. And nerdy. "I emailed you, but I know it's after school hours, and we're headed into Thanksgiving break. I thought I'd take a shot and call as well. I hope that's okay?"

The same curl kept falling into her eye, and she cursed it inwardly. "Of course, I'm happy to talk now. I'm a first-year teacher, but I've been familiar with Bandmaster's Associations for as long as I can remember. I'd love to volunteer."

"And we would love to have you!" Elle could hear his smile. This was far different than the expression he wore when Greg was speaking to him. "We always maintain volunteers from each district; it's important to have representation that way. I've had problems getting volunteers from District 6. In fact, we've had to bypass our usual term limits in favor of having a rep from there. Do you know Greg Howard?"

Elle stammered, "I... Yes, I know Greg."

"He's been overseeing Adjudication and acting as District Chair for years. The ABA would be *delighted* to give him a break. Now, I know that's two roles, and you're still getting into your teaching zone. I hesitate to have you take them both on at once, but you could pick either one as far as I'm concerned. Does that make sense?"

"It makes perfect sense, thank you. I will devote some thought to this. Um, how do I apply?"

"I know we send a ton of emails, but keep an eye out for interest emails from ABA. We send them quarterly and track them throughout the year in case we need unexpected backup. When we return from vacation, there'll be one for volunteers and getting ready for concert season."

"Is there somewhere I should have subscribed to receive emails? I don't think I'm receiving any."

Ira replied, "Let me see real quick...." A keyboard clicked in the background, then, "I see the problem. That's strange;

your email address is misspelled. I'm so sorry, Elle. I have no idea how this happened and went unnoticed. I fixed it for you, and I'll talk to our Communications Chair."

"Thank you so much, Ira."

She hung up the phone, mind reeling. *Why was my email misspelled? We're getting at least quarterly emails, but didn't Billy say he only received ones about competitions and concerts?*

The week of Thanksgiving served as a refreshing break from the grind, but Elle had to admit her schedule was filling up fast. Monday and Tuesday would be spent with Mavis and Tiny for a painting extravaganza. Tiny would park her truck in Elle's yard, and they would finish the rooms inside while Mavis tackled the truck. Derek thought they were having a Girls' getaway since she wouldn't see them on Thanksgiving. It was true-ish. When she'd told them about spending the holiday meeting Derek's family, they were excited for her but also dismayed she wouldn't be able to attend what they called "Friendsgiving." The idea of spending the early week together was both to celebrate and make headway. Wednesday and Thursday were dedicated to Thanksgiving. On Friday, she aimed to reserve time to plan the Christmas Concert, then maybe it could be a restful weekend before returning to those short school weeks before winter break.

Tiny pulled her truck into Elle's yard early Monday morning. Seeing it outside the business parking lot in this setting made it look enormous. Tiny and Mavis hopped down from the cab, and Elle joined them as they began unloading painting supplies. The side of the truck was already sanded down, which made its shabby appearance even worse. However, it had removed most of the old paint and smoothed minor imperfections.

Mavis handed each of them a can of primer hooked up to what looked like a water gun. "Instead of you two starting on the house straight away, could you help me prime it? You can pull the trigger on these, so it's easy. It'll go much faster if we all tackle it together." Elle and Tiny readily agreed and started spraying. It took an hour to complete, even with all three of them working. Elle was grateful it was cool outside but had to wipe her brow even so.

"Phew, okay, while that's drying, snacks and hydration, please!" They entered the house. Elle opened a cabinet to pull out some chips and noticed Mavis and Tiny hadn't made it into the kitchen. She popped her head back around the corner and caught them admiring the living room. Tiny whistled. "This place looks great, Elle!"

Mavis nodded. "It does. It's completely different than just a few weeks ago! You've been busy."

Elle shrugged. "Thanks, ladies! Mavis was an enormous help in getting things started with the cleaning. Once it was done, I don't know; it all started falling into place. Now all that's left is the couple rooms of paint and finishing touches."

They walked into the kitchen, a stark contrast to the completed living room. Tiny said, "Ah, this room we're painting first thing after snacks."

"Hah! Yeah, we can start here. I also have a dining room set ordered to replace this." She knocked on the old table, and it wobbled slightly. "I'm hoping we can paint here and the rest of the bedroom and the porch before Wednesday."

Tiny waved her hand, indicating not to worry. "We've totally got this."

Mavis asked, "Any more news about the whole ABA thing?"

"Actually, yes. It's more non-news, I guess. Greg canceled

the BM's next scheduled meeting, too, and said they should meet up in December for a golf match. Still came off secretive, and Chuck and Billy were creeped out. But I don't know; something is off. It doesn't seem like Greg to put off or ignore something for so long. He's usually so direct."

Tiny shivered. "Even beyond that. I'm telling you, that guy gives me serial killer vibes. Agree, though. He is definitely not the sort who would hold back on anything."

Mavis stood from the table and plucked a cobweb they'd missed in the corner. "I understand their paranoia, but could it be that he knows the effect he's having on everyone? Maybe that's the game, and he's just enjoying messing with you."

Elle tilted her head side to side, considering. "Another issue is that Ira advised me to restrict myself to one of the roles. Should it be the Adjudication or District Chair? I thought Adjudication. That's the role he holds over everyone's head and makes his threats with. However, Chuck pointed out that a District Chair may oversee the Adjudication under normal procedures. I read all the role descriptions, but it's not totally clear."

"Derek should take the other spot. Problem solved." Mavis wiped her hands against each other.

"We did talk about that," Elle pursed her lips, "It's a no for now. Derek offered to go for it immediately, but I convinced him to wait until we know more. If things go sideways, I want to be the only person in the crosshairs."

Tiny's eyebrows raised past her bangs. "Bet you didn't say that crosshairs line to him."

Elle laughed. "Well, no. It was implied."

Snacks depleted, Mavis returned outside to paint the solid base layer coat, a bright white to make the stencil design stand out. Elle poured the sage paint into a tray while Tiny oohed and aahed at the color. They used painter's tape to cover the window sills, ceiling, and floor and started rolling.

"What would you do in the worst-case scenario?" Tiny asked.

"Mmm. The worst case scenario where Greg sabotages me enough that I'm fired?"

"Ugh, when you put it like that..." Tiny stuck out her tongue in disgust, "But yeah, that's the one."

Elle sighed. "I don't know. I have trouble thinking about it... The truth is, I love teaching Music, but I wouldn't be able to do so in this region anymore. I love Derek too, and this is his home." She stared at the paint bucket for a minute, then said resolutely, "I don't think that will happen, so it doesn't matter." Elle felt Tiny's eyes on her. She knew she was thinking about Derek's past and wondering if history would repeat itself. *It won't. I can't think like that.*

As they stood back and admired their handiwork, Mavis returned. She whistled. "Great job in here! Come see the truck!"

The truck looked new. As if it had been freshly assembled from the factory. The white was shining in the evening sun. "Oh my God, oh my God, oh my Godddd!" Tiny exclaimed as she danced around the perimeter of the vehicle. "I can't believe this!"

Mavis replied, "I know. I can't wait to use the stencil, but we should let this dry today and tackle that tomorrow. I can come help with the house for now."

"We'll be quick to finish the house. I've already got the bedroom half done and fully taped. Then it's the porch, which doesn't need any tape except where it touches the house."

Mavis suggested they divide and conquer, so Elle went to finish the bedroom while Mavis and Tiny tackled the porch. Elle's prediction they'd be done in no time was accurate. The bedroom's lavender coat was completed in half an hour. Elle joined Mavis and Tiny for the last bit of whitewashing on the porch, and then they all had fun pulling down the tape from the kitchen. Tiny balled her tape up and tried to throw it up so it stuck on the ceiling, which became a game until Elle's stomach growled. "Pretty sure dinner is on me tonight. I can't thank you ladies enough."

The following day was similar, except the remaining painting that needed doing was the stenciling. Mavis grew increasingly anxious as she prepared for the work, snipping at Elle and Tiny and telling them not to help. They sat on the porch while she affixed the stencils to the truck. It was a complicated task. The logo was large and required multiple pieces in perfect alignment for the design to come out right. Once all the pieces were where she wanted them, Mavis pleaded for them to go inside while she did the painting.

Elle knew Tiny tried not to stare out the window, but she caught her eyes roaming that direction several times as they sat and visited on the couch. Elle didn't call her on it, but after the third time, Tiny huffed in frustration, snatched a wrinkled piece of paper out of her pocket, carefully unfolded it, and slapped it on the coffee table. Elle recognized it. "The design! We'll get to see it in person soon."

Tiny nodded, keeping her eyes on the image. "I get why she doesn't want an audience. Mavis is a perfectionist with her work in the first place, and I know she's putting pressure on herself to make this pristine. She's the most talented person I know. It will be incredible, and she won't be happy."

"She designed the logo, yeah?" Elle asked. It was a large pink circle with blank slats through it. A coffee mug with a swirl inside the cup was featured at the bottom center, and the top was emblazoned with large script reading "Tiny's Cafe."

"She did," Tiny confirmed, "and it's everything I could imagine wanting. I'd like to put it up in the store too, maybe on the window."

Elle agreed. "That would be awesome."

Elle started playing Top Chef episodes on her computer, and they critiqued the chef's creations through the choppy streaming service. After a couple hours, Mavis opened the door, and Tiny sprang from the couch and ran outside. Elle gave Mavis what she hoped was a reassuring look, and they followed Tiny. They found her sitting on the stairs, head in her hands, sobbing so hard her back heaved up and down. "This…" she pointed at the truck and sniffled. "This is the most beautiful thing I've ever seen." The last word stretched with her cry. She suddenly stood up and wiped her face dry. She stamped her foot aggressively and pointed to the truck again. "This is beyond my wildest dreams!" Tiny shouted at Mavis.

Mavis bit her lip, not quite repressing a sly smile. "I still have to do the other side."

"Shut up!" Tiny yelled. "I love you!" She tackled Mavis, who wasn't prepared for the full-body hug, but fortunately did manage to catch her.

Derek couldn't decide whether Elle's meeting his parents was a big deal. She was the first girlfriend he would introduce to them since Sarah and his parents and Elle seemed to think it was an event; his parents were excited, and Elle was nervous. On the other hand, they'd already spoken plenty of times through FaceTime, and it felt…. *Inevitable. Of course, my family would all be together on a holiday.*

Wednesday was spent almost entirely in the kitchen. The time zipped by, and by the end of the day, they'd made the cobbler and a cherry pie, cranberry sauce, two fresh loaves of bread which had already been diced into tiny squares for stuffing purposes, along with onion and celery. The turkey was in a brining bag, green beans and sweet potatoes were washed, and a pitcher of sun tea steeped on the porch.

They bopped around cleaning the kitchen, Derek drumming out rhythms and Elle singing to the pop music pumping into the room. The sway of Elle's hips as she scrubbed the dishes demanded his heed. Her ass was fantastic. From all that running, he knew. He spooned her from behind and swayed with her, his erection against the small of her back. Elle hummed seductively and turned to face him. She wore an apron streaked with cranberry and flour atop a floral sun dress, and her hair was back in a simple ponytail. "You've got something," Derek leaned toward her ear and whispered, "Right here." He licked the side of her neck, then gently tugged at her earlobe with his teeth. Derek grinned at the appearance of goosebumps along her neck and chest.

Elle breathed, "Catch me," and jumped, wrapping her legs around his waist. He wrapped his arms under her bum and set her on the kitchen counter. They kissed deeply. The heat between their bodies rose. He stepped back, unbuckled, and removed his belt with one hand, leaving it forgotten on the floor while he pounced back to her, a low rumble in his throat. He sidled back to her and scooched her to the counter's edge, his pants around his ankles. Elle's eyes widened. "Here?" Derek replied with a slow nod and gently pushed her panties to the side. He pulsed his thumb against her clit, and her back arched with pleasure.

She leaned back on her elbows and spread her legs wider, an invitation. Derek pushed into her, enveloped by her warmth and softness. He closed his eyes to focus on the sensation. No person felt like Elle. They were a whole greater than the sum of their parts when they were together. A hip-hop song started playing, and Derek took up the rhythm with his body movements; Elle giggled and joined. She wrapped her arms around his neck, and he half picked her up as they ground against each other. He could feel her round buttocks bumping against his thighs. The expression on her face was rapturous, and when he saw the blush on her cheeks, felt her body totally let go and heard her cry out in ecstasy, it pushed him over the edge.

Derek lost the rhythm, pushed into Elle as deep as he could, and stayed; it wasn't of his volition. His hips stopped working as the intensity of his orgasm took over. It was like lightning dancing along his skin and through his veins, starting in his pelvis and erupting through him.

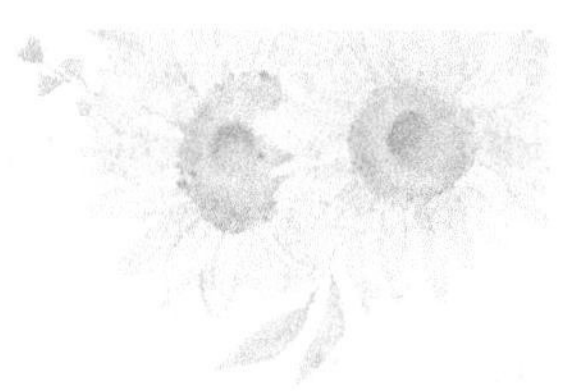

Seventeen

CRESCENDO - A GRADUALLY INCREASING SOUND.

A perfunctory knock sounded on the door before Derek's parents let themselves in. His Mom held a bouquet of flowers in fall colors, and his Dad had a bag that clanked suspiciously. Derek was sure it contained bottles of wine for the evening.

"Hi, Mom!" Derek rounded the corner to meet them in the living room, Elle two steps behind him. They embraced, though she pulled away quickly and fussed over Elle instead.

"You must be Elle! These are for you!" She handed over the flowers.

Elle smiled and said, "Thank you! These are beautiful! It's so good to see you in person." Being pulled into a hug caught her off guard, but Derek noticed her stiffness fade as she returned the squeeze.

"We're huggers." Mom offered as an explanation.

Derek cleared his throat. "And this is Dad. Of course, you already know." Derek's father offered Elle an easy side embrace. "How was the drive?"

They moved into the kitchen as they lamented Atlanta traffic. Elle trimmed the flowers and set their vase as a centerpiece on the table. Dad unpacked his shopping bag, confirming Derek's speculation. "We brought a red and a white because we weren't sure what you prefer."

"So considerate, thank you! I'm a wine fan, in general."

Dad pointed at her with a bottle still in hand. "My kinda gal."

Mom was already staring out the window at the garden. Derek put his hand on her back. "Come on. Let's go out." He turned to Elle, winked, and mouthed, "I told you so."

They all walked around the plot, Mom commenting here and there. "Your brassicas are healthy, but no spinach sprouts yet?"

Derek lowered his eyes. "I planted them a couple weeks late. They might still spring up." He was met with a reproachful hum. "The kitchen is running itself for now. Anyone interested in hiking a little?" He gave Elle another meaningful look and tried to communicate wordlessly. *See, it's all going like we imagined.*

And everything did go as planned. Or rather, the events did; Derek could have never predicted the dinner conversation. His Mom was, well, he didn't know what his Mom was doing. In the past, she had been normal, easy even, to introduce his friends or girlfriends to. Throughout Thanksgiving dinner, however, it almost seemed like the more comfortable he and Elle acted, the sharper her questioning became. Derek couldn't understand why. They already knew each other!

Things started well enough. Mom volunteered to share what she was grateful for first and included Elle's addition to their family traditions and how Derek was bursting with happiness. However, from there, she asked Elle how she was enjoying Everest, if she'd made any other local friends, and finally, pointedly, "So, where is your family?" She turned her head around the room as if expecting them to walk in. At this, Derek's Dad caught her eye and tilted his head down questioningly. Derek worried about how it would make Elle feel, but she continued to clear her plate and answered, "We aren't close. Something I'm learning now, through seeing your family support and love for each other, is missing for me."

Derek's heart fluttered in his chest but was squashed instantly by his Mom's follow-up. "That is sad. It's enough to make you wonder. With the absence of an example, if you know how to function in a committed relationship."

Derek and his Dad interjected at once. "Mom!" and "Kelly!" Rang out over each other, but Elle raised her hands, saying, "No, I get it." She held eye contact with Mom. "You're afraid I'll hurt him, judging from your other questions, in the same way that happened before."

Mom put her hand over her heart and nodded. "I'm sorry. It was rude to assert, but you're right. Seeing Derek," she turned to him, "I'm sorry, but fawn over you," her eyes returned to Elle. "I'm so happy for him. Happy for you both, but it is scary. It was a long time before he got over Sarah."

Elle put her fork down. "You're a great Mom. I wish..." She sighed, "My experience growing up... while different than other peoples, led me to crave a slower pace with deep relationships. Living in Everest has served to affirm I was right. I have never been happier. While I can't tell what will happen in the future, I can tell you what I hope happens, and that definitely includes Derek's continued well-being." Derek looked at her in awe.

Elle squeezed Derek's knee, breaking him from his trance. He spoke directly to Elle, "I know what I hope, too." A vision of what could be played in his mind, for the first time, not tainted with fear.

Mom apologized at least three times before the night was over.

Returning to school after a break made for raucous and tiring classes, and today was no exception. Elle's students were challenging to reign in as they feverishly talked to each other, comparing notes about their vacations and trading gossip. After her first two periods, she slipped into her office to enjoy a minute of silence. That golden moment was interrupted by her computer sounding. *Blasted emails!* As Ira had mentioned, an email from the ABA had arrived. Except she received two copies of the same message. She opened the first and read.

ABA Members,

We hope you all had a fantastic Thanksgiving week and have returned ready to begin Concert Season. Below is your guide to planning a successful concert. Each link will take you to the corresponding information. **Remember, you must submit your Concert Registration and indicate your approved musical selections no later than February 11th.**

We have several positions open and are seeking volunteers to fill these next year, in addition to stand-by volunteers who will help as needed or in the absence of a chairperson or committee member. Click here for a complete list of open positions. To submit yourself for consideration, please email rhonda.gilbert@aba.org with ABA Volunteer as the subject line, and indicate your name, district, school, and what position you're interested in.

Concert Season Guides

- *Selecting Challenging but Attainable Music for Your Band*
- *Approved Concert Music List*
- *Making the Most out of Rehearsal*
- *Small Ensemble Considerations*
- *Concert Etiquette*
- *Sight Reading Preparedness*
- *Understanding Adjudication Scores & Comments*
- ***Concert Registration (must be submitted by February 11th)***

Yours in Music,
   Rhonda Gilbert
   Alabama Bandmasters Association
   Communications Chair

Elle clicked into the duplicate email but found it wasn't a duplicate after all. It was similar, but some items were missing. Curious, she opened them side by side. The 2nd email didn't include the paragraph calling for volunteers and the guides for Making the Most of Rehearsal and Small Ensemble Considerations. *Weird.* She made a mental note to investigate later and left to greet her third-period class as their chatter crescendoed into the room.

Welcoming her students at the door as they arrived at class was something Elle looked forward to, even on the busiest days. It set the tone and had become almost like a ritual between them. She offered everyone high fives and fist bumps and addressed them by name. "Hey, Marcus. Lorraine! Good break, Suzanne?"

Her 8th graders put together their instruments and found

their chairs right away but were not immune from the after-vacation energy. Instead of warming up, they sat talking to their neighbors. Elle cleared her throat, but only the first row seemed to notice. She rapped her baton on the stand in front of her. Now silence spread in a wave as visiting ceased from the second row back to the percussionist. "We have a lot of energy today. Understandable, but we do have some work to do. I hope we can harness some of that spirit and get creative today. As the seniors in our school, you're the experts on our Holiday Concert. I'd like to hear how they've been, what could be better about them, and ideas on making this year's something special." She saw several students shift into what she thought of as their 'thinking face.' "Who can tell me how our performances in years past have gone?"

Hands shot in the air, and as Elle called on people, students shared everything from how finding their seats on stage was scary to the pieces they performed and even an admission of an ill-timed squawk from a clarinet player when they were in sixth grade. Elle jotted down what they said on a whiteboard.

All in all, Elle expected to hear most of the reports, though she tried to console Kayla before continuing. "I still remember splitting my reed on the way out to the stage for an honor band performance in high school. We all have experiences like that." She drew a line to make a new column on the board. "These are great, everyone! We've got some things that went well and maybe some areas we can improve. Let's use these to start planning this year. For example, getting on stage was stressful, so let's practice how we want to file on stage this year. What else can we improve?"

Some ideas were floated, including having a countdown to concert day so it didn't sneak up on them and knowing where they needed to practice most. It was here that students began to get distracted. Elle had to recenter the room several times and wondered if she should proceed to the next step in these conditions.

It was easy to determine that there wasn't enough time to delay, so she drove on and drew another column on the board. "Now, we won't be able to do everything in this column, but this is the space for our wildest dreams…"

"Santa hats!" Liam shouted from his seat next to the bass drum.

The class buzzed with talking and laughter at the outburst, and Elle had to call for their attention again. "Up here, everyone. Silencio!" Once they calmed, she continued, "That's actually a great example, Liam, but let's raise our hands, please." Several hands shot up. "I'm going to write down everything you say, but before we start, please think about how this year has been different. Several of you have told me you weren't used to learning music history or about the pieces you performed in the past, as an example. Is there a way to apply that to our performance?"

Elle wrote 'Santa hats' on the board and worked through the raised hands. As she expected, some of the ideas were cause for outbreaks of giggles or were simply impossible, like paying every performer $100. Other ideas, though, made her heart swell with pride. When a shy flutist, Rebecca, was called, she recommended they perform a piece with the high school band. This got almost as much of a response from her peers as the request for payment.

By the end of class, she had never been more thankful for a lunch break, and when Derek entered the room, hair askew and wide-eyed, Elle knew he was having a similar day. "Big productive with your kids today?" she asked with a plastic smile.

"Ha. Haha. Hahaha." Derek ran his hands through his dark waves and pulled.

Elle laughed and nodded in agreement. "Hey, have you

checked your email today? I got two from the ABA, but it's weird. One is different than the other."

Derek fished an apple out of this lunchbox. "Not sure. I'm impressed you had time to check your mail at all; it's been madness in my classes!"

"Welllll, I may have been hiding in my office between the classes," Elle admitted. "Come see." She shook her mouse to wake the computer screen, and they leaned toward the monitor.

"Bizarre. Which came first?"

Elle pointed to the timestamps. "The longer one was first. The shorter one came about 30 minutes later. It must have been the one I heard deliver when I was in here." She thought momentarily, then asked, "You'd think if it was a retraction, it would say so, right?"

"I don't know. I'll check mine as soon as I'm back. Maybe there was an error, and everyone got two. They might not have realized somehow."

Elle received a text from Derek as soon as he returned to his room. He confirmed he'd only received one email from the ABA, the shorter one, at approximately the same time she had received it.

Later that night, Elle lay in bed with a window cracked to let the cool air in and enjoyed a light breeze fluttering her newly hung curtains. The sounds of soft cooing birds outside and the gentle motions of the curtain had nearly lulled Elle to sleep when she shot up with a gasp. She announced, "It can't be!" to herself, swiftly opened the email app on her phone, and scrolled to the two strange emails. This time, noting the sender's address. The first message was from rhonda.gilbert@aba.org. The second message was from AL_Bandmasters_Assoc@gmail.com. A chill ran up her spine.

Elle took a screenshot of each and texted them to Derek.

Elle Foster

We have a problem. 11:53pm

Elle Foster

I guarantee that gmail address isn't an ABA address… It has to be him, right? 11:54pm

She made to put the phone down. Not that she expected to get any sleep now, but knowing that Derek turned in earlier than her, Elle didn't anticipate a response until morning.

Derek Michaels

Holy fuck 12:01am

Her phone rang. They didn't bother with greetings. Derek said, "I'm sure you're right. This is insane. It's INSANE."

"Has he been controlling the flow of communication to all of you? How long has this been going on? The implications… I have so many questions."

"Yeah, like how? And why? Would he really do something like this just to keep himself in those positions?"

Elle massaged her forehead. "I don't know. Ugh. We need more information. I don't know how this isn't Greg, but I don't want to jump to conclusions, either. It's early. Maybe we're overlooking a simpler explanation?" She didn't really believe they were, though.

Derek sighed. "Right. You're right. Tomorrow, we can see what Chuck and Billy received. I know some directors in other districts. I'll try to find out what they got, too."

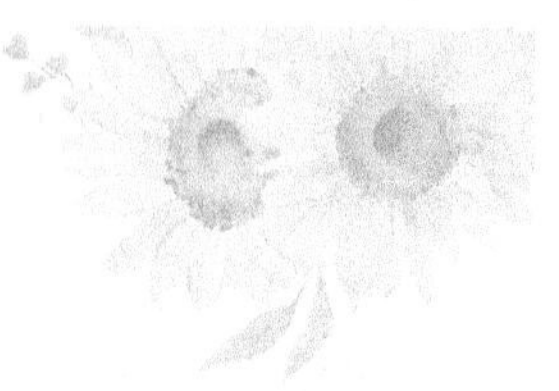

Eighteen

ICTUS - THE INSTANT AT WHICH THE BEAT
OCCURS. USUALLY INDICATED BY A DIRECTOR
WITH A SUDDEN CLICK OF THE WRIST OR A
CHANGE IN BATON DIRECTION.

The time between Thanksgiving and Winter breaks was stressful. At school, Elle felt pressure for her bands to perform exceptionally at the holiday concert. This was the first performance the community would hear since she started, and though she was less like an outsider than she once was, the memories of those initial stares and judgments still stung when she recalled them. This was her chance to prove her worth. That her teaching was effective. She could gain the trust of the people of Everest.

So, Elle pushed her classes. They used more of their class time in rehearsal. She assigned homework for the first time to write a paragraph on the origin of a song of their choosing. She even offered extra credit for additional practice hours logged at home. To her relief, getting buy-in from her students by asking for their feedback about the concert had them responding well. They seemed equally determined to give a great show.

Preparing for the concert wasn't the only thing hanging over Elle's head. She and Derek had carefully documented everything they learned about the emails from AL_Bandmasters_Assoc@gmail.com. It didn't feel like much, and some of the information was slow going. At the same time, they didn't know what else to do with their findings. It was infuriating. They'd confirmed the gmail.com address was responsible for delivering all ABA communication sent to Derek, Chuck, and Billy. This was also true for other directors in their district whom Elle hadn't met yet. Derek had also contacted five colleagues in other districts, and all five reported they exclusively received communications from addresses ending in aba.org.

Some of those colleagues forwarded their emails from aba.org, and Derek compared them to the ones he had received. In each case, the emails from gmail were missing information.

The picture was clear. Someone was editing ABA emails and sending the limited information they wanted to be delivered to the directors in District 6. How this occurred was the topic of endless speculation. If every email in an entire district was misspelled in the way Elle's had been, surely there would be some sort of alert when sending that Rhonda would have noticed. Not to mention the mystery of how the addresses would have been manipulated in the first place.

Another hot topic was what to do with all their findings. Elle and Derek discussed this casually while strolling downtown before the Holiday Concert. This would be Elle's first holiday season without snow. While she missed it a little, she had to admit Everest was positively charming. The moment Thanksgiving was over, the town transformed with sparkling lights and festive decorations. Each lamp post was wrapped in evergreen and white light. The storefronts held Christmas trees and windows painted with snowmen and sleighs. In the low light of the evening, the twinkling of string lights gave life to the air around them.

"I wish we could definitively find out who owned the gmail account. It's the biggest missing piece." Elle lamented.

Derek squeezed her hand. "Me too. I don't see how we can get any more information. I guess we could ask Chuck and Billy to reach out to any of the people they know, but I'm confident it will be the same. Now it's just... what's next?"

"It's hard because it's *so* damning. Someone is definitely tampering with the communications, and we have proof. If we give the evidence to Ira, what happens?"

"That's the part worrying everyone." Derek took a deep breath. "It's all speculative from here. If it's not Greg, or they can't prove who the culprit is, Greg will certainly know about our investigation, which scares everyone. If it is Greg, and they can prove it, I'm not sure what that means either. The ABA isn't affiliated with the school, but at the same time, they provide the necessary programs for our students. Could he be banned from the ABA and still keep his job? Would he be fired outright somehow? Maybe it's not anything? I... well... I don't like Greg's company or his power plays, but I've always thought he was probably an okay director for his school."

Elle glanced over at Derek and saw his brows knit in concern. "I understand." He looked over at her. "Our jobs are our life. It would be awful to separate someone from their calling and livelihood. Even if that person is the scum of the earth." Derek laughed, and she smiled at him, feeling good about relieving the tension in his face and dreading what she needed to add. "That said... I think this part is out of our hands. This is a huge transgression and probably wasn't easy to achieve. If he gets fired, he may have earned it, and Derek... Depending on how he did it, they may even press charges."

"Oh." Derek's face went blank, "That hadn't occurred to me yet."

Elle pursed her lips to the side. "It's more guessing, but it occurred to me last night. Trespassing, hacking, and I don't know what else could be involved that might merit legal action."

They turned a corner that revealed an enormous Christmas tree set in a small park area. It was swathed in colored lights, and a star glinted at the top. Elle's eyes opened wide, and she tugged Derek's hand as she hastened toward the display. Derek spun her when they arrived before the tree and dipped her into a kiss. He supported her to standing and said, "I think we should see what other information trickles in so we can give a complete report, then email Ira when we return after the break. You're right. What will come isn't our decision, but we're obligated to report." He twirled her into him.

Elle asked, "Are you ready for tonight?"

"Best Holiday Concert ever. Coming right up."

Everest Middle was taking the stage first. Elle had programmed the grades to perform in order, starting with 6th. After the 7th and 8th grades finished, the high school band would take the stage, then the complicated bit of them all playing the last piece together would occur. It was strange to feel both confident and nervous, but those emotions roiled through her as her youngest students found their chairs just as they'd practiced.

She gave them a reassuring thumbs-up and whispered, "We're going to do great." Elle turned toward the audience. The room was packed, which was surprising until she likened it to football games. They didn't have quite that many people turn out, but most seats were full nonetheless. Determination rooted her feet to the stage, and she began. "Hello, everyone, and thank you for coming to our Christmas Concert. I'm Elle Foster, and seated behind me is our 6th-grade band. These are our newest musicians." A light smattering of applause made her stop. "Yes! Give it up for them; this is their first time on stage." The clapping picked up. "This year, Mr. Michaels and I worked together to offer something a little different. We'll be giving you a short background story before each piece. Some of what we learned about the history of these popular pieces is fascinating."

Elle walked across the stage and stepped onto the podium. "Our first piece is considered a classic but is relatively new compared to some of the other works you'll hear tonight. In 1939, the Great Depression was waning, and World War II was impending. A department store, Montgomery Ward, wanted to create some holiday cheer in that bleak time by making a free children's book. Adman Robert May was responsible for penning this work. As Adman observed the heavy fog over Lake Michigan, he envisioned a reindeer with a nose so bright he could help Santa navigate his sleigh. This is Rudolph the Rednosed Reindeer."

She turned toward the band and lifted her baton. Students responded by moving their instruments into playing positions. She counted a measure for them and took an exaggerated breath on the 4th count, which the band mirrored, and they started together.

Elle provided the story of Good King Wenceslas, brother of Boleslav the Cruel. Unlike his brother, Wenceslas was beloved by his subjects and posthumously was declared a king and later a saint. The 6th graders did admirably on both pieces, starting and finishing together, in tune most of the time, and only a couple unfortunate squeaks. They received a lengthy round of applause, and Elle felt more relaxed after their debut went as intended. She explained their program to the audience as they exited the stage, and the 7th and 8th-grade bands came on. "Give us a few minutes as we rearrange some seating, please. Our 7th and 8th graders will be coming on next. I'll share more about these pieces, but we'll be playing a work that we don't know who to credit for and used to be called Carol of the Drums, a song originally more about the New Year featuring lines like 'Fill the madcap, drain the barrel,' which were translated into the holiday tune we know today, and finally a piece which almost never was and surprisingly came from a place of grief."

After her band played through Little Drummer Boy, Deck the Halls, and Santa Claus is Coming to Town, she gestured for them to stand up and take a bow. Attendees got to their feet and gave an ovation; whistles rang through the auditorium. It had been an exceptional performance from the middle school. Elle raised her voice to address the crowd, "I agree! What an amazing job they did. I could not be more proud of these students' hard work. And I don't want to spoil anything, but hint: you'll hear from them again! For now, we'll turn the stage over to Everest High." She helped the kids grab their stands and guided them into the front section of reserved seats. When they were settled, Elle crept back to the side of the stage behind the curtain to watch Derek.

Thanks to the stage lighting, the v of his back beneath his shirt was visible when Derek was turned away from her. He teased and joked with his students, speaking softly so only they could hear him, setting them at ease before addressing the crowd. "I believe this piece is the newest song we'll play tonight. It was released in 1966, and while I'm sure you'll recognize it, you might not know the singer is also the original voice of Frosted Flakes Tony the Tiger." The high school band moved to position as one. Derek simply breathed and gave the downbeat, You're a Mean One, Mr. Grinch began.

Elle was transfixed with Derek's interactions with his students and the audience. His familiarity with each person on stage made admiration swell in her chest. When he addressed the spectators with such confidence and humor, they hung on his every word. He joked about Welkin Rings when introducing Hark the Herald Angels Sing, shared the shockingly bleak original lyrics to Have Yourself a Merry Little Christmas, and used his students to share three fun facts about Jingle Bells before playing Jingle Bell Rock.

"We're coming to the end of our program." There were hisses and boos. "Yes, I know, but we still have two extraordinary things to share. Both unprecedented. Neither attempted in Everest before." The crowd quieted. "This next piece is one of the most challenging holiday pieces a group can play. It topped the US Christmas Music Charts every year between 2009 and 2012 and did so again in 2015. Pretty impressive for a song that never even mentions the holiday in the lyrics. We know from the composer's wife, who said, 'Leroy didn't set out to write a Christmas piece, but rather his intentions were to convey the entire winter season through the imagery of a sleigh ride, much in the way Mozart did with his piece of the same name.' This is Sleigh Ride by Leroy Anderson." When Derek turned to face the band again, he winked at Elle before raising his hands.

Wow, he is an excellent conductor! Elle had never realized. Now she thought of it, most of her time viewing Everest High was with the marching band, which was always led by the drum major. Sleigh Ride was a complex piece that involved repeated cueing, phrase shaping, and challenging syncopation. She marveled at the snappiness of his ictus, which was the perfect match for the jauntiness of the tune and kept them up to tempo. His body moved in and out or side to side with the musical phrases depending on what section had the melody. He cued the well-known slapstick part perfectly. Ben, the percussionist playing the slapstick, leapt back and forth at each slap, causing the audience to chuckle and a joyous smile to take hold of Derek's face.

At the final cutoff, the audience stood and cheered loudly, and for such a time, Derek had to motion for them to sit back down. "That was the most fun I've ever had conducting these insanely talented kids, which is really saying something." The audience began to applaud again, but Derek held up a hand. "They absolutely deserve it, but please hold. I promised you two unprecedented events." Elle began leading her band in a line, spacing out the students so they were up and down each of the aisles amongst the onlookers. "As far as we could find, Everest Middle and High bands have never performed a piece together. That is going to end today. It's worth noting that this idea came from an 8th-grade student, Rebecca Washington. Thank you, Rebecca. We invite you all to sing along to this piece from the 16th century, which embodies the spirit of caroling. We Wish You a Merry Christmas."

Elle jogged back on stage. Derek scooted to the front of the podium, facing his band, while she stood back to back with him, facing the crowd and her students. They started as one. Music filled the entire hall, not solely from their bands but the voices of the audience as they sang with abandon. Elle felt they might shake the dust from the rafters, and it was all she could do to keep conducting and fight the lump in her throat.

After the show, Elle found herself surrounded by parents.

"You're Eli's favorite teacher."

"I need to thank you. Stella is practicing all the time. She's never been so engaged with anything."

"Adam tells us about what he did in a band every day."

"You must be doing a great job because I've never seen Maddie happier."

She fielded compliment after compliment, trying to memorize the parent's faces and names and tie them to their student. After a few minutes, most people exited. Only Derek remained, with a couple parents on stage and a few stragglers standing beside the main entry to the hall.

Elle turned to help Derek clean up but stopped as a voice called to her. "Uh. Ms. Foster, could I talk to you for a minute?" She didn't recognize the man, whose tone differed from the excited, praising folks she had just met.

"Yes, of course. How can I help you?" She traversed the distance to him.

"I, uh. You don't know me, really. Gosh, this is hard." He dropped his hand, which had been massaging his opposite shoulder. "I made a mistake withdrawing Robert from your program earlier this year, and I'm hoping it's not too late to re-enroll him?"

Recognition clicked into place. "Mr. Brown? It's nice to meet you." Elle held out her hand, and they shook. "It's never too late to learn. I'm sure we can have Robert start next semester." Though full of righteous vindication, Elle held back her euphoric emotions, not wanting to misstep.

"That's great!" Relief washed over Mr. Brown's face. "Thank you, and I'm sorry."

"No, thank you. Robert will have a wonderful time with us next semester. I look forward to having him in class."

Mr. Brown walked out of the auditorium, and Elle spun on her heel to the stage. Derek was there eyeing her. She glanced around to ensure they were alone, then shouted, "Did you hear that!?"

Derek smiled, his eyes crinkling and reflecting in the stage light. "Leave it to you. Outstanding performance tonight, by the way."

Elle yelled in triumph and ran to the stage. "And you! Your conducting was... Wow. It took my breath away."

It only took them a few minutes to clean the stage and lock up their classrooms. Derek could tell Elle was soaring. She deserved it. It was hands down the best performance he'd heard from the middle school, and he understood what it meant to have the conversation with Mr. Brown. His own emotions were up, too. Her concert was more important than his own in many ways, but Everest High had shown out. He couldn't believe they did Sleigh Ride!

Elle positively waltzed to the parking lot. She grabbed something out of her car and held it behind her back. "I have a surprise for you... If it's a good time?"

Derek shrugged and basked in her playfulness. "I don't have anywhere to be."

"Great!" She took the blindfold from behind her back.

"Uh... What did I agree to?"

Elle sang, "You'll seeeee..." as she tied the blindfold around his eyes and led him to her passenger seat.

Derek tried to track the vehicle's turns to see where Elle might be taking him. After they turned onto the dirt road, he was reasonably certain they were headed to her home. Anxiety made his stomach squirm. He was triggered the last time he was here and admittedly responded poorly. If he saw her home again, how would he feel? They'd come so far; seeing a sign of detachment would be even more devastating. *Remember, she wants to stay. We know more now.*

The car turned off the road and onto the lawn. The engine quieted, and Elle's keychain rattled. He felt hollow as she grabbed his hand and led him out of the car. She walked him a couple slow steps to the right. Without a word, she removed the blindfold.

The porch was freshly whitewashed. Derek noticed right away; the white popped even in the darkness of night. Elle held his hand and said, "Come on," while gently tugging his arm. They stepped through the door, and it was like stepping into another world- some house miles away or across the globe- definitely not the neglected place he'd seen before.

It was clean, and bright colors were on the walls and shelves. There were shelves! The room was furnished, and there was a rug. He could see one side of the kitchen ahead, and it was clearly also freshly painted, and a new table had replaced the rickety one he'd tried to eat breakfast on. "Elle..."

"Go look." It was permission and command. Derek ran to the kitchen. He swiftly came out and inspected the bathroom, then her room. It was a home. A real home. There was no pit in his stomach. He was full. He was... picking Elle up and spinning her around in her living room while she told him, "Merry Christmas."

"When did you do all this?"

"Late nights, on the girl's days, Mavis and Tiny helped. You like it?"

Derek couldn't move his eyes from Elle, still wearing her black slacks and red satin top from the concert, her light locks pinned back with a giant poinsettia clip, and her eyes. Hopeful and nervous. "This is the best gift anyone has ever given to me." He weaved his fingers through hers. Between kisses, he whispered, "Thank you."

Nineteen

LEGATO - IN A SMOOTH FLOWING MANNER,
WITHOUT BREAKS BETWEEN NOTES.

G reg Howard

> Long time no see for the Band Misters. It's
> time for us to go to the greens, fellas. I
> reserved us a game on the 19th. 2pm.
> 12:39pm

"Greg messaged the group!" Derek aimed his phone screen at Elle. They were finishing lunch at his kitchen table.

"That's tomorrow. Love that he assumes you're all free."

"This is what he always does. This is normal Greg behavior... Which is now weird."

Matt Norris

> See you there. Bring your A game. 12:41pm

Billy Thompson

Alright 12:41pm

Elle played with the fork in her hand. "Are you going to respond?"

"Oh. Yeah." He took his phone back.

Derek Michaels

Sounds good 12:42pm

Elle watched him type, swallowed the bite of kale salad she had taken, and teased, "Liar." Then, more seriously added, "It's going to be strange, isn't it? Knowing we're sitting on all this scandalous information."

"True. Chuck will be alright; his strategy of being silent is enviable. Billy... I'm a little worried about Billy now you mention it."

Derek, Chuck, and Billy ensured they entered the club at different times, wanting to purposefully avoid the appearance of communication between them. Derek was the last to arrive and found all the men leaning on the bar across the room. Greg slid him a glass of brown liquor as he joined. "Wild Turkey."

"Thanks." He picked up the glass and tipped it toward Greg. Derek noted that he looked different. Drawn. Tense in a way he'd not been before. He hadn't seen Greg in nearly a month; what happened during that time?

Greg noticed Derek observing him and sharply questioned, "What?"

It was probably the low light of the bar making his eyes dead and dark. "Nothing." Derek downed the rest of his bourbon. "Ready to play? It's five 'til." The men grabbed their golf bags and filed out the back door to claim their carts and make it to their first tee.

Things were awkward immediately. For the first few holes, he thought it may be the usual feelings of not fitting in and dreading Greg's commentary. It was the fourth hole when Greg put his finger on the difference. "You're as quiet as Chuck today, Billy. You sick or somethin'?"

Shit. He was right. Derek had been so busy trying to act normal he didn't notice that Billy was utterly withdrawn. He couldn't blame him. His own head was racing with the information he knew they would turn in to Ira in a few short weeks, searching for more clues in the conversation and ignoring unsettling remarks. None of them were exactly actors, either.

Derek tried to think of a way to help Billy; he'd indeed begun looking sick at being questioned. "How'd everyone's holiday concerts go?"

Greg leaned on his driver, still inspecting Billy, but Matt answered. "It was good. Same old, same old." As he answered, his eyes nervously shot to Greg. *Does he also look strained?*

"We gave a little background on each of the songs this year. Great feedback from the audience about that, and it wasn't hard to research some fun facts if anyone wants to try it. My band did Sleigh Ride justice, too. I'm proud of that."

Derek's account of the concert earned Greg's attention. "Heard about that. Y'all are having a banner year at Everest High. Accolades for your marching and a Grade 4 piece midseason. Gotta give it up to ya." Derek waited for him to say something cutting or doubtful, but it never came. Instead, he noticed Greg acting antsy. The darkness in his eyes had not abated when they left the bar, and Derek wondered again why they hadn't met in November.

They were halfway through the course, and Derek didn't know how they could possibly finish. Time dragged dangerously. The conversation was minimal, and the tension in the group was becoming unnerving. Chuck and Billy were largely silent and only spoke briefly when directly addressed. Matt seemed to be purposefully maintaining a distance from Greg. He continued to glance at him anytime he went to talk as if seeking approval. Greg's behavior was alarming and hard to watch. His fidgeting had become wilder, more violent movements that he performed incessantly: kicking his clubs or the bag, swinging the clubs into the bag, kicking the cart tires. Derek had the notion he was under growing pressure and trying not to explode.

All of this was most unlike the Greg he knew. It would have been a fight if anyone else handled his precious clubs like he treated them now. And when had Greg ever been concerned about blowing up? Confrontation, shouting, getting in people's faces... These were not things he'd ever shied away from previously.

On the 10th hole, Derek couldn't stand the growing stress anymore. Instead of introducing innocent small talk that fizzled out, he took a deep breath and asked, "You okay, Greg?"

Greg stilled for the first time since the beginning of their game, but it did not bring solace; it was deadly. He spit on the manicured grass. "Now, what in the world would you ask me that for?"

"It just seems like you're nervous or something." Derek

gestured to the club in Greg's hand. "I've never seen you kick at your clubs before."

Greg hoisted the driver over his shoulder, and for a split second, Derek thought he would strike him, but then he moved to the tee. It was his turn. Greg planted his feet carefully, pulled it back, and swung, connecting with the ball. It veered too far to the left and landed in a sand trap. Greg didn't move. His club still hung above his head. Even the birds were silent. Derek glanced at Chuck. He shook his head left to right the slightest bit. Then Greg screamed. It was the sound of a wild animal. Matt and Billy took a step back.

"Nothing is okay!" Greg turned and stalked toward Derek, who raised his hands as if surrendering. Greg pointed his finger and poked Derek in the chest. "Of course, I'm not okay. And you know it more than anyone because it's your fault." Derek's mouth dropped, and he stuttered, but before he could form a reply, Greg was yelling again. "The Band Misters are ruined! You think I don't know about the kiss heard 'round the world?! You and that fucking whore are destroying everything, and you don't even have the balls to come out and tell me you're together."

Derek's entire body sweltered in an instant. His blood rushed through him, making his heartbeat pound in his ears. His vision narrowed, so all he saw was Greg. All he could think about was how good it would feel when he buried his fist into that face. His right hand twitched.

Chuck was suddenly between them, pushing Derek and Greg apart. His ears started picking up sound again. Chuck said, "You can't do that, Greg. You can't call Elle, or anyone else, a whore."

Greg gaped at Chuck as if seeing him for the first time. "The shit, I can't." He turned back to Derek. "She's only with you because she needs protection. Too bad she chose someone so weak."

Billy stepped forward. His words came out hesitantly, "Greg... I've met her. She's a good director. You know. She seems like a good person."

Greg spun his head, looking at each of them. He bared his teeth, and spittle flew from his mouth as he growled, "I knew you were meeting behind my back! You think this bitch deserves to be here? Maybe the problem is you don't know what excellence is. That's it. You're lacking, and it makes her more proficient by comparison!" His eyes popped madly, and his fist was clenched tightly around the club he still held in his left hand.

Greg started a sentence, "We've just got to..." but was interrupted by Matt.

"Greg." Matt barely spoke over a whisper. "Set aside everything about Elle individually. This type of behavior. The language you use. It's... It's similar to what Principal Locke has talked to you about, right? Those complaints?" Matt's eyes darted to and from Greg.

A few seconds of silence passed as Derek, Chuck, and Billy stealthily regarded each other. Derek could tell this was their first time hearing about trouble at Darton. Greg roared. He threw his club on the ground. "WHAT COMPLAINTS?!" He stormed toward the cart, Matt jumping out of his way, slung his bag and driver into the back of it, and sped away.

It was difficult for the four men to fit on a single golf cart with their bags. Matt drove slowly. Nobody spoke. Derek was sure they were all reeling internally, as he was. He'd never seen anyone so unhinged before. Visions of Greg's veined neck and screaming face kept replaying in his mind. He could still feel his finger jabbing into his chest. *And what complaints was Matt referring to?*

When they pulled the cart back into its space, Derek looked around for signs of Greg, but it appeared he'd left. As they unloaded, Derek suggested, "I think it's time we all talked together." He saw Matt nod his head out of the corner of his eye.

The group returned to the club and settled into a dark corner booth. Derek sat across from Matt. "This is awkward, but..."

A waitress appeared at the table, happily bouncing on the balls of her feet. "Short game today. Didn't I see you leave out at 2?" When no one answered, she continued, "Umm, what can I get you?"

Derek closed his eyes, summoning patience. "Water for me."

Chuck's voice was flat, "Nah. We're going to need something stronger than water for this." Billy turned up his lips and nodded his agreement. "I'll get us a round of Gulden Draak."

"Coming right up!" She floated away to the bar.

Derek leaned against the cushion of the booth, not wanting to start the conversation just to be interrupted again. "Thanks, Chuck."

"No problem."

Once everyone had their first sip of what would likely be a meal in a bottle, Derek began again. "I think it's time we looped you in, and I hope you can share about whatever is happening at Darton."

Derek explained from the beginning. As he described his general discomfort with Greg's behavior and how it had peeked, he glanced at Chuck for an indication that he should skip his part of the tale. To his astonishment, Chuck took over the narrative and explained their late-night park conversation. Billy began to punctuate the story with his own observations and experiences. The longer they spoke, the less stifling the air around them felt.

"When Elle and I saw Greg and Ira's interaction, it gave us the courage to carefully reach out to him. Elle volunteered to do it in case anything got back to Greg. The conversation with

Ira led to a big discovery." Derek pointed around the table to each of them. "We aren't receiving official ABA emails. Nobody in the district is. Someone, we think Greg, is receiving the actual emails, deleting information about volunteering for positions and other things, then sending the rogue messages to us."

Matt took a healthy swallow of his beer, then leaned onto his elbows and pulled at the hair around his temples. Derek expected him to ask questions, maybe even to be disbelieving. He didn't anticipate the wreck on his face. "Why didn't you tell me?"

"Oh. Matt. I'm sorry. I guess we were afraid. You work so closely together at Darton, and we did try to find an in. A sign or something that might indicate you weren't friends, but we never saw it."

Matt rolled his eyes. "Well, you should have looked harder. I'm alone with him, you know?"

Chuck's face fell. "I do know. Goddamnit, I know the feeling. Should have recognized it in you." He swigged from his mug.

Billy added. "I never thought about it that way. Which... I should have put myself in your shoes. We all should have. I'm sorry."

Matt sighed. He winced before saying, "Things the past few months have been especially bad." He threw his hands up. "Now, I don't know everything. The information is being controlled, but I do know there's an investigation because I was questioned." He focused on the table where his finger idly traced in a circle, looking miserable. "I don't know how much to say."

Derek longed to give him relief. "Only say as much as you're comfortable. We understand if that's nothing." Chuck and Billy nodded, brows furrowed.

"You all just said when you started coming together and

talking about Elle, you figured Greg was a fine director, that his habits didn't extend to the school. I used to think so, too, but now I don't know. Mind you, he's always pushed his students hard and maintained a wall between himself and them, more like a commander. But that's his style. Then, earlier this year, I heard there were some complaints against him from a girl in his band. I didn't think much of it. I figured he'd cussed at the wrong student, you know?" Derek, Chuck, and Billy remained rapt as Matt swallowed several times. "But it was like the complaint never went away. I heard rumors that more than one person was coming forward, and they were sayin' he harassed 'em. I'm an idiot, though, because it still didn't seem like anything to write home about until the last few weeks. Me and some of the high school teachers, anyone who may have worked with Greg, were called in for questioning. They didn't really tell me nothin', but it was obvious by what they asked. Things like if I ever saw him say anything or act inappropriately. If I ever noticed he was closer to some students." Matt shuddered and closed his eyes tight.

"That's horrible, Matt... I'm..." Derek started.

"It ain't even done." Matt shook his head and continued. "Greg, you know how he's connected to damn near everyone. He found out I was interrogated. He cornered me in my room after school. No idea how he got there so fast; my school is a ways away from the high school, and we'd just dismissed. Anyway, he said I needed to tell him exactly what they asked, if they hinted at anything. If anyone else was there. He was scared, I could tell, but he never asked me what I told them. When I realized that... I don't know; it hit me. He did something. Today was the first day I've seen him since then."

The table was speechless. Each of them stared at their drinks for several long minutes, grappling with what they'd heard.

"It's monstrous," Billy mumbled. "If a teacher did anything. Said anything to my daughter…"

Derek added, "This is why he canceled our meetings. He must be tied up with all this going on."

"And trying to control the rumors," Chuck offered, "I'm shocked at… Geez, the whole damn thing, but how have we not heard about this in Stoville and Everest?"

Derek puffed a "Huh." at the question. "Maybe he is innocent? I mean, if he's still working, right? Wouldn't they at least put him on some sort of forced leave while they investigate?"

Matt shook his head. "I don't know. That sounds like the TV shows. Might not happen like that here. Maybe in the city."

Chuck waved his hand across the table. "Maybe it's a sign they couldn't prove anything, but even if that's true, if he has done something to the emails, he's toast. Best case scenario for him is the ABA doesn't sue. He'd still lose his job."

"Elle brought that up too, Chuck. It's hard for me to think about the emails with this new information. What he may or may not have done with his students. I'm horrified, but I wish I knew more at the same time. I don't prefer his company, but I never would've believed… his kids?"

Matt shook his head again. "He doesn't think of them as his kids. They're more like employees."

"This is awful." Billy was staring off into the distance. "I don't know if he did it. Anything. But I think he's capable of it. Seeing how he's controlled the communication for so long now, It goes together, doesn't it?"

His sentence hung over them. It's what they were all thinking.

"Why was he acting like that?"

"He called me a whore?! Wow."

"Oh, my God!"

"Oh, my GOD!"

"Chuck!"

"What?"

"No. No. Come on."

Elle had been following along excitedly as if watching a reality TV show drama unfold, but her mood sobered the instant Derek explained what Matt had shared. She slumped onto the couch. "What if he hurt them? Tiny always warned she thought he was dangerous. I should have told someone."

Derek gently lifted her chin with his finger and looked into her eyes. "You should have told someone your friend had a vibe? Elle." He said her name like a legato; the soft L sound held longer than typical, and it was like a salve. "I don't want to downplay Tiny's intuition, but this isn't your fault. Having a feeling isn't actionable." She nodded.

"We don't honestly know anything for certain. Only that investigators asked those questions. I hope it's nothing because nothing happened. Can you imagine one of ours?"

"No. Never." Derek paused. "The other thing is, the guys wanted me to tell you sorry we had this whole conversation without you and asked if you wanted to go ahead and send the findings to Ira. We wouldn't hear back until after vacation, likely, but given Matt is a known entity and the news about the investigation. I think we're all itching to do something."

"I literally have it ready to send. It's in drafts. I can do it right now." She walked to the kitchen table and brought back the laptop. "Nice of them to think of me being absent." She passed Derek the computer to proofread the email.

He smirked. "I thought so, too. That wasn't from me, by the way. Chuck was the one to bring it up. Full of surprises, that guy, now that he talks."

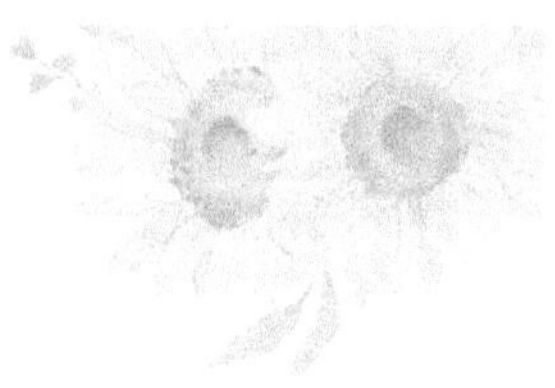

Twenty

PARADIDDLE - A RUDIMENTARY DRUMMING
PATTERN CONSISTING OF FOUR EVEN STROKES
PLAYED IN THE ORDER OF LEFT-RIGHT-LEFT-
LEFT OR RIGHT-LEFT-RIGHT-RIGHT.

They'd sent the email and all their findings to Ira, and the news about Greg's investigation had reached the general populace. According to Derek, Mavis, and Tiny, this had to be the slowest-spreading event in regional history. Once it broke, however, Elle couldn't escape the buzz of rumors. She was grateful it was Christmas break because at least it was easy to avoid public areas; Elle and Derek were cozy in their now-decorated homes. Still, anytime she went to Green's or Tiny's Cafe, it was impossible to avoid overhearing people trade their version of events.

Some of the things Elle heard seemed plausible, and others were so outlandish they couldn't be true. It was an accepted fact that Greg was under investigation for sexual assault. Many people also claimed he wouldn't return to Darton High in the new year, though his position had not been listed on any job board. On a recent date to Katie's Deli, Derek and she had been low-key eavesdropping on a couple a few tables away. The woman's sharply cut blonde bob moved slightly with each gesticulation. It swung violently when she proclaimed Greg was the leader of a secret sex cult. Derek turned his laugh into a cough, but not before the couple glared suspiciously in their direction.

Elle was determined to put the heaviness of the recent weeks aside. She and Derek had decided to go to the annual Everest Christmas Bash, and she hoped it would be a place to let their hair down. The Christmas Bash sounded a little like a block party, except it occurred in a barn outside of town. Derek explained that it was a huge gathering and people came from miles around, but he refused to tell her more, insisting he didn't want to spoil it for her.

She pulled back from leaning over the dresser mirror, applying mascara. Elle asked, "You don't think Greg will be there, do you?" It seemed infeasible. Surely not.

Derek sat on the bed behind her, wearing fitted jeans and a ribbed tan sweater with elbow patches that hugged his muscular shoulders and tapered around his waist as if it were made for him. He rubbed the stubble on his chin. "I don't think so, though he has always come in the past. He goes to all the local events; that's how he stays so intertwined."

"Bizarre, how he's so much a part of the community, and yet something like this is happening, and nobody suspected."

"I've been grappling with that too. But then, it's because most people are generally trusting and believe others are doing their best- or at least not the worst... And that's a good thing. Imagine if we all suspected the worst of everyone." Elle felt a gentle pressure on her back. She adjusted her focus in the mirror to see Derek looking lovingly at her from behind. "You're too cute!"

Elle wore jeans that rolled at the cuff with tiny white hearts speckling them, Doc Martins, and a forest green chunky knit sweater with gold threading throughout. "As are you!" She turned around to face him- challenging in the tight space. His hands slid down to the small of her back and pulled her closer against him. They kissed, and she reached beneath his sweater.

Derek leapt back with an "Eeep!" He looked at her incredulously. "How are your hands literal blocks of ice?! We're inside!" He stepped closer to her and enveloped her hands in his. "I must break this curse." He lifted her hands to his mouth and breathed into them.

"They're not cold to me. Maybe you have a low tolerance, being from the South and all."

They teased each other as they drove to the Bash. Elle stealthily found places to lay her cool hands on Derek. Derek promised her a bevy of gloves for Christmas. "Gloves of every color. Gloves in each package. Gloves decorating the tree!"

Getting to the Christmas Bash was an adventure in itself. For one thing, there were many cars and apparently not great places to park them. They had left paved roads behind and driven on the orange clay for 10 minutes before parked vehicles started lining both sides. Derek pulled into a small open space between two trucks, and they started walking. After what must have been a quarter mile, oak trees on the left side of the road gave way to reveal now-fallow fields. They turned left onto a long driveway that reminded Elle of a wagon trail. It winded to a cute farmhouse decorated simply with white lights lining the door frame and windows. Nobody was visible, but the sound of a crowd was growing from somewhere beyond the house. Elle heard their crunching shoes less and less with each step, and when they passed the home, she had to admit the reveal was grand.

The Bash was still off in the distance, but even from this view, she knew this was no simple barn party. There was a barn, and it was glowing with light, but there was also an enormous bonfire, stacks of hay bales, and an area with at least 30 picnic tables with string lights zigzagged above it. She spotted Tiny's truck with a queue in front of it. There were pickup trucks on either side with their tailgates down, offering other food and drinks. After taking in the scene, Elle exclaimed, "This is enormous!"

"Wait until you see what's in the barn," Derek smirked.

They walked to Tiny's truck first. Elle popped her head into the door and waved at Tiny and Mavis, who were working the window. Tiny was serving cocoa as a special menu item for the event, and it was clearly a hit as Elle saw them spray whipped topping on the drinks they passed over. Tiny pushed back the sequined Santa hat she was wearing and waved back at Elle.

The trucks lined beside Tiny's were regular pickups selling goods out of the back. There were apple ciders, beers, s'mores kits to bring to the bonfire, and homemade baked goods. Derek picked out two brownies with pecans, which they munched on while walking to the fire.

The blaze roared, flames licking 8 feet into the air. It let off incredible heat so that, though a crowd of merry people surrounded it, there was a ring several feet in diameter that only those trying to make s'mores entered, arms outstretched and wincing slightly in the brightness. Elle basked in the warmth and people-watched. She was surrounded by smiling faces and people gesturing freely. *This is precisely what we all need.*

Someone was waving at them from the opposite side of the circle. Elle didn't recognize them; shadows were criss-crossing their face. She pulled on Derek's sleeve and pointed.

He peered in the direction and announced, "It's Mark. Let's go say hi."

Elle hadn't spoken with the Everest High principal since the beginning of the year. She followed Derek to him and found many other high school teachers visiting with each other. Derek greeted them with nods and waves.

"Good vacation so far?" Mark asked. Before Derek could reply, he added, "Considering."

Elle admired how smoothly Derek declined the bait. "It has been good! How's the family? Steph is at that prime Santa Claus age, I imagine?"

"Boy, is she ever! Already requesting us to read The Night Before Christmas before bed. Which reminds me that the concert was incredible. Congratulations!" He turned toward Elle, "How are you getting along so far?"

Elle couldn't help but smile at the innocent chit-chat. It felt untainted and airy. "Really well, thank you for asking."

Derek and Elle mingled with the teacher group until Elle could no longer dampen her curiosity about the barn. Derek was laughing at something Coach Williams said when Elle whispered in his ear, "I'm going to check out the barn if you want to come." Derek excused himself. Coach waved farewell to them, and they started the trek through the crowd. They'd finally broken free from the throng of people surrounding the fire when Elle heard, "Wait!"

She turned to see a woman jogging toward them the best she could, her high heels sinking into the soft earth. When she caught up to them, Elle recognized Liz from the Homecoming dance. Liz grasped Elle's shoulder to help balance herself on the balls of her feet. "Elle. I've been looking for you." Liz glanced around them before continuing. "Listen, I just wanted to apologize. When you came along, it must have been hard. There was a lot of talk about you, and now, with everything going on. I guess I realized the source wasn't trustworthy."

A memory of their first meeting flashed through Elle's mind. She'd forgotten until now. "Darton First Baptist?" She asked.

Liz bobbled her head from side to side. "Yeah, kind of. I know we were... hesitant about you, but you know, it all kinda came from him, and we trusted him."

Elle didn't know how to reply. A part of her wanted to shout at how ridiculous it was to believe rumors about someone you'd never met, yet Liz's face was wrought with remorse. "I... It was tough to integrate here. I don't want to lie." The corners of Liz's mouth tightened. "But that's in the past. Maybe when someone else new moves in, we can all do better to welcome them."

Liz exhaled, and her expression slackened. "Thank you so much. You know, it's a very welcoming community at DFB. Biggest church in the area if you want to come check it out." Elle blinked. "Just think about it." Liz patted her arm before tip-toeing back toward the fire.

Derek had stepped away to give them space to talk but listened to the conversation. "That was... something." He said as he took her hand.

"I guess I can confirm who caused some of the strange looks and whispers I got at first."

"Yeah. Now all the looks and whispers are ones you've earned." Derek smirked, his dark eyes twinkling in the remnants of firelight.

"Hey!" Elle bumped him hard with her hip and laughed. "True, though."

As they neared the barn, it became clear this was where the dancing occurred. The thrumming beat reached Elle before she could see inside.

The same large hanging string lights above the table area were used in the barn, but there were so many they gave the appearance of a false ceiling. Elle expected the floor to be dirt or straw, but when she stepped inside, it was finished. A DJ was set up on the far side, and hundreds of people were line dancing. There was another small cluster of people to the right of the entrance. Derek pointed toward them, and they walked over. She didn't realize until they drew closer that kegs were being manned in the corner. They helped themselves and watched the dancers.

Derek commented on the music. "Hear the drum kit? It's

called a Train Beat, and he's using paradiddles to execute it. Super common rhythm in country music."

Elle grabbed his beer from his hand and placed both their beverages on the table before them. "Are you as good at line dancing as shuffling?" She lowered her brows in challenge.

Derek's expression opened. "I guess we should find out." He walked out to the dance floor without hesitation, and Elle jogged a few steps to keep up.

He was immediately incredible. *Of course.* Derek did the first sequence of steps with the crowd, but they were crisp and perfectly timed. His talent ensured he stood out from the surrounding dancers, but then the second sequence began. He started adding graceful motions with his arms, kicks, and side steps not included in the original choreography. Some of the other more talented dancers around them spotted his ad-libs and began copying Derek while Elle tried to keep up. After the song finished, he received a smattering of cheers from the people around him, and they returned to their beer.

"You're so good! I've got to get better at dancing to keep up with you."

"This calls for private lessons. Are you free, like right now? Or anytime later would be fine." He winked at her.

Derek showed her a few steps he "liked to keep in his back pocket" before they returned to the floor. "Just follow my lead when we're out there. I've got to run to the bathroom real quick first. Be right back!"

Elle brought out her phone and filmed some of the next dance. Now that Derek had shown off, other people were taking up the mantel, and she wanted to show him what he had inspired. A flash of bright red caught her eye across the barn; someone was dressed up as Santa. Seeing Santa at the Christmas Bash should have been lighthearted and fun, but something was off. The suit was dirty, and there was a bubble around him.

People were moving away from Santa as he moved. Elle followed him with her eyes until he was close enough to recognize. Greg. It occurred to her that she didn't know where the bathrooms were. Wishing she did, Elle inspected the door Derek had gone out. Unease roiled in her stomach, but she had decided to move too late. Santa stood directly in front of her.

"Well, if it isn't Ellie- I'm sorry, I mean Elle. Old habits. I really am sorry. Actually, that's what I wanted to talk to you about. I owe you an apology. I know I've done things that hurt ya. It's been weighin' me down heavy. If you could allow me just one single minute, somewhere quieter, to apologize. Please? One minute to get everything off my chest?" Greg's face was hard to read. Elle felt sick and weak with anxiety. She wiped the sweat from her brow. "Are you hot? Let's come outside to cool down there, sweetheart."

Greg put a supportive arm around her. The world looked like she was underwater. She searched for Derek- Greg had led her out the same exit, but everything was blurred together. *Something is wrong.* She tried to shout but couldn't muster her voice. It was as if her body was no longer under her command.

Greg was nearly carrying her as they rounded the dark side of the barn. He propped her against the rough wood and leaned over her. His breath was hot on her face. She hated the feeling of him on her. "I know what you did, you cunt." He whispered in her ear.

No, no, no. Elle tried to push him away but had no strength.

"You thought I wouldn't know it was you? It doesn't take a genius to figure out the person who volunteered to take my positions was the person who figured out my little email game."

A tear slid down Elle's cheek. *Stay awake! You at least have to remember everything. You have to remember every detail. If you live...*

Greg ran his hand under her sweater and groped her breasts. "Not much there. I don't know what Derek sees in you." He lifted a finger to her face and brushed away her tear. "Aw, don't worry, doll. You won't remember a thing."

Elle's legs gave out, and she fell to the ground.

Derek made the long trek back from the row of portable toilets, thinking about another easy step he could fit into most line dances to teach Elle. When he walked into the barn, he could tell something was wrong. Elle wasn't there. She really wasn't there, and he knew it because her phone was sitting next to their empty cups. She would never leave her phone. He looked around frantically before picking it up. The camera app was filming. He pressed the code to unlock it and stopped the recording so he could play it back.

Elle had filmed the dancers, but Greg was in the background. Derek's heart stood still. After seeing it these last years, he would know that ratty Santa costume anywhere. He pocketed the phone. Assuming the worst, he ran out of the barn.

He stopped every group, asking, "Have you seen Santa?" Many of them thought he was joking and laughed him off. Derek didn't have time to argue with them. He'd made it 20 feet when he forced himself to stop. *Where would Greg take her? Not far. I haven't been gone that long.* Derek's desperation grew with each inhale. He nodded to himself, deciding to search in the immediate area.

One side of the barn was practically unusable. There was only a small cleared path between it and the cornfield. When Derek rounded the corner, he saw two people making out. *Go figure.* Except... was that a red suit? It was so dark he couldn't tell. Derek walked toward the people as silently as he could. He held his breath and listened hard. He heard the drawl as soon as his vision caught the red color of the suit, and he launched himself at Greg.

It wasn't planned. Derek had never tackled anyone before but was suddenly on top of Greg. There was blood seeping out of Greg's nose, and Derek's hand was numb, but Elle was on the ground.

"HELP! SOMEBODY HELP! HELP ME!" Derek screamed, his voice raw. Several silhouettes appeared at the end of the alley.

"Things okay back here?" They called hesitantly.

"NO, PLEASE COME HELP!" Derek sobbed. Every iota of his body needed to check on Elle, but he would not stop pinning Greg, passed out or not.

The silhouettes became larger. Derek didn't care who they were. As soon as he saw faces, he said, "Keep an eye on him." Then he was over Elle, who also appeared to be unconscious. *Please be alive. Please be alive.* He swept her body, but she was uninjured. She was breathing, thank all the gods.

One of the people stood over him. "I called 911. What happened?"

"I don't know." Derek laid his head against her chest and listened to Elle's heartbeat. He jostled her head gently and yelled her name, but she didn't show any sign of life, so he kept listening to that beautiful, reassuring song in her chest. He could tell many people were behind him because it had gotten so loud. There were meaningless shouts and anxious voices.

Someone grabbed his arm firmly. "You have to let me look at her now." Derek reluctantly sat up and nodded. Another paramedic approached him. "Let me see that hand."

"What? Is Elle okay?"

"Your hand, sir. I need to make sure it's not broken. You might need stitches."

Derek looked at his right hand. It was bleeding freely. Suddenly, all the sound came into focus. Sirens were blaring, and police officers were on megaphones, commanding the area be cleared. Officers were talking to the first people who had shown up, gesturing to Greg, who was still on the ground. Medical professionals hovered over him, too. "I need to talk to the police."

"I'll get one if you let me assess your hand." Derek thrust his hand out to the man who briefly inspected it. "It'll be stitches." Then, under his breath, he said, "You got him good. I hope he deserved it." He turned and called to the officers.

Elle woke in a strange place. It was bright; she could tell even with her eyes closed. Her head was pounding. She dared to open her eyes, only into a squint, and found she was in a quiet white room. *The hospital?* She opened her eyes fully and saw Derek asleep, propped up on his hand, in a small green armchair. His other hand was wrapped in gauze.

A tsunami of panic flooded her body. *What happened? I was supposed to remember. I know I was supposed to remember, but I can't. We were dancing in the barn...* Elle sat upright and put her head in her hands. Something had happened. Her shifting in the bed roused Derek, who flew to her side.

"Elle!" His voice was raspy and broken. She reached for him, and they embraced, rocking back and forth on the bed. Elle never wanted to move, but too quickly, Derek leaned back, holding her shoulders and appraising her. "Are you okay? How do you feel?"

"I... My head hurts and... All I remember was telling

myself I had to remember, but Derek, I don't." Hot streams of tears rolled down her cheeks.

She could see the heartbreak on his face. He pressed the call button for the nurse and hugged her close, stroking her hair. "You don't have to. We're pretty sure we know what happened. I'll tell you everything."

A nurse came through the door. She smiled kindly. "Glad to see you awake, Ms. Foster. I'm going to take your vitals and give you some pain medication if you want. I'll also be ordering a psych consult for you. Standard procedure for what you've been through. I'm sure the police will also want to talk to you." She made notations in her chart, gave Elle acetaminophen for her head, and insisted on ordering her breakfast.

Elle looked at Derek, waiting for the story. He took a steadying breath, blowing it out through his mouth. "Do you remember filming this?" He handed her phone to her. "I had gone to the bathroom."

She watched the happy dancers, willing herself to remember. "Vaguely." She nodded. "The last thing I remember was Greg. It's fuzzy. He was in a Santa suit, and I was nervous, but then he apologized and... and... My drink must have been drugged when we were dancing. We set them down to go!"

Derek nodded sadly. "We think so. The police were able to collect our cups and put them in evidence. They're going to test them."

Elle turned back to the video. "Greg did it? Did he... Did he..."

"No. I think he might have tried, but I found you before he could. He... He had his hands on your breasts, but we don't think he touched you anywhere else, and your clothes were normal." He swallowed. "They said they would ask you to do a rape kit. So, that's coming."

"Tell me the rest," Elle demanded, her face stony.

Derek nodded. "I came back, and you were gone, but your phone was still on our table. I knew something was wrong, and the video you just watched confirmed it. It was still filming when I picked it up, and when I watched it back, I saw Greg. He's been wearing that damned felt Santa costume for years." He licked his lips. "The rest was luck. God, if it had gone any other way." Derek wiped at his eyes.

"Your hand!"

Derek sighed and continued. "Yeah. Well. I was trying to find you and knew you couldn't be far. I wasn't gone for long, so I ran all around the barn first, and luckily, he had taken you along the back side. He was pinning you against the wall. As soon as I saw him I... I lost it. I tackled him from the side and punched him. He has a concussion, they think from the tackle, and a broken nose, which my hand is payment for. As soon as he was off of you, you dropped. It was like he was holding you up. I called for help, and some people came. They called 911. You were..." His shoulders shook, and she pulled him back onto the bed. "I didn't know if you were alive. I've never been more scared in my life. But then I could hear your heart." He squeaked out the last words and closed his eyes tight.

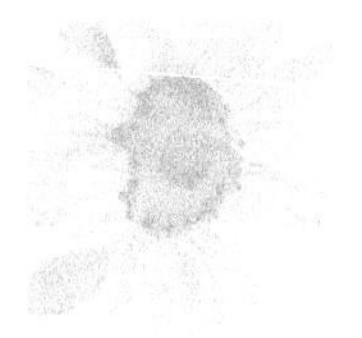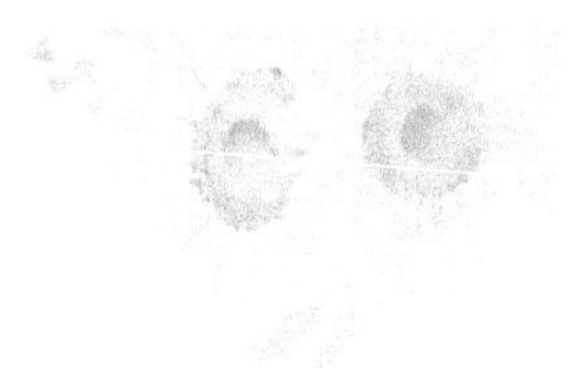

Twenty-One

ALLEGRO - AN INDICATION TO PLAY QUICKLY
AND BRIGHTLY. OFTEN USED IN THE FINAL
MOVEMENT OF CLASSICAL ERA SYMPHONIES.

S ix months later...

The heat of July's sun pressed on Elle's neck. She sat on Derek's porch stairs, watching small pale yellow butterflies flicker in and out of a clover patch. Sweat dripped from her arms down to her pinky fingers and splashed on the wood beneath her.

The screen door squeaked open behind her. "Good run?" Derek held out a glass of ice water.

"Yeah, it was. It's a beautiful day." Elle accepted the glass. "Thanks! Beautiful but hot!"

"Just like you, then." Derek quipped and lowered himself to sit beside her. Elle smiled and gave him a playful nudge. "Are you ready?"

Elle kept her eyes on the butterflies and nodded. "Definitely. This is the weirdest party I've ever heard of."

"In Florida, they have hurricane parties. Those are weird." His hand slid down to the small of her back.

She shrugged. "That's Florida. Let me shower off, and I'll help set up."

Many things had changed since Greg's arrest. Some were logistical. Matt was now the band director for Darton High School. Darton Middle hired a new director, Chloe Higgins. The ABA had formally investigated the rogue emails in District 6, finding video and a digital trail of evidence proving that Greg was the culprit. He'd even created email rules preventing automated responses and bounce messages from regular delivery. Essentially hiding that anything was amiss. The ABA declined to press charges in lieu of the sexual assault investigation and ensuing trial. When they announced their findings to the organization, it resulted in multiple volunteers from the district. Elle was appointed Adjudication Chairperson, while Mack Casey of Brookfield took on the District Chair position.

Other changes were less tangible. Elle's experience at the Christmas Bash was no secret. At first, renewed stares seemed to follow her everywhere. The nature of these looks was different, however, and nearly immediately gave way to care from the community. In the weeks after, daily care packages were delivered to her doorstep from concerned neighbors. A caroling group had even driven the dirt road to her home on Christmas Eve and regaled her and Derek with hymns. Chuck, Billy, Matt, and Chloe had also become close friends. Elle had a soft spot for Billy's firecracker of a daughter, Eva. Chloe had been welcomed into the fold with great purpose.

Elle replayed the last year as she rinsed off. Ultimately, she had arrived at her long-sought dream. She was stable, doing what she loved. She had close friends who were more like family, and Derek... Derek was the rhythm her soul kept.

It had been a stressful and sometimes terrible path that led here. Elle was still in counseling and glad for it. Greg's trial had unveiled horrors that were impossible to anticipate, but it was finally over. With it came a depth of serenity.

"Breaking news this evening. Local band director Greg Howard was found guilty of seven counts of sexual assault. Mr. Howard was under investigation after several students came forward reporting curious events such as mis-buttoned clothing and reports of headache, nausea, and even memory loss after private lessons with him. Police were initially frustrated with the investigation and unable to secure enough evidence to proceed. However, that changed after Mr. Howard was caught drugging a local woman's drink with gamma-hydroxybutyrate, more commonly referred to as GHB. That discovery enabled them to get a search warrant for Mr. Howard's home and workplace, where they found a glass jar of reeds soaking in an unknown liquid."

"Now, wait, Nancy." A co-host with slicked-back brown hair interrupted. "For those of us unfamiliar, what is a reed?"

"Great question, Ryan. A reed is a thin strip of material used on the mouthpiece of instruments which vibrates to produce a sound. These particular reeds were made of cane, and the liquid they were suspended in was laced with GHB. Mr. Howard was arrested at that time. During testimony, each student confirmed they recalled Mr. Howard offering them a new reed or, in some cases, even breaking their reed and replacing it."

The camera panned out to include Ryan. "So he was drugging these students through their instruments?"

Nancy nodded. "It does appear so. Parents reported that, in most cases, he drove their children home, claiming they fell asleep at practice. They believed him to be a caring teacher, and by all counts, Mr. Howard was a trusted member of the Darton community."

"This is... unimaginable. What can we expect to happen now?"

Nancy turned her head back toward the camera. "His sentencing will occur tomorrow, but experts say he may be looking at life in prison."

"And we'll keep you up to date with sentencing." Ryan chimed in. "If you or someone you know has been the victim of sexual assault, help is out there. Call the number below..."

"Well, I guess it's official." Billy pointed at Elle across the table. "You're 'local woman' now."

Everyone laughed, and Elle was grateful for the humor during what was a grim reason to have gathered. Elle and Derek were joined by Mavis, Tiny, Chuck, Billy, Matt, and Chloe. They'd been following Greg's trial closely. Having a support system through all that unfolded had been vital for each of them. Elle shot back, "I've been here almost a year now! We should really review the policy for what makes a local, a local."

Chloe pointed at Elle and gave her a knowing look. "I actually refuse the initiation if it involves being drugged."

Matt shook his head at Chloe. "You aren't allowed to leave. I mean, maybe after I retire, but I'm going to need you to sign some legally binding paperwork now that you mention." Chloe and Matt had almost instantly become something of a dynamic duo.

Chuck cleared his throat. "Whelp. It's done. Is everyone as relieved as I am?" Heads nodded in agreement around the room, but there were no tears. The raw emotionalism and utter shock were behind them. Only revulsion for what he'd done and the hope for whatever justice could occur remained. The guilty verdict was a relief still working its way through Elle.

Mavis and Tiny joined the kitchen crowd from their places

on the couch. Mavis raised her hands, "Everyone up. It's time for cathartic screaming."

Chloe tipped her head to the side, "Cathartic screaming? I like it."

They arranged themselves in a circle, Chuck and Billy looking apprehensive. Tiny caught their faces and said, "We all deserve this. You BMs-of-old and Elle the most of all. Trust me."

Mavis explained, "It's easy. I'll count us in. Surely you conductors know about that. After three, we scream. Don't hold back. One. Two. Three."

A sound unlike anything Elle had ever heard erupted from the circle as they all inhaled and shrieked with abandon. A discordance of deep and high voices from the depths of each of them rattled the windows. She felt as if the scream siphoned off some of her anguish.

Elle glanced around the circle and saw surprised and smiling faces. Familiar faces. She'd celebrated the New Year and Easter with them, enjoyed picnics and game nights, and had a very memorable Valentine's Day with Derek. The school year had concluded with her conducting Everest High during their graduation ceremony so Derek could shake the hand of his seniors as they walked across the football field and accepted their diplomas.

Elle suddenly became aware that all eyes were on her. Derek squeezed her hand. "Whatcha thinking about?"

She felt her eyes brighten as the right corner of her mouth twitched up. "I was thinking about what this next year will bring. You know, I think we should officially retire the name Band Misters."

Chloe rolled her eyes. "I can't believe you called yourselves that." She clicked her tongue. "Embarrassing, really."

Matt offered, "Southwest Alabama Directors?" and was met with a shove from Chloe.

"You really want us to be SAD?"

"Oh. Ha! No."

The evening progressed over boisterous rounds of Rat Race and pizza with occasional shouted proclamations of, "I've got the perfect name," invariably followed by the worst options they could think of.

Elle wasn't sure what they'd call themselves or if they would adopt a new moniker at all, but she was certain about one thing. She was finally home.

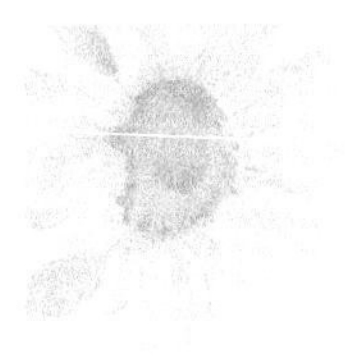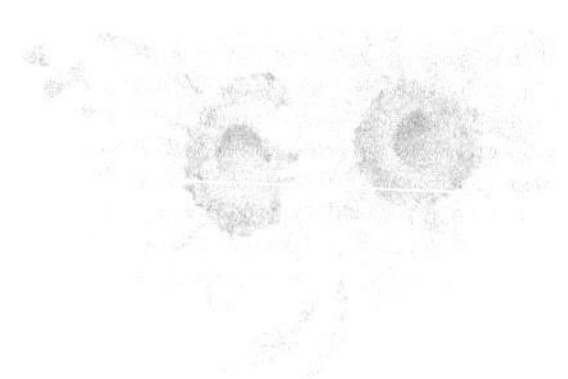

Encore

- AN ADDITIONAL PERFORMANCE DEMANDED
BY AN AUDIENCE.

S even years later...

"Are beverages a love language?" Elle extended her arm to accept the Pinot Grigio Derek offered.

"They're our love language!" He laughed but then straightened his face most seriously. "Cheers to you, Elle. Congratulations." They clinked glasses in front of their kitchen island. "What do you think you'll do next?"

A dreamy look crossed her face. "I don't know." She fussed with one of the tulle tiers of her bright pink dress. "Apply to a bunch of administrator positions?" She laughed, and Derek smiled at her sweetly. Proudly. Elle officially graduated with her Master's in Education earlier that day. Her school was remote, so instead of a graduation ceremony, they were headed to Atlanta to celebrate her accomplishment. It was a hard decision to step away from music and into administration. Her love of music brought her here, but she found that her love of the kids and education kept her going.

"Mom! Jamie keeps stealing my blocks!" Long raven hair flashed between the counter and island before halting in front of Elle. "Oooh! Your dress is pretty!"

"Thank you, Isa. Remember, Aunt Tiny is coming over to watch you two, so we should probably clean up the blocks anyway."

Isa's mouth turned down in a frown. "Yeah, or else Danielle will eat them."

Derek leaned over and snatched Isa into the air; the action met with a riot of giggling. "When you were a baby, you tried to eat everything, too."

Jamie, not quite as fast as her sister rounded the corner. "Isa won' lemme play!" She stopped short at the sight of her parents dressed up. "Where are you going?"

"We're going to a fancy dinner with Grandma and Grandpa to celebrate Mommy's graduation." Elle had loved Derek completely before they were parents, but the way he looked at their girls somehow did the impossible of making those emotions run even deeper.

"I wanna come!" Jamie exclaimed.

Elle chuckled, "Well, they don't exactly serve chicken nuggets, I'm afraid." Jamie was their picky eater. "But you'll have so much fun with Aunt Tiny and Danielle, and we'll be back tomorrow." This would be their first night away since having Isa. An overnight getaway five years in the making.

"Tomorrow?" Isa questioned. Elle briefly wondered if there would be a meltdown, but Isa continued, "It's my first slumber party!?"

Derek bit his lip in excitement. "Yep! And you're getting pizza and popcorn, too!" Both girls cheered.

The sound of the front door opening caused the girls to take off, followed by Elle and Derek. "Elle, can you take this?" Tiny called. Elle extended her arms, flexing her fingers in a gimme motion, and received the 6-month-old Danielle.

Tiny hurried back out the door without explanation but returned balancing pizza boxes. "Thank you!" She turned to the girls. "Are you ladies ready to party?"

"Yeah!"

"Awesome! Take these to the table, Isa." Tiny handed Isa the pizza, who hung a right back through the kitchen, Jamie hot on her heels. "I'm so glad you're celebrating! You look beautiful!" Tiny crooned. "And very handsome, Derek."

Derek clutched his chest dramatically. "I, what? Are you not blinded by Elle's radiance? How did you even see me?" He winked at Elle.

"Thanks for watching the kids. How was the competition?" Elle bounced Danielle and cooed at her between conversation.

"Biggest one yet! We took all three trucks. The event was so huge, the entire downtown was blocked off for it, all three nearly ran out of supplies, plus..." Tiny fished around in her diaper bag and extracted a thick paper, "Second place for baked goods! Not too shabby!"

"Wow! Congratulations! Gosh, remember that first little table of coffee at the football game? Now you're traveling and placing in food truck competitions!"

Tiny's smile widened as her eyes drifted up. "Yeah, wow. Mavis sends her congratulations, by the way. She wanted to be here for the sleepover."

"She's told me a hundred times, don't worry. I swear it's like she doesn't realize getting commissioned for her art is a huge deal! We'll have more time to celebrate all our achievements next week when she's back." Mavis had resigned from teaching and became Tiny's business partner as Tiny's Cafe took off. Their business kept them both busy and traveling. Recently, other food truck owners had begun inquiring about Mavis doing the art for their operations. She was currently in Virginia consulting with a well-known BBQ Chef.

The unmistakable cardboard-on-cardboard sound of an opening pizza box floated to them from the kitchen. Tiny scooped Danielle from Elle and shot her eyes toward the kitchen. "You two should get outta here while they're distracted."

Elle nodded, but her brows furrowed. Derek rubbed her shoulder and whispered, "They'll be fine."

"I know they will! It's just a complicated feeling, sleeping away from them. We'll obviously have our phones if you need anything at all..."

Tiny smiled, and Elle knew she understood. "We'll Face-Time you before bedtime. Go have fun!" She kicked her feet at them, shooing them toward the door, but they took the long route to the kitchen to say goodbye first.

Isa had served Jamie a slice of pepperoni, and both girls wore marinara evidence on their faces. Isa said, "Daddy, this cheese is better than the other cheese."

Derek sighed. "I know!" He swooped down to kiss each girl's head, ruffling their hair. "You girls have fun. Don't do anything that I wouldn't do."

Elle followed behind him. "We love you so much, and we'll see you tomorrow."

"Love you, Mommy." Jamie managed a full-mouthed reply.

Driving toward Atlanta, a journey they made regularly, felt different to Elle this time. It was not only about leaving the girls. She was reminded of another day, nearly nine years ago, when she was driving toward something exciting and unknown. There were some differences. This time, she had a support system, a family, that was everything to her. She wasn't uprooting her entire life but rather changing career trajectories. What position would open, at what school, and when it would happen were the mysteries. Her colleagues would change her pattern of living, but these were unknowable for now. For now, it was time to enjoy her husband's company. She reached across the middle console and weaved her fingers through Derek's.

Afterword

Dearest Reader,

Thank you so much for reading Crescendo: A Musical Love Story. I hope you loved it.

As a special treat, I humbly offer you a bonus chapter that takes a peek into Derek's past. Derek is not always a perfect character, but he has come a long way.

Check out Derek & Sarah's Finale here- https://bit.ly/crescendobonus or scan below.

Happy Reading!

Acknowledgments

Towards the end of writing Crescendo, I was laid off from my corporate job. It happened too soon. My husband, Tim, and I had set goals about me writing full time, but we didn't expect that to be possible for years.

When my position was eliminated, it was heartbreaking and scary, but from my first tearful, shocked moments, Tim was the image of a supportive spouse. Now, thanks to him, I get to pursue my passions both in my career as an author and in other work. He is my partner in everything, my forever love, the father to my children, my glass half full, and my alpha reader (and a million other things). Though he seems to think all these positions are a pleasure, I can still never thank him enough.

I've had many band directors in my life; sadly, none of them were women. When I attended the USF School of Music, there were times that I questioned my major because of my gender. It pains me to admit it now. I wish I were more aware of gender equality then, but that is where I was. This is part of the reason representation is so important.

The lack of representation doesn't mean I didn't have incredible directors, and though he won't read this, Tony Taylor was the finest director who instilled the love of music and band in me. A huge thanks to him for seeing whatever he saw in me, but even more for being the teacher and friend we needed.

I'm also so grateful to my parents. Again, for countless reasons, but what comes to mind here is raising me in an imperfect small town. I will always appreciate the stars, close friendships, and the ability to just be because of it.

My beta readers stunned me with their thoughtful feedback. They helped make Crescendo the best version of itself. Thank you, Karen, Heather, Megan, Brooke, and Ally, for your time and thoughts.

Finally, thank YOU for reading. There are so many talented authors and never enough time to read all their amazing works. Your spending time with my book is a gift. I appreciate you so much!

About the Author

Lori Thorn writes romances featuring realistic characters finding their way into healthy relationships and hosts Page Rebels, a podcast spotlighting indie authors.

She draws inspiration from her life, including growing up in a small town in the country and her BA in Music Studies, which she attained hoping to teach music but went in a completely different direction.

Lori lives in Florida with her husband, Tim, and their three kiddos. She enjoys playing clarinet (and bass clarinet and tenor sax) in the local community band and preparing scrumptious vegetarian meals.

tiktok.com/@glorylace

instagram.com/author_lori_thorn

facebook.com/authorlorithorn

About the Illustrator

Heather Balcerek is a passionate creative and lover of books. While her design experience has been born out of necessity in her past roles, she eagerly learns new programs and tricks of the trade whenever she can. Whether she is drawing Zentangles or noodling around on ProCreate or designing in Canva, Heather puts all her love and energy into each piece. Aside from visual creativity, she also hosts the Connect the Dots podcast, which focuses on career development.

Heather lives in Clearwater, FL with her husband. Together they run the food and travel blog, It's a Salty Life.

Connect with Heather
    @msheatherbdot
    @connectthedots_podcast
    www.thepolkadotdesk.com
    @saltylifefft
    www.itsasaltylife.com